Praise for Peg Cochran's
Cranberry Cove Mysteries

"A fun whodunit with quirky characters and a satisfying mystery. This new series is as sweet and sharp as the heroine's cranberry salsa."
—Sofie Kelly, *New York Times* bestselling author of the Magical Cats Mysteries

"Cozy fans and foodies rejoice—there's a place just for you, and it's called Cranberry Cove."
—Ellery Adams, *New York Times* bestselling author of the Books by the Bay Mysteries, the Charmed Pie Shoppe Mysteries, and the Book Retreat Mysteries

"I can't wait for Monica's next tasty adventure—and I'm not just saying that because I covet her cranberry relish recipe."
—Victoria Abbott, national bestselling author of the Book Collector Mysteries

"First-class mystery fun."   —*Suspense Magazine*

NO FARM,
NO FOUL

PEG COCHRAN

BERKLEY PRIME CRIME
New York

BERKLEY PRIME CRIME
Published by Berkley
An imprint of Penguin Random House LLC
375 Hudson Street, New York, New York 10014

ISBN: 9780425282021

First Edition: September 2016

Printed in the United States of America
1 3 5 7 9 10 8 6 4 2

Book design by Laura K. Corless.

To my wonderful agent, Jessica Faust,
who had a brilliant idea and let me run with it.
Thank you!

ACKNOWLEDGMENTS

I would like to thank my brainstorming buddies—Janet Bolin, Laurie Cass, Krista Davis, Kaye George, Daryl Wood Gerber, and Marilyn Levinson for coming to my aid whenever I was stumped! You guys are the best. Also thank you to my editor, Julie Mianecki, who catches all of my mistakes and helps me fix them.

1

Shelby McDonald stood in the midst of row upon tidy row of lettuces, a woven willow garden basket over her arm. Dew, shimmering like diamonds on the delicate leaves of the plants, was evaporating rapidly in the rays of the sun. The rich, dark earth was cool against Shelby's bare knees as she knelt between the two rows and began picking. She plucked some merlot lettuce from the ground, shook off the excess dirt, and placed it in her basket. It would go into the salad she was making for the St. Andrews Church potluck later that day.

She moved to the next row and chose some heads of butter lettuce. Its smooth, buttery taste would be the perfect complement to the full-bodied flavor of the merlot. Plus, the pale green of the butter lettuce and deep burgundy of the merlot would look beautiful together in the bowl.

Shelby had taken over Love Blossom Farm ten years

ago, when her parents retired to spend their time traveling the country in their secondhand RV. She'd headed to Chicago after college, but city life hadn't suited her, and she'd been glad to return to Lovett, Michigan, and the place she loved more than anywhere else on earth.

Shelby grew lettuces and herbs that she sold to the Lovett General Store and also cultivated a kitchen garden, which provided her and her children with vegetables all year long—fresh in the spring and summer and canned or pickled the rest of the year. The speck of red in the distance was an old barn, where Patches, an aging calico cat, who was still nimble despite her advancing years, kept mice and other small critters at bay. Next to it was a chicken coop. Shelby kept a flock of cantankerous Rhode Island Reds that squawked for their feed every morning but presented her with a stream of large brown eggs. Jack Sparrow, a bantam rooster inherited from an elderly farmer her parents knew, strutted among them, keeping order.

Her basket full of lettuce, Shelby headed back to the farmhouse. It was old, with worn gray shingles and plumbing that was in a constant state of disrepair, but Shelby loved it. She pushed open the back door and went through the mudroom and into the kitchen.

She put the basket on the counter and filled the kitchen sink with cold water. Although she grew everything organically, it was still necessary to make sure the lettuce was free of any dirt or sand. She separated the leaves and put them in the water to soak.

Her computer was on a small table tucked into a corner of the kitchen. Shelby slipped into the chair she'd picked up at a going-out-of-business sale and powered on her laptop. She put her fingers on the keys and began to write.

Dear Reader,

Today is the church potluck fund-raiser. Poor St. Andrews is desperately in need of a new roof. Last Sunday it rained more inside the church than out. The St. Andrews Youth Group, under the direction of the Reverend Daniel Mather, who is beginning to look slightly harried, is erecting a large tent here on the grounds of Love Blossom Farm, and his wife, Prudence, is helping the Women's Auxiliary as they prepare to set up long folding tables for the food.

As I write this, my house is filled with the fragrance of a cottage cheese pie baking in the oven and a huge pot of dill and wax bean soup simmering on the stove. I made the cottage cheese earlier this morning, and used the whey in the soup instead of some of the stock. There are dozens of uses for whey, a by-product of making cheese, and it's packed with protein and vitamins and minerals.

The house is so peaceful. The children are quietly occupied in the living room. Amelia is practicing her piano and Billy is working on his latest model airplane. It is amazing how well they get along even though Amelia is about to turn thirteen and her younger brother is only eight . . .

"Mom!" Amelia screamed suddenly in the tone of utter disdain that only a preteen girl can achieve.

Shelby took her fingers from the keyboard and rushed out of the kitchen to see what was wrong. Because Amelia's tone made it very clear that something was wrong—of course, it could be anything from a wild bear breaking into the house and attacking them to the fact that she was down to one bar on her cell phone.

Shelby stopped dead in the hallway. "Not again!" She cried.

Dear Reader, Shelby composed in her head, *I lied. The children are not playing happily together in the living room. No, indeed. Billy has gotten his head stuck in the banister railing again, and Amelia is amusing herself by taking pictures of him and texting them to her friends.*

If she was going to write a blog, Shelby decided, she might as well be honest with her readers about the crazy, tumultuous, sometimes frustrating, and often wonderful life she was leading on Love Blossom Farm—give them the good with the bad, because that was life.

"Billy, didn't I tell you not to do that?"

"Aw, Mom, I didn't mean for my head to go all the way through, honest."

"I don't think you're going to be able to get it out this time," Amelia said without taking her eyes from her phone. Her curly blond hair and blue eyes made her look like an angel, which Shelby knew was a highly misleading resemblance.

"We've done it before, we can do it again. The ears are always the biggest problem."

Unfortunately, Billy's ears provided no hindrance to getting his head through the bars, but they sure did when it came to pulling it out. It was a matter of tilting his head at exactly the right angle. After all, if he got it in, surely they could get it out again?

Shelby studied her son. Exasperation combined with a tidal wave of affection washed over her. She loved every inch of him—from his dirty feet that looked too big for his body to the freckles scattered across his nose, the tiny chip in his front tooth from the time he fell off his bicycle, and the cowlick in his blond hair that was as stubborn as he was.

Shelby put her hands on either side of his face and turned his head slightly.

"Ouch," Billy yelled.

"He's faking," Amelia said with her eyes still glued to the phone in her hand.

Shelby grabbed the wooden railings on either side of Billy's head and put as much pressure on them as she could. If they moved even a millimeter, it would help.

"Come on, pull," she said. "Harder."

"Owww," Billy yelled again, but his head finally came free and he staggered backward. He rubbed the back of his head briskly, making his hair stand on end.

"Where are you going?" Shelby grabbed him by the strap of his overalls as he turned and tried to head back to the living room. "Not so fast."

"But cartoons are on."

"It's time to get ready for the potluck." Shelby gave him a gentle push toward the stairs.

"I am ready," Billy protested.

"You're not wearing those dirty old things." Shelby pointed to his stained and torn overalls. "Go wash your face and hands and put on a clean shirt and pair of pants."

Billy grumbled, but he did as he was told. Shelby let out a sigh. That would end soon enough, when he reached Amelia's age. Her daughter refused to listen to anything she said, and they argued more often than not. Shelby knew it was a stage. She just wished it would hurry past.

If the children's father were still alive, perhaps things would be different, Shelby thought. William "Wild Bill"

McDonald had lived up to his name—dying in a motor-cycle accident on a rain-slicked road one night several years ago. At the time, Shelby thought she would die from the pain of her loss, but over time the pain had lessened until it became a dull ache. Much to her surprise, entire days went by now when she didn't think about it.

Shelby went back to the kitchen, hit SAVE on her computer, and powered it off. She would finish her blog later. She'd started writing *The Farmer's Daughter* during the long, lonely winter nights mostly to amuse herself and chronicle her little family's life on the farm, but the blog had taken off and she now had a respectable following. She loved sharing recipes and cooking and gardening tips along with the challenges and joys of being a single parent and running Love Blossom Farm. If she didn't post for a day or two, readers would actually e-mail her to ask if everything was okay.

iiiiiiiiiiiiiiiiiiiiiiiii

Everyone at St. Andrews had prayed for good weather for the potluck, and it looked as if they'd been successful. Only the faintest wisps of clouds floated in the blue sky, and the breeze was soft and gentle. Shelby paused on her front steps. Even though she'd grown up on Love Blossom Farm, she never tired of the view of the rolling green hills of southwestern Michigan.

She took a deep breath, savoring the scent of newly mown grass and fresh hay mixed with the faintest hint of manure. That last wasn't a scent most people cared for, but to Shelby it smelled like home. And if the wind was coming from the east and Jake Taylor's dairy farm, there would be more than a mere hint of manure in the air. It was possible to have too much of a good thing, Shelby thought.

Next to the farmhouse, with its welcoming front porch cluttered with wicker rocking chairs and pots of flowers, was a large pasture that Shelby leased to Jake. He kept a herd of black-and-white dairy cows and, in exchange for a reduced rent, provided Shelby with enough milk to make the cheeses she sold to the Lovett General Store.

When Prudence Mather had approached Shelby about holding the potluck at Love Blossom Farm, she had readily agreed to the plan. When Shelby's husband died four years ago, members of the church had wrapped their arms around her and her family, bringing them dinner every night for weeks, stopping by to keep her company in those early days, running errands when she was still too dazed to drive. She was glad she could now return the favor in some small way.

The farmhouse was set far back from the road with a sweeping and fairly level front lawn bordered by a white fence. It was the perfect venue for the dozens of people expected to attend.

"Whoa," someone yelled suddenly.

Shelby looked in the direction of the shout. The tent was tilting precariously to the right. The women scurried out of the way, chattering like Shelby's chickens when she came out with their feed in the morning.

Daniel Mather, the newly appointed rector of St. Andrews, was gesturing wildly. He was decidedly sweaty now, and Shelby was pretty sure that he was muttering a couple of choice words under his breath, despite being a minister. She knew she would.

"Grab that rope." He gestured frantically to one of the

members of the youth group, a skinny kid with glasses. "No, the other one. No, that one over there."

The young boy hesitated like a baseball player trying to decide whether to steal second base as he attempted to make sense of the reverend's contradictory instructions.

The tent listed farther and a high-pitched scream went up from one of the women.

"Daniel, please be careful. You could get hurt." Prudence Mather scurried over to where her husband was trying to deal with the uncooperative tent.

Daniel gave Prudence the same sort of look that Shelby's husband used to give her whenever she told him to be careful. She'd seen other men do it, too. It was their *I am a man and therefore invincible, so please don't emasculate me by telling me to be careful* look.

Prudence was wearing powder blue capris, with a flowered top and matching blue sandals. She would have been homely if not for her eyes, which were large and deep sapphire blue.

"Need some help?" Jake stepped over the fence separating the front lawn of Love Blossom Farm from the pastures beyond and strolled over to the group. He looked more like a cowboy than a dairy farmer—dressed in worn jeans, a faded blue work shirt, and cowboy boots.

"Thank you," Prudence gushed, squeezing Jake's arm before scooting out of the way.

Jake studied the tent, then grabbed one of the ropes and pulled. Slowly the tent righted itself and a sigh of relief went up from the crowd.

"Got a hammer?" Jake held the rope with one hand and untied the knot anchoring it to the stake with the other.

Daniel rushed over to Jake and handed him a large hammer with a red handle. He stood back and ran his finger around his collar. He wasn't wearing his clerical collar but was dressed informally in a short-sleeved shirt and khakis.

"Thanks. I want to hammer this stake in a little further. If you'll hold this rope . . ."

Daniel grabbed the rope with two hands while Jake pounded the stake a couple of inches farther into the ground. Daniel handed him the rope. Jake quickly tied it to the stake and gave it an extra tug for good measure.

"We can't thank you enough," Daniel said.

"My pleasure." Jake stood up and brushed some bits of grass from the knees of his jeans.

He ambled over to where Shelby was standing.

"You need any help with anything?" He shaded his eyes with one hand and smiled at Shelby. She noticed that the expression created attractive crinkles around his blue eyes.

She gestured toward the crowd on her front lawn. "Thanks, but I haven't been given any jobs to do besides bringing the dishes I'm contributing."

"I'm afraid I wouldn't be of any help to you there." Jake laughed. "My cooking skills consist of microwaving, opening take-out containers, and peeling the plastic off frozen pizzas."

The thought of someday inviting Jake to dinner flashed through Shelby's mind. She knew he found her attractive, by the way he looked at her and how he was always offering to do little things to help her out. She certainly found him more than attractive. Someday. She wasn't quite ready yet.

Prudence came over to where Shelby was standing. "What have you made for the potluck, dear? I read your blog all the time, and those recipes!" Prudence clasped her hands together and rolled her eyes heavenward. "They all sound so delicious."

Shelby told her about the cottage cheese pie she had baked earlier that morning and the various salads she'd put together with produce from her own gardens.

"That sounds wonderful. I can't wait to try everything."

By now the women had the tables set up and covered in plastic cloths. Napkins, paper plates, and plastic silverware were set out, along with some flowers Shelby had picked earlier.

Prudence glanced at her watch. "I guess we should start bringing out the food." She looked toward the group of women for confirmation. One of them, an older woman with tightly permed gray hair, nodded approval.

"I need to know where your outdoor outlet is," Prudence said, looking down at Shelby.

Prudence was of average height, but Shelby barely made five feet and even soaking wet wasn't much over a hundred pounds. Amelia was already almost as tall as her mother, and Shelby knew Billy wasn't far behind.

"It's over here." Shelby led Prudence across the lawn toward the side of the house. "I have extension cords and a couple of surge protectors, too."

"I'll need to plug in my slow cooker," Prudence said. "I've made some meatballs." She frowned. "I do hope they'll be okay. The telephone rang while I was making them and in the end I couldn't remember whether I'd put any salt in them or not."

"I'm sure they'll be fine," Shelby said.

She left Prudence to deal with her slow cooker and scurried away as quickly as she could. She noticed Billy had come out of the house and was wearing a fresh outfit. Never mind that the shirt and pants clashed wildly—at least they were clean. He was amusing himself by weaving in and out of the tent poles. Shelby looked around, but Amelia was nowhere to be seen. She was probably still in her room, polishing her nails or fussing with her hair.

A woman was headed across the grass toward Shelby. She was clutching a bowl covered in plastic wrap.

Shelby waved to her. "Hi, Jodi."

"Hey," Jodi said. She held the bowl out toward Shelby. "I brought some potato salad. I hope it's okay—it comes from the General Store here in town. I just didn't have time to make anything. I felt kind of bad when I saw what everyone else brought, though." She jerked her head in the direction of the tables.

"It's perfect. Everyone loves the General Store's potato salad."

"If you're sure. You're always posting those great recipes. Someday when I have time . . ."

Jodi Walters had a full-time job in the local dentist's office, a husband who was a long-distance trucker, and three young boys to look after. It was hard to imagine how she found the time to sleep, let alone cook something for a potluck.

Cars were beginning to pull into the empty lot next to Shelby's house. Among them was a small truck with LOVETT GENERAL STORE written on the side. It maneuvered into a space next to a red pickup. Shelby noticed Matt Hudson get out of the driver's seat, walk around to the back, and open the double doors. He wrestled several large coolers from the truck. A couple of men rushed to help, and they carried them over to Shelby's front lawn.

"Any particular place you want these?" Matt asked when he came abreast of Shelby.

"What are they?"

"Popsicles for the kids. Compliments of the Lovett General Store." Matt grinned.

Shelby looked around. "Maybe under that tree?" She pointed toward a large maple whose branches would provide some shade.

It was so like Matt to think of the kids. She walked alongside him as he made his way to where she was pointing. He bent and put the cooler down with a grunt.

"We're almost out of your herbed yogurt cheese," he said, stuffing his hands in his pockets.

Matt had purchased the Lovett General Store from the previous owner who had operated it ever since Shelby could remember. He was slowly introducing some gourmet food items—particularly Shelby's homemade cheeses and homegrown lettuces and herbs—among the packages of macaroni and cheese and canned spaghetti and rakes, snow shovels, kayaks, and all manner of other things the store carried. The nearest big-box store was forty miles away, so people depended on the Lovett General Store to meet their needs.

Matt always had a slightly sad look about him, but Shelby thought it was slowly lifting. He had come to Lovett to escape from memories of September 11. At that time, he had been working as an investment banker at a firm in Lower Manhattan. He counted himself lucky to have survived when some of his friends hadn't been as fortunate. He had stayed in Manhattan for almost another ten years before deciding that he needed to get away in order to heal completely.

Shelby knew he liked her and that with a little bit of encouragement would probably ask her out. Someday, she said to herself again.

"Looks like you've got a good turnout." Matt shaded his eyes and looked around at the growing crowd. A line was beginning to form at the food table.

"Yes. I think Reverend Mather is going to be quite pleased."

2

Dear Reader,

Our church potluck is well under way. The front lawn of Love Blossom Farm is crowded with people chatting and enjoying the food. Several of the men brought their barbecue grills, and the scent of hamburgers and hot dogs sizzling over the coals is filling the air. Fortunately the breeze is coming from the west, so the odor of manure from Jake's farm is mercifully faint. The kids are running around the lawn playing tag, their faces colored red, purple, and orange from the Popsicles donated by the Lovett General Store. . . .

The sound of someone calling her name brought Shelby out of her reverie. Her good friend Kelly Thacker was hurrying across the lawn carrying a large dish holding a quivering green gelatin mold. Kelly was the local vet—her specialty was farm animals, but once a week she set up a clinic in a trailer in downtown Lovett and treated the residents' dogs and cats. She was considerably taller than Shelby and had curly carrot-red hair. True to form, she was wearing jeans that looked as if she'd slept in them, a T-shirt advertising the Lovett Feed Store, and no makeup—not even a hint of lip gloss.

"Hi," she said when she caught up to Shelby. "Is there somewhere special I should put this?" She held out her dish and made a face. "I'm afraid a gelatin mold was all I could manage. But I did mix in some mandarin oranges to make it fancier. I hope that counts. Perhaps I can get an A for effort if nothing else." She grimaced again. "I was called out early this morning to the Clarks' farm over on Bridge Road. One of their heifers was about to calve. She's a little young—only a year—and has a rather narrow rump. Plus the calf was in a posterior position—" Kelly stopped abruptly. "You're looking a little pale." She slapped Shelby on the back.

"TMI," Shelby said. "Too much information."

"But you've had babies," Kelly countered.

"Yes, but they were barely seven pounds each, not half a ton."

"The calves aren't that big." Kelly laughed. "They're rarely over a hundred pounds."

"Please." Shelby held up a hand. "I don't want to think about it." She brushed a strand of hair out of her eyes and looked around. "Where's Seth? Isn't he coming?"

"I don't know. He said he'd be here. But you know what the doctor's life is like."

Kelly was engaged to Seth Gregson, who had set up a family medicine practice in Lovett.

"So, tell me about your dinner last night—did you wow your future in-laws?"

Kelly snorted. "The main course was fine—I did a roast chicken and a salad with some of your delicious butter lettuce—but dessert was a complete disaster."

"Oh no. What happened?"

"I know I should have listened to you and done something simple like your tiramisu sundaes—I mean, even I can scoop ice cream and soak some ladyfingers in coffee." She looked thoughtful for a moment. "Although I'm not sure I could find ladyfingers at the Lovett General Store."

"You can't. But I've found that lightly crushed vanilla wafers work just as well." Shelby swatted at a fly that was attempting to land on her arm. "But why did you change your mind?"

"Prudence Mather heard me talking about the dinner and insisted on giving me her recipe for a foolproof chocolate cake." Kelly put air quotes around the word *foolproof.* "You know how earnest she is. I tried to say no, thanks, but she looked so crestfallen that I found myself agreeing to try it. Besides, Seth's father adores anything chocolate."

"What went wrong?"

"She must have left something out of the recipe! The cake came out nearly flat and as hard as a rock." She shook her finger at Shelby. "I've heard that women do that—omit an important ingredient so that your recipe doesn't turn out as well as theirs."

"Somehow I can't imagine Prudence doing that."

Kelly tilted her head. "Neither can I, but you never know about people. I imagine you're right, though. I suppose I must have done something wrong. Like forgetting the baking powder." She laughed and shrugged. "Oh well. I think Seth will marry me anyway. It's not as if he's going to be surprised by my lack of cooking skills."

iiiiiiiiiiiiiiiiiiiiiiiiiii

"I think our little potluck is a success." Daniel came up to Shelby. He was smiling broadly. "We can't thank you enough for your generosity in letting us use your property like this." He stuck his hand in his pocket and jiggled his change. "And it's not only that we're raising money. Events like these bring our little church community together, and that's even more important."

A little girl whose face was all red and whose pigtails were quickly coming undone ran up to Daniel. "Come play tag with us, Reverend Mather. Please?"

Daniel gave Shelby an apologetic look. "Never turn down an invitation from a lady," he said, starting across the lawn.

Shelby headed toward the far corner of the yard where a group of men were playing a rousing game of horseshoes. The clank of metal against the stakes and the dull thuds as the horseshoes hit the ground rang out among the triumphant shouts and groans of the players.

A fellow in jeans and a short-sleeved plaid shirt was bent over slightly, a horseshoe in his hand. He swung it a few times as if judging its heft.

"Come on, Earl! We haven't got all day," a man wearing a Detroit Tigers baseball cap yelled. He was sipping from a can of Dr Pepper.

Earl swung the horseshoe. It made a loud clang as it hit the stake and bounced off.

"Better luck next time." The man in the cap handed

his can of pop to the guy next to him, picked up a horse-shoe, and got into position.

"Earl," Shelby called out.

Earl swung around and, when he saw Shelby, smiled shyly.

"I haven't seen you in church lately. Is everything okay?"

Earl's face turned slightly red. "Sure, sure, everything's fine. The kids are growing. Earl Jr. is off to college next year. The wife is still working part-time at the feed store. Everybody's fine."

"Are you still an usher at St. Andrews? The last couple of Sundays we've had someone else."

"Nah, I've been doing it for ten years. I thought it was time to give someone else a chance."

"Oh." Shelby was surprised. It had always been obvi-ous that Earl took great pride in his role in the Sunday service. It was odd that he had decided to give it up.

"Hey, Earl," the man in the cap yelled, holding out a horseshoe. "It's your turn."

"Nice to see you," Earl said before scurrying back to his game.

Shelby took the opportunity to check on the food to see what needed refilling. Prudence's meatballs were almost gone, so they must have turned out okay after all. Someone had brought a tray of miniature quiches. They were certainly more elegant than any of the other fare. She plucked one from the tray and took a bite.

"What do you think?" a woman who had come up to the table asked. It was Liz Gardener, whose husband was an orthopedic surgeon at the regional hospital. Her blond hair was perfect as always and she was wearing a pink-and-green-flowered cotton dress.

"Very good," Shelby said, somewhat indistinctly as she swallowed the bite of quiche.

"Really? I'm so glad you like them. They're mine." Liz clapped a hand to her chest. "I follow your blog religiously, and I love your recipes. And everything else, too. That tip you had for getting stains out of suede absolutely saved my life."

"I'm glad."

"There are so many people here today," Liz said, looking around. She pointed to a woman in a flowered sundress and squinted. "Is that Lisa?" She fluttered a hand in the air. "I'm afraid I'm very naughty and don't always wear my glasses."

They chatted for a bit longer and then Shelby touched Liz's hand lightly. "I'd better replenish this salad." She picked up a serving dish.

Shelby was on her way back to the kitchen with the nearly empty bowl of salad she'd made with roasted beets and red onion from her garden sprinkled with her homemade feta cheese when Prudence ran up to her and grabbed her by the upper arm. She began to tug Shelby back toward the tent.

"What are you doing?" Shelby asked as she tried to wrench her arm free from Prudence's grip.

"You've got to help," she begged. "I don't know what to do. It's the dogs. I'm afraid of them."

By now they had reached the tent, and Shelby saw what had Prudence in such a tizzy.

"Oh no!" Shelby yelled. "Bad doggies, bad."

Her West Highland white terrier, Jenkins, and her

mastiff, Bitsy, were feasting on the remains of a platter of hamburgers. The tablecloth covering the spot where the hamburgers had been was bunched up, and it was obvious that Bitsy had pulled the whole plate right off the table and was sharing the spoils with Jenkins.

Both dogs looked at Shelby with quizzical expressions while they chewed the last of the meat and then licked their lips happily.

Shelby put her bowl down and grabbed the two by their collars—not easy given their disparate sizes—and dragged them away from their ill-gotten gains.

"Thank you so much," Prudence said. "I didn't know what to do."

Shelby could see Prudence's hands were trembling. She was tempted to laugh. There was nothing to be afraid of. Knowing her dogs, Bitsy would have knocked Prudence down and the two of them would have licked her face until she cried *uncle*. Vicious attack dogs, they were not.

"How did you two get out?" she scolded affectionately as she made her way toward the back door.

Suddenly she noticed Amelia walking toward her, wearing a sundress and a pair of ridiculously high wedge sandals. That was one mystery solved, Shelby thought. Amelia must have left the door open . . . again. Normally it didn't matter—Bitsy and Jenkins roamed the property but always stayed out of trouble and came when called—but obviously the lure of a table filled with food had proven to be too much for them.

Shelby called to Amelia. "Please take the dogs back inside for me. And be sure you close the door."

Amelia complied but with a sulky look on her face as she tottered back toward the house with the two naughty canines in tow. Shelby watched her go. Where on earth had she gotten those sandals? She must have bought them with the Christmas money her grandparents sent. They were in Oregon the last she'd heard, but they never forgot holidays or Amelia's and Billy's birthdays.

Shelby retrieved her dish and went into the house to refill it. She checked the refrigerator and noted that there was one pitcher of iced tea left and two of lemonade. That ought to last them for a bit longer. Matt had also brought a cooler filled with cans of pop. There was a nice breeze, but the sun was warm, making everyone thirstier than usual.

Her salad bowl newly refilled, Shelby headed back outside. As she got closer to the tent, she noticed a heavy floral scent in the air that hadn't been there before. It was too intense to be coming from the pink climbing roses along the fence.

She noticed Daniel talking to a woman in a short, strapless sundress and wide-brimmed straw hat. She was wearing a pair of stiletto sandals, and Shelby couldn't imagine how she had made it across the lawn in those heels. She hardly ever wore heels herself, and she found it rough enough walking around inside. The closer Shelby got to the couple, the stronger the flowery scent became. The woman must have drenched herself in perfume.

Kelly came up alongside Shelby. She had a plate in her hand and was finishing the last bite of pie. She held the dish toward Shelby. "Was this your pie?"

"Yes. I made it this morning."

"It's delicious." Kelly licked the last bits of pastry off her fork. She tilted her head in Daniel's direction. "Isn't that the woman who always lingers after the church service on Sundays?"

Shelby nodded. "She seems to be making a big play for Daniel. He doesn't look very happy about it."

Kelly frowned. "Neither does Prudence."

"That's for sure."

Prudence was standing several feet away, twisting a handkerchief around and around between her fingers. Tears clung to her lashes, and her mouth was downturned. Shelby didn't think she had anything to worry about—Daniel looked decidedly uncomfortable and appeared to be trying to edge away from the woman, who had put a hand on his arm as if to restrain him.

Shelby turned to Kelly. "Did you say anything to Prudence about the cake recipe?"

Kelly made a face. "I did. She got all flustered the way she does and apologized over and over that my cake hadn't turned out." She laughed. "But despite all the hand wringing and tut-tutting, she never really acknowledged that her recipe might have been at fault. It was pretty obvious that she thought I had either copied it down wrong or that I had made a mistake in putting the cake together."

"No offense, but . . ." Shelby punched Kelly's arm.

Kelly laughed. "I know, I know. I'm not the greatest cook in the world. But I still wonder if she didn't leave something out of the recipe on purpose."

Dear Reader,

Our potluck is a success. Although the money we're raising will be a mere drop in the proverbial bucket compared to what is needed to repair the church roof. And after the roof is fixed, there will still be the issue of the ancient electrical wiring in the older wing of the church.

The children are all running around kicking a soccer ball. Billy is right in the middle, of course. I swear, my son is a dirt magnet. His shirt has come untucked, and the knees of his pants are green from grass stains. He will definitely need a bath tonight, although I know it will be a struggle to get him into the tub. He wears dirt like it's some sort of badge of honor.

I don't see Amelia . . . oh, there she is over by the house. She is talking to a . . . boy!

For a moment Shelby felt as if a stake had been driven through her heart. Amelia was a month away from turning thirteen—hardly old enough to date. At her age, Shelby had been more interested in catching frogs than catching boys. *Not so fast,* a little voice whispered inside her head. Even back then she'd been aware of the charms of Bill McDonald, although her idea of flirting had been to throw paper airplanes at him in English class.

Shelby saw Amelia reach out and touch the boy's hand. She frowned, ready to head over there and break things up if they went any further. Who was that boy anyway? She squinted. He had floppy bangs that he kept brushing out of his eyes and was wearing black high-top sneakers. She didn't recognize him, but not everyone at the potluck was from St. Andrews. Prudence had persuaded all the shops in town to put up posters advertising the event and had even taken an ad in the local weekly paper.

Shelby noticed someone waving at her and turned to see Prudence coming toward her.

"There you are," Prudence exclaimed when she reached Shelby, as if Shelby had been purposely hiding from her. "We've certainly got quite the crowd, haven't we? I'm so pleased. I put a lot of effort into this event."

Shelby could recognize a hint as well as the next person. "You really have done a spectacular job," she said on cue.

"Why, thank you." Prudence beamed. "It's not easy when you're new to a parish and have all these unknown personalities to deal with. Being a minister's wife is far from easy. Of course, I knew what to expect when I married Daniel. My brother-in-law was a minister at a church in North Dakota, and I know how much work that was for my sister, even though he was the one employed, not her. He's retired now, thank goodness. They bought a very nice home in Florida. We hope to visit them one day, but it's so hard for Daniel to take any time off."

Shelby nodded, looking around for an avenue of escape. Once Prudence got going, she was hard to stop.

A shout from the far corner of the yard drew both Prudence's and Shelby's attention. A couple of boys Shelby recognized from the Sunday school class she taught had opened the Plexiglas doors to the bright red-and-yellow popcorn machine the church had rented for the event. The corn hadn't finished popping, and it was now spewing out over the grass. The boys had their cupped hands out, catching handfuls of popcorn and shoving it into their mouths.

Prudence and Shelby both headed in their direction, steaming along like a ship going at flank speed with all engines running at capacity.

"Boys, boys," Prudence yelled weakly.

Shelby had had more experience with mischievous little boys. And big boys, she thought to herself, flashing back on some of her husband's escapades. She put her index and middle fingers in her mouth and let out a piercing whistle. The boys froze instantly.

Prudence and Shelby reached them just as another couple did. Shelby recognized the woman from church, although she looked different in her plaid Bermuda shorts and yellow golf shirt. She had her arm linked through that of a man whom Shelby had never seen before.

By now the popcorn had finished popping. The grass near the machine was littered with the fluffy kernels.

"Boys," the fellow said sharply, but with a twinkle in his eye, "you're going to have to clean this up." He reached over and shut the doors to the popcorn machine, although the damage had already been done.

The boys looked sulky, but they obeyed, looking over their shoulders as they snuck handfuls of popcorn into their mouths.

The woman in the plaid shorts laughed. "They're going to have stomachaches tonight." She turned to Shelby and Prudence. "I'm Grace Swanson, by the way."

"I'm Shelby McDonald." Shelby held out her hand. She hated introducing herself for the first time. It wasn't lost on her that she lived on a farm and her last name was McDonald, but so many people still found it necessary to point it out, as if it couldn't possibly have occurred to her.

"Alan." The woman reached for the man, grabbing him by the arm. "This is my husband, Alan."

The man turned around and smiled at them.

Shelby waited for Prudence to introduce herself, but she didn't. Instead she said, "You'll have to excuse me," and turned on her heel. Shelby saw her dig her cell phone out of the pocket of her capris as she walked away.

Shelby was shocked. That wasn't like Prudence. Had she and Grace had a run-in over something? Shelby couldn't imagine Prudence having a run-in with anyone.

Shelby didn't have time to think about it anymore. She headed back toward the tent to check on things. The food set out on the tables was almost gone—a couple of bites remained here and there, although a few of the dishes were still full. Her pie plate was empty—people had obviously enjoyed her cottage cheese pie. The recipe originally came from her grandmother on her mother's side, and was an old German one handed down through the generations. She planned to share it on her blog as soon as she had the chance.

Shelby picked up her empty plate and started toward the house. She might as well get it washed now. She had the feeling that after the potluck was over, all she would want to do was put her feet up and read. She sighed. It didn't matter what time she went to bed—the chickens expected to be fed bright and early every morning. She'd tried getting Amelia to do it—using everything from bribes to threats—but so far she had been unsuccessful.

Shelby was about to open the back door when Prudence caught up with her and tapped her on the arm. She was clutching her empty slow cooker.

"Yes?" Shelby asked, trying unsuccessfully to disguise the weariness in her voice.

Prudence's mouth moved for several seconds before she actually spoke. "I was wondering if there was somewhere I could rinse this out before I take it home." She held the slow cooker toward Shelby.

Shelby almost said she would wash it out for her but then bit her tongue. She was too tired. She'd been on the go since five o'clock in the morning. Running a farm was a twenty-four-hour-a-day job.

"Come on in." She held the door for Prudence and led her into the combination utility room, mudroom, and gardening room. Hooks along one wall held a selection of yellow slickers, and three pairs of rubber boots in various sizes were lined up underneath. A rough wooden worktable was cluttered with terra-cotta pots, bags of potting soil, clippers, and soiled gardening gloves.

"There's a sink over there." Shelby pointed to a large tub with a high-arc faucet.

She left Prudence to it and went through to the kitchen. The clock over the sink read ten minutes after five. Shelby was surprised—it felt later. Her back was starting to ache, and she longed to kick off her shoes and stretch out on the sofa.

Instead she rinsed out her pie plate and put it in the dishwasher. She glanced into the living room, where Jenkins was asleep on the back of the couch and Bitsy was sprawled out on the couch itself. Shelby had been determined to train them to stay off the furniture, but a lot of luck she'd had with that one. At first she had draped the sofa and chairs in old sheets, but soon realized that was pointless. The furniture was already old and worn—what difference did a few more stains make? She gave one last look around and went back out through the front door.

The crowd on the lawn was diminishing. The children had slowed down and were sitting on the grass playing quieter games while their mothers packed up their dishes and began carrying them to the cars, which were parked in the empty lot next door.

Grace and her husband came up to Shelby to thank her for hosting the potluck. Shelby was embarrassed and apologized for Prudence's uncharacteristically abrupt behavior earlier, but Grace just laughed it off. Shelby noticed that Grace's husband's pristine white polo shirt had a smudge of sauce of some kind on it. She herself had long ago made it a rule to never wear white to a picnic, a barbecue, or an Italian restaurant. Odds were good she'd end up ruining her outfit.

The older boys were breaking down the tent under Daniel's supervision. Taking it down was going better than putting it up had gone, although Daniel was still running to and fro like a terrier chasing a mouse.

Finally the tent was collapsed on the ground, the last

poof of air bellowing out as the fabric settled on the grass. Daniel looked around and then, spying Shelby, walked over to her.

"Have you seen Prudence?" He pulled a handkerchief from the pocket of his khakis and swiped it across his brow. "The ladies need some help with the tables."

"She was washing out her slow cooker." Shelby gestured toward the house. "But she ought to be finished by now."

Was Prudence one of those women who liked to snoop? Was she checking out the contents of Shelby's medicine chest?

Daniel ran the handkerchief over his face again. He looked over his shoulder, where a handful of women from the Women's Auxiliary were standing around idly, waiting for directions.

"Would you mind checking on her? She really needs to handle this."

Shelby smiled. "Not at all."

Shelby went back through her front door. Jenkins and Bitsy lifted their heads, but, with their tummies full and a soft place to sleep, they weren't about to rouse themselves any further. Shelby went over to give each of them a pat, relishing the silence of the old house after the hubbub outside. Jenkins tried to prolong the moment by rolling onto his back so Shelby could rub his tummy. She gave him a few more pats, then went out to the kitchen.

She groaned when she saw the dirty dishes littering the counter. She'd been in too much of a hurry to get ready for the potluck to clean up from breakfast. There was a cereal bowl and spoon sitting next to the range. Obviously Amelia had decided to help herself to something to eat but had found it too burdensome to put her dirty plate and cutlery in the dishwasher. Shelby sighed and rolled her eyes.

She didn't hear the sound of running water coming from the mudroom, so Prudence must have finished washing out her slow cooker. It was now almost twenty-five minutes after five. It shouldn't have taken Prudence that long. How funny it would be if she had been going out the back door while Shelby was coming in the front?

Shelby stuck her head into the mudroom but didn't immediately see anyone. The water was off and there was no sign of Prudence's slow cooker. Shelby was about to leave when something caught her eye.

It was Prudence—she was crumpled on the flagstone floor. Shelby's first completely irrational thought was that Prudence would hate to be caught in such an immodest position—her blouse had bunched up to show a broad swath of her midriff.

Shelby knelt on the floor next to Prudence and was about to feel for a pulse when she noticed the electrical cord embedded in Prudence's neck.

Shards of ceramic glazed pottery were scattered across the floor. It looked as if someone had strangled Prudence with the cord from her own slow cooker.

Shelby stumbled to her feet and ran through the house. She nearly tripped on the throw rug by the front door but managed to grab the banister at the last minute. She threw open the front door and dashed down the steps to the porch.

"Someone call nine-one-one!" she yelled to the astonished crowd.

4

Dear Reader,

Our potluck, which had been going so well, came to an unexpected and tragic close. I will spare you the gruesome details, but Prudence, the wife of the rector of St. Andrews, met with an unfortunate end in my mudroom.

Our peaceful little existence here on Love Blossom Farm has been interrupted by a swarm of police and Detective Frank McDonald, my brother-in-law. Billy is, of course, fascinated by all the goings-on and tries to tag along behind the officers, but they shoo him away like a pesky fly. As you can imagine, Amelia is feigning boredom, but there is one young policeman—so young he is still wet behind the ears—who is awfully cute and has attracted her attention. It reminds me of when I was thirteen and mooning over rock stars twice my age.

Hopefully they will put a swift end to this mystery. Who would want to kill a harmless woman like Prudence Mather?

Shelby collapsed onto the front porch steps as people began rushing toward her in a hazy wave. Sound was muted, and she felt as if she were viewing everything in slow motion—old Mrs. Willoughby pulling her purse out from under one of the tables, Jake reaching into his pocket for his cell phone, Daniel dropping the folding chair he was holding.

Suddenly her vision cleared and noise rushed back at her like a tsunami.

"What's happened? Is someone ill? Has there been an accident?" Everyone was talking at once.

Jake brandished his cell phone above the heads of the crowd. "Ambulance is on the way."

The beautiful, blue-skied, fresh-aired day had suddenly turned ominous, and the landscape tilted precariously. Shelby felt herself sway.

"You're white as a sheet," Matt said, pushing his way through the people crowded around Shelby.

Mrs. Willoughby marched toward them, her red patent leather purse hung over her arm, her gray curls quivering in excitement with each step. She undid the clasp on her capacious handbag and pulled out a handkerchief and a small vial.

"Make way, make way," she said, her considerable bulk cutting through the crowd like an ice cutter through frozen water. "Here." She shoved the vial under Shelby's nose. "Take a deep breath."

Shelby pushed the bottle away. "I'm fine. I am not

Champlain Library 613-678-2216
15 Aug 2019 03:22 pm
LIBRARY RECEIPT

CURRENT STATUS

02015
NAME: Seguin, Gabrielle

Loans: 3

044349
Due: 05 September 2019
Knit, purl, die: bk. 2

059165
Due: 05 September 2019
Yews with caution

055693
Due: 05 September 2019
No farm, no foul

Summer Reading Club de lecture !

going to faint." She coughed and raised her chin as if to say *so there*.

"What's going on? What's happened?" Grace Swanson's querulous voice rose from the back of the group gathered around Shelby.

"It's Prudence," Shelby managed to choke out. Her mouth had become as dry as Texas during a drought.

Daniel rushed over to Shelby. He grabbed her by the arm. "Is she sick? Is there something wrong with Prudence?" He looked around him distractedly. "I must go to her." He squeezed Shelby's arm again. "Where is she? Where is Prudence? Tell me what's happened."

"She's in the . . . the . . . the mudroom." Shelby pulled her arm away and rubbed the spot where Daniel had been clutching it.

Daniel began to mount the front steps.

Shelby held up a hand. "You might not want to—" she began, but Daniel wasn't listening.

She felt a hand clamp down on her shoulder and looked up to see Jake standing over her.

"I'll go with him," he said, taking the front steps two at a time.

Kelly sidled through the crowd that had gathered and plopped down on the steps beside Shelby. She didn't say anything but put an arm around her friend and squeezed protectively.

It wasn't long before the men returned, Jake supporting a clearly distraught Daniel.

"I don't think we need an ambulance," Jake said to Shelby. "I think we need the police."

As if on cue, a patrol car pulled into the driveway. The front doors opened, and everyone watched as the two officers emerged—one short and stubby and the other tall and lanky. They both trotted across the wide lawn toward the crowd that was still gathered around Shelby.

Billy, who had been uninterested in what was going on and who was busy flinging the horseshoes the adults had abandoned at a tree, flew at breakneck speed toward his mother.

"Whoa," Matt said, grabbing Billy by the shoulders. "Why don't we go see if there are any more Popsicles left? Assuming that's okay with your mother?"

Matt smiled at Shelby, and she managed a smile back. She waved her hand. "Sure."

Billy obviously did not want to leave the excitement, but he capitulated under Matt's firm grip. Shelby breathed a sigh of relief. How horrible if Billy was to witness something as awful as the sight of Prudence lying dead on the mudroom floor.

The two officers stood in front of Shelby, feet braced apart, arms folded across their chests. The shorter one had a buzz cut and muscles that bulged out from beneath his short-sleeved shirt. The taller one was much younger—so young Shelby wondered if this wasn't his first day on the job. His dark hair was carefully slicked back, making him look as if he was ready for picture day in grade school.

"Ambulance should be here shortly," the older officer said, still slightly breathless. "Where's the victim?"

"I'll show you." Jake stepped forward and ushered the officers up the stairs and into the house.

Shelby sagged against the steps. The day had turned surreal. Daniel, who was the one usually comforting others, was being comforted by the formidable Mrs. Willoughby.

She worked part-time as a secretary at St. Andrews and presumably knew Daniel better than anyone else.

The younger policeman came back out of the house. His face was ashen, and for a moment Shelby wondered if they were going to need Mrs. Willoughby's smelling salts after all. He spoke into his shoulder radio.

"Cancel the ambulance. We have a homicide on our hands."

〽〽〽〽〽〽〽〽〽〽〽〽〽〽

For the next several minutes, people stumbled around in shock, not able to settle to anything. Earl sorted through the trash—putting aside cans and bottles for recycling. Grace was folding the dime store plastic tablecloths that they had planned to throw out anyway. Jodi had corralled the remaining children as far away from the scene as possible. They were all tired, dirty, and sticky from the Popsicles, but she managed to engage them in a game of duck, duck, goose. Their laughter sounded odd ringing out in the air that had suddenly become so somber.

A car came down the road, and everyone froze. The dusty and battered blue pickup truck turned into the long driveway and rattled toward the farmhouse. Everyone swiveled in that direction and watched as a man got out. He was wearing worn jeans, a plaid shirt, and a Lions baseball cap. He was Shelby's brother-in-law—Wild Bill's older brother—and a detective with the Lovett Police Department.

Shelby began walking toward him. He saw her and started in her direction.

"You okay?" he asked when they came abreast of each other. His face was pinched with concern.

"Yes. At least I think so."

He put an arm around Shelby's shoulders. "It must have been a shock. But I know you're tough. That's one of the things Bill liked about you."

Shelby smiled. Frank had the same blue eyes his younger brother had—so light they were almost transparent. Bill had been taller, though, with darker hair and a passion for danger that drew him to motorcycle riding and fast driving. Frank, on the other hand, found his thrills chasing down criminals.

Billy came running toward them. "Uncle Frank, Uncle Frank," he yelled.

Frank grabbed Billy around the waist and swung him up in the air before giving him a big hug.

Frank had done his best to take Bill's place in Billy's life—teaching him how to fish, taking him camping and out on the lake in his boat. Frank would have loved kids of his own, but so far it hadn't happened for him and his wife, Nancy.

"Can I watch? Can I?" Billy danced from one foot to the other in excitement.

"I'm sorry, buddy, but this is police business. It's off-limits, I'm afraid." He dropped his voice to a whisper. "But I promise to fill you in later, okay?" He winked.

"Sure." Billy shrugged. He dragged his feet as he went back to the circle of children playing on the lawn.

Frank turned to Shelby. "Do you mind showing me where the incident took place?"

Incident? What a funny word to use for murder, Shelby thought. "Sure. It . . . the body, that is . . . is in the mud-room." It felt wrong to be referring to Prudence as *it* or *the body*, but she didn't know how else to put it.

Shelby wasn't anxious to go back into her mudroom. She had loved working out there at the long, rough-hewn gardening table her father had made out of found pieces of wood. She could spend hours separating overgrown plants, rooting cuttings, and starting seedlings. Now she didn't know if she'd ever want to use the room again.

"Don't let anyone leave," Frank called to the young policeman, who looked as shell-shocked as anyone else.

Shelby led Frank around to the back of the house. The door to the mudroom was open and yellow police tape with POLICE LINE: DO NOT CROSS on it in black had already been strung across it. The other policeman—the short, stocky one—was waiting outside. Frank lifted up the tape and ducked underneath.

"It might be better if you waited out front," he called to Shelby.

Shelby joined the crowd milling anxiously on the lawn. They quickly gathered around her, everyone murmuring in low voices. Mrs. Willoughby's purse hung from the crook of her arm. Shelby supposed she wanted to be ready with the smelling salts in case someone developed the vapors.

Dear Reader, the thought of that old-fashioned phrase—the vapors—almost made me laugh and now Mrs. Willoughby is looking at me strangely.

"It's the shock, dear," Mrs. Willoughby said, her tone doubtful, as if she was looking for an explanation for Shelby's strange behavior.

Shelby quickly assumed a more somber expression, which certainly matched how she was feeling inside.

"That policeman says we can't leave," Alan said, maneuvering his way to the front. "Grace isn't feeling well." He gestured toward his wife, who looked just fine to Shelby—she had a paper plate in her hand and was eating the remains of a piece of cake. "I'd like to take her home. This has been a terrible shock."

"It's been a shock for everyone," Mrs. Willoughby said firmly. "We'd better obey the authorities."

"I think there's some iced tea and lemonade left in the fridge," Shelby said, turning toward the house. "I'll bring them out. Maybe a cold drink will make Grace feel better— no doubt she's a bit woozy from the sun and the heat. Obviously no one can leave until the police say it's okay."

Shelby almost apologized for the inconvenience, but then realized how ridiculous that was. None of this was her fault, although maybe if she had refused to let Prudence use her mudroom? She shrugged off the thought. If someone had been intent on killing Prudence, they would have found a way no matter what.

Another car had pulled into the long driveway leading to the farmhouse when Shelby came back out with two pitchers of iced tea and one of lemonade. The car was black and looked quite new but had already gathered a layer of dust from the country roads. It hadn't rained in almost a week and when it did, all that dust would turn to mud.

Jake rushed over to take one of the pitchers from Shelby.

"The medical examiner is here." He cocked his head in the direction of the newly arrived car.

Shelby shuddered. She'd seen enough police shows on television to know what indignities were coming. Poor Prudence.

A few minutes later, Frank came around the side of the house. He was frowning and tugging at his lower lip. Bill had often done the same thing. A wave of longing for her late husband swept over Shelby, and she wiped a tear from the corner of her eye. If he were here right now, she would collapse against his broad chest, and he would make everything all better again. But that wasn't going to happen—she was on her own. She stiffened her spine and stood up a little straighter.

Frank walked over to where Shelby was standing. Jake hovered nearby—like a sheepdog protecting its flock.

Frank took off his hat and ran a hand over his head before clapping the cap back down again. He looked at Jake. "Mind giving us a minute?"

Jake hesitated, his black eyebrows drawn together in an almost straight line.

"It's fine," Shelby said to him. "Frank is my brother-in-law. I don't think he plans on arresting me." She smiled to show Jake that everything was all right.

Frank waited until Jake was beyond earshot. "Can you give me any information on the victim?"

"Yes. It's Prudence Mather. She's the wife of the rector of St. Andrews." Shelby looked around and spotted Daniel sitting in a chair under the shade of a tree, Mrs. Willoughby standing protectively by his side, her red patent leather handbag still slung over her arm. "That's her husband there." Shelby pointed toward Daniel.

"Was this some kind of party?" Frank waved a hand encompassing the stacks of folding tables and chairs, the ice chests from the Lovett General Store, and the popcorn machine that was now turned off. "I don't remember getting an invitation."

He smiled, and Shelby gave a weak laugh.

"We were having a potluck fund-raiser for St. Andrews Church. For a new roof," Shelby added.

Bill and Frank and the McDonald clan had frequented the Catholic church in town growing up, but Shelby had had strong ties to St. Andrews, and Bill had started going with her after they married.

Frank nodded. "Do you have any idea why Prudence was in your mudroom? Did you let her in? Or are you two friends, and she comes and goes when she wants?"

"Prudence wanted to rinse out her slow cooker, so I took her inside to let her use the sink in the mudroom."

Frank pursed his lips. "Any idea what time that was?"

"As a matter of fact, I looked at the kitchen clock on my way back out. It was ten minutes after five."

"I don't suppose you happened to glance at the clock when you found the body?"

Shelby nodded. "Yes, it was almost five thirty. Prudence had been gone more than long enough to clean out her slow cooker, and the Women's Auxiliary was waiting for her to tell them what to do with the tables. I went looking for her, and I found . . . found . . ."

"Of course." Frank put a hand on Shelby's shoulder. "I'm sorry—I wish you didn't have to go through this, but there's no other way. Why don't you get yourself a drink of water while I talk to some of the other guests?"

Frank walked away, and Shelby saw him approach Kelly, who was sitting on the ground, leaning against a tree, her eyes half-closed. Shelby supposed she must be exhausted after her early-morning trip to the Clarks' farm.

Shelby looked around for Amelia. She was sitting on the old swing hanging from the apple tree—the one Shelby used to swing on when she was a kid. And she was sitting with that boy. Shelby supposed there wasn't much she could do about it—at least not without making a scene. That would embarrass Amelia and accomplish nothing.

Jodi came up behind Shelby. "They look cute together, don't they?" She pointed toward Amelia and the young boy.

Shelby turned toward her. "Do you know who that boy is?" She looked back at the couple and frowned.

Jodi laughed. "That's my son, Ned. And I assume that's your daughter."

"Yes. Amelia," Shelby said through tight lips.

"He's a good boy," Jodi said.

"How old is he?" Shelby thought he looked older than Amelia. There was a hint of baby-fine hairs on his chin.

"He's fourteen. Going to be a freshman at Lovett High School next year," Jodi said with a hint of pride.

"Amelia's only turning thirteen. She's too young for someone that old," Shelby protested.

Jodi laughed. "There's only a year's difference between them."

"Yes, but he's going into high school. She's only in middle school."

Jodi looked at Shelby and gave a half smile. "You can't hold on to them forever."

5

Dear Reader,

Our little world here at Love Blossom Farm is still rocking from yesterday's tragedy. The police were here until
late last night taking pictures of my mudroom, dusting
for fingerprints (there will be a ton, considering how
often we go in and out of that room), and generally
looking for clues.

I hardly slept at all last night, but of course I managed to fall asleep an hour before my alarm went off.
I wanted nothing more than to silence it (preferably by
throwing it across the room), pull the covers over my
head, and go back to sleep. But the chickens will be
squawking to be fed and besides, today is my cheese-
making class and I have to get ready. A number of
women have shown an interest in learning how to make

fresh cheese. We are starting with ricotta cheese, which is incredibly easy to make and so delicious—far tastier than the containers you buy in the supermarket.

Jake promised to leave the milk we'll need by the front door. Normally he delivers it to the back door, but the mudroom is still out of commission because of what happened yesterday.

Shelby slipped her feet into the gardening clogs she'd left by the front door. It was still fairly dark out as she made her way around the house and toward the ancient barn, whose outline she could barely make out in the distance. At this hour it was still cool, and the grass was wet with dew. She ran a hand through her tangled curls and felt the damp from the morning air.

She'd made this same journey so many times that a slightly indented path had been worn in the ground. Shelby didn't need a flashlight—she knew where every hole, tree root, and rock was by heart.

The chickens began to squawk as soon as they heard her coming. Shelby pulled open the door to the barn, which groaned like an old man getting out of bed first thing in the morning. Shelby felt along the shelf next to the door until she found the flashlight she kept there. It was shaped like a lantern and threw a bright patch of light in front of her as she crossed to the corner of the barn. She put the flashlight on the floor and picked up the rusty tin bucket they had been using at Love Blossom Farm for as long as she could remember. She filled it with feed from an open burlap bag propped in the corner.

Patches wound in and out between Shelby's legs as she walked toward the door. She bent down to scratch the cat's back. Patches swished her tail back and forth, gave an indignant meow, and streaked off, disappearing into the shadows.

Shelby carefully navigated the darkened barn—skirting the small hole in the dirt floor that was just big enough to catch your foot in and twist your ankle. She had learned the hard way to avoid it, having stepped in it more than once already. One time she went flying, landing on her knees and scattering the bucket of chicken feed all over the barn floor.

By now the chickens' squawking had reached a frantic crescendo. "I'm coming, I'm coming," Shelby called to them as she briefly put down the bucket to turn off the flashlight. She put it back in its place on the shelf and went outside. The sky was getting lighter by the minute, and the air was slightly warmer.

The chickens immediately surrounded Shelby, dancing from one scrawny leg to the other as she tossed the feed in a wide arc away from the birds clustered around her. They scattered in all directions, pecking at the ground with their sharp, pointed beaks. One of them—who was slightly bigger and therefore felt entitled to boss the rest of them around—pushed the others out of the way, giving a loud squawk and flap of her wings to warn them off. She had never produced any eggs, and more than one person had suggested that she would make an excellent chicken dinner, but Shelby couldn't bring herself to do that.

All the feed scattered, Shelby returned the bucket to the nail in the barn wall and headed back toward the house. The house was quiet—it would be hours yet before Amelia and Billy woke up. Shelby tiptoed through the living room—although she didn't know why she bothered, because both kids could sleep through a nuclear explosion—and out to the kitchen.

She avoided looking at the door to the mudroom as she put on a pot of coffee. As soon as it had brewed, she poured herself a cup and got to work. She was making a sour cream coffee cake to serve the ladies while they waited for the cheese they would be making to drain and the curds to separate from the whey.

Shelby got the cake into the oven and began to set the kitchen table. She had a hand-embroidered tea cloth that had been her grandmother's and a tea set left by a great-aunt who'd never had any children of her own. She enjoyed making everything look nice even though it didn't happen often. Although she and the children sat down for dinner every night, either Amelia or Billy was always in a rush and finished eating by the time Shelby had her napkin in her lap. Amelia was in charge of setting the table, and Shelby was positive she made a mess of it on purpose—the knife to the left of the plate, the forks tossed anywhere, the napkins left in a pile in the center. Shelby had decided long ago that it wasn't worth fighting over, but still . . .

She stood back and admired her handiwork. Everything looked so pretty. She caught sight of the mudroom door out of the corner of her eye. The house was still hushed, and it was hard to believe such ugliness had happened here.

A few minutes before nine, the front doorbell rang. Shelby dried her hands on a kitchen towel and went through to the foyer. Jenkins and Bitsy were there ahead of her, pressing their noses to the glass panels alongside the door, adding to the collection of nose prints and paw prints that already blurred the glass and which Shelby kept meaning to wipe off.

Mrs. Willoughby was standing on the front steps. She'd exchanged her red patent leather purse for a navy blue one that matched her shoes and the belt around her shirtwaist dress.

By the time Shelby ushered Mrs. Willoughby inside, the other women began arriving. Punctuality was considered a virtue in Lovett, although some people took it too far, arriving twenty to thirty minutes ahead of time and occasionally catching their host or hostess in the shower.

Shelby led the way through to the kitchen, the women chatting about the previous day's events as they followed her.

"I almost didn't come today," Valerie Young said, "but I wanted to find out if there was anything new about the . . . the . . . well, you know."

Valerie was the junior warden at St. Andrews. She had a round, bland face, rather like an unbaked biscuit, that belied her sharp nose for gossip. Shelby doubted she would have missed this morning's class for anything and the chance to have a firsthand look at the scene of the murder. Indeed, as soon as they entered the kitchen, Shelby noticed Valerie's head craning in the direction of the mudroom door.

Liz Gardener had brought a friend with her. They were both immaculately coiffed, made up, and dressed, even though they were going to a cooking class.

Dear Reader, Liz always manages to make me feel unkempt and slightly sloppy. Well, what can I expect, I suppose, when my wardrobe consists of T-shirts with stains on them and worn-out jeans and shorts? I'm sure Liz sleeps in pretty nightgowns and probably even has special clothes just for gardening.

Olivia Willoughby, Valerie, and Mrs. Willoughby's neighbor Karen, whom Mrs. Willoughby had persuaded to come, stood on one side of the kitchen island, while Liz and her friend Hope stood apart from them on the other side.

"We're all here, so let's begin," Shelby said, grabbing a half gallon of the milk Jake had delivered earlier from the refrigerator. "I'm only making a small amount of cheese today, so you can see how easy it would be for you to do this at home."

Shelby planned to mix the finished ricotta with cooked pasta, meat sauce, and shredded mozzarella for dinner that night. It wouldn't need more than half an hour in the oven to become deliciously browned and cheesy.

Shelby poured the milk into a large pot she had ready on the stove.

"Is that whole milk?" Liz frowned. "Can you use low-fat?" She patted her flat stomach absentmindedly.

"You can use two percent," Shelby said, turning the burner under the pot to a medium flame. "But I wouldn't try it with skim or nonfat. Your curds and whey wouldn't separate."

"Makes me think of Little Miss Muffet." Mrs. Willoughby laughed.

"As soon as your milk reaches two hundred degrees," Shelby said, inserting an instant-read thermometer into the pot, "it's time to remove it from the heat." She turned the burner off under the pot. "Now we are going to add one-third of a cup of lemon juice or, if you prefer, distilled white vinegar." She poured in the lemon juice she had squeezed in advance.

Valerie peered into the pot. She pointed at the mixture. "It's beginning to form curds."

Mrs. Willoughby jostled into position so she, too, could have a look. "What's that yellowish liquid?"

"That's the whey," Shelby said. "Don't throw it out. It's so healthy. You can use it in baking instead of water when you're making bread or pizza dough." Shelby stuck a spoon into the pot and poked around. "It takes about ten minutes for the curds to form." She peered into the pot again. "This looks good."

"What do we do now?" Mrs. Willoughby asked, casting a glance at the coffee cake sitting out on a cake stand on the counter.

"Now we drain the mixture." Shelby set a strainer in a large bowl and lined it with the piece of cheesecloth she had cut earlier. She spooned the larger curds into the strainer first, then upended the pot and poured out the rest. "This will need to drain for anywhere from ten minutes to an hour depending on how wet or dry you want your ricotta."

Liz rubbed at an invisible spot on her white linen blouse. "So we wait for an hour?" She frowned and looked at her watch.

She was probably late for some committee meeting, Shelby thought, but she had been clear when Liz signed up that the class would take approximately an hour and a half.

"How about we have some tea and coffee cake?" Shelby said, gesturing to the kitchen table with its embroidered cloth and fancy dishes.

Mrs. Willoughby was the first to take a seat. She patted the chairs on either side of her, and Karen and Valerie slipped into them.

"Do you need help pouring, dear?" Mrs. Willoughby half rose from her seat.

"If you wouldn't mind," Shelby said. She knew Mrs. Willoughby was one of those people who liked to have a task to do.

She bustled around filling the delicate china teacups with enough pomp and circumstance to be worthy of an English royal.

Liz and Hope shook their heads when Shelby offered up the sour cream coffee cake.

"Have to count my calories," Liz said with a stiff smile. "Do you have any artificial sweetener?"

Shelby pushed a bowl filled with blue and yellow packets in Liz's direction.

Mrs. Willoughby looked as if the very concept of calorie counting was completely alien to her and managed to snare the piece of cake that was infinitesimally larger than its mates.

"So, what about the elephant in the room?" Liz asked, slyly looking around the table.

Shelby stopped with her fork halfway to her mouth.

"Oh, come on," Liz chided, "we're all just dying to talk about the murder, aren't we?" She looked around the table again, finally glancing at her friend, who looked suitably enthusiastic.

Mrs. Willoughby pointed her fork at Liz. "I think it was that hussy who comes to eleven o'clock Sunday Mass smelling like she poured an entire bottle of scent over herself."

"Isabel Stone?" Valerie asked. "She's always wearing such inappropriate shoes—those stilettoes make such a racket when she walks down the aisle for Communion."

"Yes, that's the one," Mrs. Willoughby said, helping herself to a second piece of coffee cake. "Have you seen the play she's been making for our rector? Disgusting, if you ask me."

"I'm sure we can rest assured that Reverend Mather is above all that," Shelby said.

Valerie sniffed loudly. "With that wife of his, maybe not. Maybe he was tempted," she said. "Not that I want to speak ill of the dead."

Dear Reader, everyone is clearly dying to do just that.

"Prudence always seemed so nice to me," Shelby said, feeling the need to rise to the poor woman's defense.

"There was more to Prudence than met the eye," Mrs. Willoughby said. "She picked at her poor husband something fierce."

"But in the nicest possible way, of course," Valerie added with a snicker.

"That's true. But he was still henpecked, no matter how nicely she pretended to do it," Mrs. Willoughby said, eyeing the remaining cake on the stand. "And who knows what went on behind closed doors?" She adjusted the navy patent leather belt around her broad waist. "Men don't like being treated like they're slightly dim-witted children."

Shelby pushed the cake stand toward Mrs. Willoughby. "Please, help yourself."

"I don't mind if I do," Mrs. Willoughby said, brushing some crumbs from her top.

"That's true," Liz said. "They like to think they're king of the jungle."

"Or at least king of their own little household kingdom," Karen added. "So maybe Prudence did drive him into the arms of another woman?"

"That other woman being Isabel Stone." Mrs. Willoughby wet a finger and picked up the crumbs on her plate.

"I still can't see someone like Isabel Stone stooping to murder. Who is she, anyway?" Liz asked.

Mrs. Willoughby finished chewing her piece of cake. "She's divorced. No children." As church secretary Mrs. Willoughby was privy to a number of details about the parishioners.

"Does she work?" Liz arched a perfectly plucked eyebrow.

"Not that I know of." By now, Mrs. Willoughby had finished her third piece of cake. "She's on the Garden Committee at St. Andrews, and I often see her working in the garden during the afternoon. She has quite a way with the roses. The groundskeeper was going to dig up this one bush that appeared to be quite dead, but Isabel brought it back to life again."

"If she's doing all that, she obviously couldn't have a full-time job. Unless she works nights." Liz raised her eyebrows suggestively.

"She probably got a good settlement in a divorce." Karen wiped her lips with her napkin.

"Maybe not," Liz's friend Hope spoke up. "And that's why she wants to snare a new husband—for the money."

Mrs. Willoughby gave a loud laugh. "Then she's barking up the wrong tree. Church rectors barely make a living wage."

"But maybe Isabel Stone isn't our murderer. Maybe Daniel Mather decided he'd had enough of Prudence." Liz turned toward Shelby. "Could he have snuck into the mudroom when no one was looking?"

Shelby thought back to the previous afternoon. "It's possible. There were still so many people milling about. No one was really paying much attention to what everyone else was doing."

"It's shocking, I can tell you that." Mrs. Willoughby puffed out her chest.

Shelby thought this was the perfect time to bring this conversation to a close. "Let's check on the cheese, shall we?"

The women looked disappointed, but they obediently trooped over to the counter and peered into the strainer Shelby had poured the curds into.

"Look at that." Mrs. Willoughby pointed toward the strainer. "It's turned to cheese."

Shelby smiled. "I told you it was easy."

"Seems like an awful lot of work to me when I can go to the Lovett General Store and pick up a container there," Valerie said.

"That's perfectly true," Shelby said through gritted teeth. "But there is a certain satisfaction in knowing you made it yourself."

"I do read your blog every day," Valerie said. "But I never try the recipes. I guess you could call me an armchair cook." And she laughed.

6

Dear Reader,

Today was my cheese-making class—we made fresh ricotta. There is such a difference between the fresh and the store-bought kind. . . .

Shelby paused with her fingers hovering over the keys—*no matter what Valerie Young says,* she thought to herself.

I've posted the recipe below for those of you who would like to try it. I'll be making a pasta casserole tonight with mine, but you can use it in lasagna, ravioli, cannoli, and other delicious dishes.

The ladies all wanted to gossip about the . . . murder. I can hardly say the word. It's so at odds with the peacefulness of Love Blossom Farm!

Billy is off for his Cub Scout meeting and Amelia has gone to visit her friend Kaylee—they've been friends since nursery school. I have to get out and do some work in the garden. I don't want the tender lettuces I've planted to be choked out by weeds. And some should be ready for picking and delivery to the Lovett General Store.

Shelby said good-bye to the ladies from her cheese-making class and watched as they slowly drifted down the path to their cars, their chattering voices rising and falling on the warm air. She closed the front door and headed back to the kitchen.

She spooned her fresh ricotta into a container for her casserole for dinner that night and cleaned up the rest of the kitchen. She was hanging up the dish towel when Billy appeared, still rubbing sleep from his eyes. He was dressed in his Cub Scout uniform and had managed to slick down his cowlick with water. Shelby had to resist the urge to grab him and give him a huge hug and big kiss. She knew that would not go over well—talk about the understatement of the year.

"Hungry?"

"Yeah, can I have some cereal? Zack's mom will be here soon, so I'd better hurry."

Shelby got the cereal box out of the cupboard along with a spoon, bowl, and milk from the fridge.

Billy downed his cornflakes and put the bowl on the counter just as a horn blared from the driveway.

"Gotta go, Mom." He aimed a kiss in Shelby's direction and ran out the front door.

Shelby watched him climb into Zack's mother's station wagon. His father would be surprised to see how big he'd become, Shelby thought, and he would be proud, too.

Shelby headed back to the kitchen and was about to step into the mudroom when the black-and-yellow police tape brought her up short. The room was still off-limits. Shelby bit her lip. Her favorite trowel was in there—she could see it sitting out on the wooden table. She would have to make do with the old one she'd tossed in the barn.

Fortunately she kept most of her gardening equipment in the barn, where it was closer at hand.

Patches rubbed against Shelby's legs as she gathered her things together. Patches had been part of the family for so long that no one could remember exactly how old she was. She spent the spring, summer, and fall on critter patrol in the barn but lately, as she'd gotten older, Shelby was able to entice her into the house during the colder months, where she gloried in the warmth of the fire and curled up nose to tail on the throw on the sofa.

The sun was high in the sky and felt good against Shelby's back as she knelt between the rows of lettuce. The ground was still cool, though, and the breeze was fresh. Patches strolled over as Shelby worked, and lolled in a sunbeam, leisurely grooming a front paw.

Shelby was yanking out a large clump of weeds when Bitsy and Jenkins bounded over. Jenkins had bits of hay caught in his white beard, and his paws were muddy. He grabbed the weeds from Shelby's hand and shook them vigorously—as he would a mouse—sending clods of dirt flying into Shelby's face.

She laughed and brushed the bits of earth from her

cheeks and forehead. Seemingly tired of his game, Jenkins bounded off again with Bitsy, who was not far behind.

Shelby was nearing the end of the row when a dark, human-shaped shadow blotted out the rays of the sun. She turned around to see Frank standing behind her. For a crazy moment, with the sun in her eyes, she thought it was her husband, Bill, and she felt a wave of longing rush over her. She shook it off.

"I didn't hear you coming." Shelby always lost track of the world when she weeded. There was something relaxing about the activity and about having your hands in the warm earth.

"I'm sorry. I didn't mean to scare you."

Shelby got to her feet and stripped off her gardening gloves. She must look a sight—dirt on her face and her hair tangled even more than usual by the breeze.

"I need to ask you a few questions." Frank rocked back on his heels. Like the day before, he was wearing jeans, a checked shirt, and work boots.

"Why don't we go inside? That sun is starting to get hot."

Frank followed Shelby back to the house. He stopped at the door and looked down at his feet. "I don't want to drag any dirt inside. That always gives Nancy fits."

Shelby smiled. Nancy was extremely good-natured, and Shelby doubted that she gave Frank any grief at all. "We can sit on the porch if you like. There's usually a cool breeze out there."

"Fine."

Shelby led the way around to the front of the house and left Frank sitting in one of the rocking chairs while she went inside to get them something cold to drink. She couldn't imagine what kinds of questions Frank had for her—she'd told him everything she knew the day before. But she supposed it was routine, and Frank had to follow protocol.

Shelby pulled a pitcher of lemonade out of the fridge, grabbed a couple of glasses, and headed back to the porch. She had just poured Frank a glass when Jenkins and Bitsy appeared around the corner of the house.

Bitsy galloped up the steps toward Frank. She went over to him and laid her head on his knee, her drool leaving a wet patch on his jeans. He scratched behind her ears absentmindedly. Jenkins was too busy snapping unsuccessfully at a fly to pay any attention to their visitor.

Bitsy finally moved to the corner of the porch and Frank leaned back, stretching out his long legs.

"What is it that you wanted to ask me?" Shelby said, handing him a glass of lemonade.

"I had a few questions about your potluck yesterday." Frank began unconsciously rocking the chair.

Shelby smiled to herself. Rocking chairs always put people at ease. Whenever she was upset as a child, her grandmother Jenny would tell her to go sit in the rocking chair and rock her troubles away.

Frank took a long pull on his drink and then wiped the back of his hand across his mouth. "Did people pay for the potluck at the door?"

Shelby shook her head. "No. We sold tickets in advance at the church. That way there would be no need to worry about having change."

"So no one paid when they got here? Maybe they decided to come at the last minute and hadn't purchased a ticket?"

"There were a handful of people who did that, but not very many."

"That's curious."

Shelby raised an eyebrow. "Why?"

"We found a thousand dollars in Prudence Mather's purse."

Shelby gasped. "What would Prudence have been doing with that amount of money in her handbag?"

"I don't know. I was hoping you would be able to tell us."

iiiiiiiiiiiiiiiiiiiiiiii

Shelby went back to her weeding after Frank left—his pickup kicking up dust as he backed down the long driveway leading to Love Blossom Farm—but the calm she usually felt out in the fields eluded her this time.

She'd been shocked when Frank told her about the money in Prudence's purse. She couldn't imagine what on earth Prudence had been planning to do with it—it certainly wasn't the cash from the handful of tickets they'd sold at the last minute at the potluck. She wondered if robbery had been a motive in Prudence's killing, although that didn't make sense because surely the killer would have taken the cash.

Obviously they didn't know as much about Prudence as they thought if the women in her cheese-making class were to be believed. Shelby had always regarded Prudence as something of an open book—a fidgety old fussbudget to be sure, but essentially harmless. The others seemed to think that Prudence was far more sinister than that—that Daniel was so unhappy he would consider adultery or murder . . . or both!

Shelby finished weeding another row—this time a crop of tender red-leaf lettuce. She glanced at the last few plants and frowned. Some of the leaves were turning yellow. There were a number of possible causes, but one of the most common was powdery mildew. She lifted up one of the leaves and sure enough, there was a white, powdery fungal growth on the top and underside of the older leaves. Powdery mildew thrived in warm, dry conditions—exactly what they'd been having lately. Shelby bit her lip. She couldn't afford for this to spread.

Fortunately there were a number of organic solutions to the problem, including mixtures made with milk, garlic, baking soda, or canola oil. It sounded like a witch's brew, but it worked. The last resort was sulfur or copper, but only after all other measures failed to stop the spread of the fungus. Shelby made a mental note to treat all the lettuce with a solution of canola oil, water, and a dash of liquid dishwashing detergent—her go-to blend for dealing with this problem.

By now the sun was straight overhead, and Shelby could feel beads of perspiration forming on the back of her neck and running down her back. Her stomach was rumbling, too—time for lunch and a cold drink. It had been hours since breakfast.

She had just stepped into the kitchen when her phone rang. Shelby grabbed the receiver with one hand and the handle to the fridge with the other. "Hello?"

"Hey, girlfriend, it's Kelly. Are you busy?"

Shelby looked at the clock. She had planned to spend the afternoon starting some yogurt since Matt said they were running out of her herbed yogurt cheese at the General Store. And then she wanted to take care of the mildew on the lettuce before it spread any further.

Kelly must have sensed her hesitation. "If you're busy, just say so, and I'll call someone else. I'm over at the Mingledorffs' farm, and I need a hand with something."

Shelby couldn't imagine how she could lend a hand with anything veterinary-related.

"My assistants are both tied up over at the Clarks' place. Another heifer is giving birth, but it's an uncomplicated one this time, so I'm letting them handle it. It's the only way they're going to learn."

"What do you need me to do?"

"The Mingledorffs' mare, Lorelei, has colic again. It seems to strike her as regularly as the full moon, poor thing. I keep telling them more fiber in her feed, but . . . anyway, I want to administer some mineral oil via a nasogastric tube, and I need someone to hold the twitch for me."

Shelby knew a little about horses—she'd been riding since she was five years old—but they'd never kept horses on the farm. She did know that colic was potentially very dangerous, though. But what on earth was a twitch?

"Where do the Mingledorffs live?" Shelby asked as she scrounged around in a junk drawer for a piece of paper and a functioning pen or pencil.

Kelly gave her the address.

Shelby scribbled it down and hung up. She opened the refrigerator and grabbed a hunk of cheese, but a real lunch would have to wait until she got back. She tucked the scrap of paper with the Mingledorffs' address on it in her purse and headed out.

The Mingledorffs weren't far, and Shelby was pulling into their drive barely ten minutes later. She parked her car in front of their weather-beaten farmhouse and began walking across the field toward the stable in the distance.

As she got closer, she heard neighing overlaid with Kelly's soothing tones. The stable was in considerably better condition than the house had looked to be—it was obvious where the Mingledorffs' priorities lay. Shelby pushed open the door. All the stalls but one were empty—Shelby had noticed the other horses out in the field on her walk over.

"Is that you?" Kelly's head, with its mop of unruly red hair, popped out of one of the stalls. "Thanks so much for coming."

"I hope I can help. I know next to nothing about horses."

"You don't need to. I just need an extra pair of hands." She gestured toward the horse. "Lorelei has colic, and I need to administer a dose of mineral oil, but I need someone to hold the twitch for me."

"Twitch?"

Kelly waved what looked like a stick with a loop on the end of it at Shelby. "This. It attaches to the horse's upper lip and applies pressure. It's hard to believe, but for some reason it calms them down."

Kelly attached the twitch to Lorelei's upper lip. "Here, hold this."

Shelby did as she was told and held on to the rod while Kelly began threading a nasogastric tube through the horse's nose. The mare stood patiently while Kelly worked.

"I hope it's not an impaction," Kelly said as she readied the mineral oil. "That might require an enema."

Shelby felt herself go pale. She really wasn't up for that. Kelly would have to wait for one of her assistants if she was planning on that procedure.

"Seth's mother has been asking me when I'm going to start looking for a wedding gown."

Shelby made a face.

"We haven't even set a date yet. I can't imagine myself in a gown—jeans and a T-shirt are more my style. I'll probably trip and fall flat on my face at the altar."

"I suppose you could get married in jeans if you really wanted to shock Seth's mother. But I'm sure you'll find something that suits you. There are a lot of cute short gowns out there now."

Kelly snorted and it was obvious she wasn't convinced. "Have you heard anything new about Prudence's murder?"

Shelby told her about her cheese-making class and the women's gossip about Prudence.

"Doesn't surprise me," Kelly said, tight-lipped. "I always thought she had a mean streak underneath that holier-than-thou exterior."

"Oh, and I had a visit from Frank."

"An official visit?"

"Yes."

Kelly paused. "Really? What did he want?" She stroked the horse's velvety brown neck. "All done, sweetheart," she murmured in its ear. "You should feel better soon." She turned to Shelby. "It seems to me Frank already asked every question in the book on Sunday."

"It's very odd. He said that they found a thousand dollars in cash in Prudence's purse. He wondered if I had any idea what she was doing with so much money—that maybe it was the money we'd collected from the potluck."

Kelly's hand jerked, and the horse tossed its head. Shelby turned to look at her, and Kelly's face had drained of color.

"What's the matter?" Shelby asked.

7

Dear Reader,

The last thing I expected to find myself doing today was helping Kelly with the Mingledorffs' colicky horse. I was a bit nervous, but the procedure went smoothly, and there was nothing particularly gross or disgusting about it. I just felt very sorry for the poor horse. I hope it feels better soon.

I used to ride when I was younger, but it's been ages since I last did it. Billy and Amelia have had lessons, but neither of them really took to it. Amelia is far more interested in counting down the years, months, days, and hours until she is old enough to start driving. Don't worry—I will warn you to get off the roads in plenty of time! Hopefully by then the farm will be doing a little

better, and we'll be able to afford a second car. Last
year was tough, and we're still recovering.

Kelly is acting rather oddly, and I don't know what
to make of it. We've been friends ever since she opened
her veterinary practice here in Lovett and I had to take
Bitsy in the time she caught that toad and it made her
sick to her stomach.

Shelby looked at her friend. "What's wrong? You look
terrible."

Kelly gave a weak smile and brushed a hand through
her hair. "It's nothing."

"It's not nothing. You got all white all of a sudden.
Something's wrong."

A tear escaped Kelly's eye and slid down her cheek.
She brushed at it impatiently. "That Prudence is a horrible woman," she said, and burst into tears.

Shelby searched the pockets of her cutoffs, but all she
could find was a used tissue that had obviously been
through the wash a couple of times. She was always forgetting to check pockets before doing the laundry. One
time Billy had left a green marker in one of his, and their
clothes had come out looking like some form of pop art.

Kelly gave a final sniffle and smiled at Shelby. "I guess
I'd better tell you the whole sordid thing."

"I'm sure it can't be that bad."

Kelly laughed. "I'll let you be the judge."

"Why don't we go outside? The air is getting rather
stuffy in here."

"Good idea." Kelly gave a smile—a genuine one this
time. "We definitely don't want to be in here when that
mineral oil does its job on old Lorelei's internal plumbing."

Shelby shuddered. "Definitely not." She did not even want to think about what that would entail.

They opened the stable door and stood, breathing in the fresh air.

"Should we go sit down?" Shelby gestured toward an old bench that sat rotting in the sun.

"Think this will hold us?" Kelly asked as they perched gingerly on the worn wooden slats.

Shelby waited, but Kelly didn't immediately say anything. Finally Kelly gave a small groan and turned toward Shelby.

"It all started with Prudence's cat. A Cornish rex."

Shelby raised her eyebrows. "What's that? It sounds fancy." She was used to the common garden variety of cat, like their calico, Patches.

"Cornish rexes were first bred in Cornwall, England, in the early 1950s," Kelly explained. "They have a very distinctive coat—short and slightly curly. Not exactly your run-of-the-mill barn cat." Kelly massaged her forehead with the tips of her fingers. "Anyway, Prudence found the cat through a breeder in Bloomfield Hills and brought it to me for a checkup. She was shelling out some big money for it and wanted to be sure it was healthy. Not that it would really have mattered—Prudence was already crazy about it—named her Cleopatra and bought her toys, a fancy bed, a scratching post, and one of those cat-condo things."

Poor Patches, Shelby thought. She had to be content with napping on their old sofa and sharpening her claws on their already tattered armchair.

"Prudence was obviously going to keep the cat no matter what I said about its health, and I don't blame her—it was a sweet little thing and so pretty." Kelly chewed on her bottom lip. "Unfortunately I was distracted—Seth and I had had an argument the night before and after sleeping on it, I'd decided he was right after all. I couldn't wait to call him and apologize."

Kelly scratched at a spot on her faded T-shirt. Shelby noticed there was a small hole by the hem—had a dog or cat gotten its claws into it, protesting having its temperature taken or the indignities of some other procedure?

"So obviously I was distracted. It's no excuse, I realize that. But I completely missed the fact that poor Cleopatra was deaf."

"Is that such a tragedy?" Shelby didn't understand. Kelly said Prudence already loved the cat.

"Prudence accused me of being in cahoots with the breeder—I had recommended them—another client had purchased Rexes from them and had been very satisfied. She claimed the breeder was paying me to give a false report."

"But you said Prudence kept the cat anyway. . . ."

Kelly sighed. "I know. It doesn't make any sense. All I know is that Prudence threatened to ruin my practice if I didn't pony up the money she'd spent on the cat and then some . . . for pain and suffering, as she put it."

Shelby thought of the money found in Prudence's handbag. "Did you—"

"No," Kelly said immediately. "I wasn't about to let Prudence blackmail me—because that's what it was—blackmail. Although she felt she was merely getting what she was owed."

"But no one would blame you—"

Kelly spun around toward Shelby. "But don't you see? It makes me a perfect suspect for Prudence's murder."

She stifled a sob. "And even worse, I told Seth about it, and I think he . . . he . . . might have given her the thousand dollars that was found in her purse."

"Do you really think Seth would go so far as to do that?"

"I'll admit, it's not like him. We're a lot alike, and I expect he would refuse to let Prudence blackmail me. But what other explanation could there be for Prudence running around with so much money on her?"

Shelby ran her fingers gently over the rough boards of the bench, feeling the shards of splinters beneath her touch. "Let's say Seth did give her the money, just for argument's sake. Then you'd have no reason to be suspected of killing Prudence, right? She promised not to say anything as long as she got her money."

"But what if Seth never planned for her to keep the money? What if he followed her to the potluck and killed her? But then you found Prudence's body before he had the chance to retrieve his cash?"

"But Prudence didn't have her purse with her in the mudroom."

"Exactly. Seth could have killed her there and been looking for her purse when you found Prudence dead and all hell broke loose."

Shelby threw back her head and laughed out loud. "Honestly, Kelly, you've been watching too much television. Besides, Seth is your *fiancé*. Surely you know he's not capable of something that . . . that heinous?"

Kelly stuck her finger in a hole in her jeans and ran it around and around the frayed edges. "You'd like to believe you know someone. I certainly thought I knew Seth. But when I asked him where he was during the potluck—why he didn't come—he . . . he refused to tell me."

Kelly clasped her arms and hunched over as if in pain. "You've got to help me, Shelby."

"Me?" Shelby pointed at herself. "You know I'd do anything for you, but what on earth could I do?"

Kelly turned her head so she was looking at Shelby. "I may be the dog whisperer, but humans talk to you— they tell you things. Maybe you can find out who did kill Prudence."

The thought of playing detective would have amused Shelby if she hadn't been so worried about Kelly. Her friend was still looking rather shaken when Shelby left her.

Shelby had read all the Nancy Drew books as a child— the long winter nights in Michigan were conducive to reading, especially since they hadn't had cable and the selection of shows on the television was quite limited.

But Shelby had no illusions about her detective skills. Besides, this wasn't a book—this was real life. She had no idea how to go about searching for clues and questioning people. She was quite certain the police would solve the mystery of Prudence's murder all by themselves without any help from her.

Bitsy and Jenkins came running down the drive as Shelby pulled in. They followed her into the house and headed straight for the large metal bowl of water Shelby kept in the kitchen. She had water dishes on the porch, by the back door, and in the barn, but the dogs seemed to prefer the one in the kitchen. And of course Bitsy always had to shake her head vigorously after a good long drink, sending water and saliva spraying all over. Shelby had long since given up on keeping the kind of spotless kitchen you saw in magazines and on television sitcoms. Besides, she suspected those people never used the stove or microwave to do anything messier than heat up takeout or boil water.

Shelby rummaged in the fridge, found some leftover tuna salad, and grabbed a fork from the silverware drawer. She sniffed the container briefly—it smelled okay—and took several bites before picking up the phone and dialing Amelia's cell phone number.

"What's up?"

"Amelia?"

"Yes, Mom, it's me. This is my cell phone you dialed— were you expecting someone else?"

Shelby gritted her teeth. It was a stage, she reminded herself. One she'd most likely gone through herself. No sense in making a big deal of it—keep that for the important stuff.

"I wanted to remind you that you have choir practice tonight. I'll need to pick you up around five so you have time for dinner."

There was a long silence on the other end of the phone, and then Shelby heard a voice—a boy's voice—in the background.

"Amelia? Amelia, who is that? It sounds like a boy. You told me you were at Kaylee's house."

Was she getting paranoid? Shelby wondered. Just because Amelia had been talking to Jodi's son at the potluck didn't mean she had progressed to sneaking around.

Amelia's exaggerated sigh was loud and clear. "Mom," she said in that tone that never failed to set Shelby's teeth on edge. "Kaylee has a brother, okay? We're playing a game together. Okay?"

Shelby immediately felt foolish. "I'm sorry, honey. I didn't mean . . . Anyway, I'll pick you up at five, so be ready."

"Fine." The line went dead.

Shame on her for being so suspicious, Shelby thought as she rinsed out the tuna container. She stopped with her hand halfway to the faucet. Amelia had never mentioned Kaylee's brother before. Why not? She gave herself a shake. She was being ridiculous. She had no reason not to trust Amelia.

Shelby pulled her slow cooker out of the cabinet and set it up on the counter. She poured in a gallon of milk and turned it to low. As soon as it reached the right temperature, she would add some starter—half a cup of yogurt she'd saved from a previous batch—and then wrap the pot in a large towel and let it sit overnight. Tomorrow she would strain it and add herbs to make yogurt cheese.

Shelby was wiping down the counter when the front doorbell rang and the door opened almost immediately afterward.

"Yoo-hoo, I'm here," a voice came from the foyer.

"In the kitchen, Bert," Shelby called back.

A tall, spindle-thin woman with steel gray hair bustled into the room. Shelby had known Roberta "Bert" Parker for as long as she could remember. She'd been coming around to Love Blossom Farm ever since Shelby was a little girl, helping out with whatever was necessary, whether it was running the vacuum cleaner or planting seedlings. She was a widow now—her husband had died a good ten years ago of a heart attack. He had been called Ernie, and Bert had never failed to get a kick out of introducing the two of them as *Bert and Ernie*.

Bert was born and raised in Lovett and liked to brag that she'd never been outside the state. As far as she was concerned, you could find anything you wanted in

Michigan—from the Big Lake, as Lake Michigan was known, to the wilds of the Upper Peninsula to college towns like East Lansing and Ann Arbor. Shelby's father used to joke that Bert had been born with gray hair, and no one knew how old she really was. Shelby guessed her to be in her late seventies at least, although she had the bustle and energy of someone much younger.

Today she was helping Shelby with canning. Love Blossom Farm had produced a bumper crop of beets this year and Shelby wanted to put some of them away for the winter. Fortunately, as the children had been eating beets since they were babies, they didn't protest like many of their peers when they appeared on the dinner table.

"What are we doing today?" Bert asked, reaching for the apron Shelby kept on a hook by the refrigerator. She tied it on over her elastic-waist jeans and her T-shirt that read GREAT-GRANDCHILDREN ARE A GIFT FROM GOD.

"Canning beets."

Bert rubbed her hands together. "Excellent. Getting ready for the winter, are you?"

The thought seemed absurd given the warm, sunny day, but Shelby knew the first snow would be falling in a few short months.

"Sorry I missed the church potluck," Bert said, standing at the sink scrubbing her hands with soap. "The neighbor kid, Rusty—he's a daredevil in the making if I ever saw one—fell off his bike and chipped the bone in his elbow. His mama's pickup wouldn't start, so I drove them to the ER. By the time we got out of there, the potluck was nearly over."

Shelby began prepping the beets she'd piled on the counter. They still smelled like the warm earth she'd pulled them from not too long ago.

Bert pointed at the knife in Shelby's hand. "Leave a good two inches on those stems and don't cut off the taproot," she said. "That way your beets will keep more of their color when we boil them."

Bert had told Shelby that dozens of times already—every time Bert helped her can beets, as a matter of fact—but Shelby always pretended that it was news to her.

She slipped the beets into the large pot of boiling water on the stove. Bert stood watch over them like a nanny over her charges.

"Don't want to let them boil too much," she said, stirring the pot. "Just enough so that their skins will slip off and then you'll know they're done."

Shelby nodded. She was getting the jars that they would need later out of the cupboard.

"Quite some goings-on here yesterday apparently," Bert said, fishing a beet out of the water and testing the skin. "Olivia Willoughby called me and told me all about it. I couldn't hardly believe my own ears."

Shelby made a noncommittal sound. She placed the clean jars, one by one, upside down in a pot with a couple of inches of boiling water and turned off the gas. In a few minutes, the jars would be hot and ready for the beets.

Bert faced Shelby with her hands on her hips. "St. Andrews hasn't been the same since Reverend Bostwick retired. Something like this would never have happened if he'd been in charge. I heard this Reverend Mather has had three churches in as many years."

Shelby agreed that Reverend Bostwick had run a tight ship, but she doubted that even he could have prevented a determined killer from murdering Prudence.

"Reverend Mather's sermon yesterday," Bert said as she lifted the cooked beets out of the pot and plunged them into cold water, "was too wishy-washy for my taste. I don't go for all this permissiveness. That's what's wrong with the world these days."

Shelby hadn't interpreted Daniel's sermon as encouraging permissiveness, but she held her tongue. When Bert was on a roll, there was no point in trying to stop her.

Bert jerked her head toward the beets floating in their cold-water bath. "You want these sliced or left whole?"

"Let's slice them. They're on the large side."

Bert grunted. "And now look what's happened—the reverend's wife murdered," she said, returning to the topic of Prudence's death.

"I don't think you can blame Reverend Mather's sermon for that," Shelby said as she filled the canning jars with the cooked beets Bert was methodically slicing.

"I blame Reverend Mather himself," Bert said, plunging her knife into the beet on her cutting board so vigorously that it shot off the counter and rolled under the kitchen table.

Bitsy and Jenkins, who had been sound asleep in opposite corners of the room, both sprang to attention and ran over to ascertain whether this sudden missile was edible or not.

Bert dove under the table with incredible alacrity considering her age, but she was too late—Bitsy had already swallowed the beet whole.

"That's one less for your dinner table, I guess," Bert said, straightening up. Her knees gave a loud crack.

Shelby began pouring boiling water into the prepared

jars. "I don't see how you can blame Reverend Mather for Prudence's death," Shelby said, carefully topping off the last jar.

"I think him taking up with that hussy had something to do with it," Bert hissed as she helped Shelby put the lids on the jars and began placing them in the pressure canner.

"What? What hussy?" Shelby asked, although she could guess who Bert was talking about easily enough.

"Isabel Stone—the one who wears all that gardenia perfume. You can't get within half a mile of her without smelling it. It gets so I can taste it in my mouth."

"Don't you think it's more a matter of her throwing herself at poor Reverend Mather? He doesn't seem to be encouraging her."

Bert was already shaking her head. "That's what we're meant to think."

Shelby frowned at her. "What do you mean?"

Bert began rummaging in the cracked leather handbag she'd deposited earlier on one of the kitchen chairs. She finally pulled out a yellow sticky note with an air of triumph. "Just you read this and see if you don't agree with me."

She handed the note to Shelby. It said—*Isabel, I'll see you at 3 p.m. on Thursday.* It was signed *Daniel.*

"See what I mean?" Bert said, looking over Shelby's shoulder as she read. She poked a long, crooked finger at the slip of paper. "They were planning a rendezvous. That's French for an affair," she whispered even though there were no young, innocent ears anywhere in the vicinity.

"How . . . where did you get this?"

"I found it stuck to the bottom of my shoe when I left church yesterday. It must have been tucked between the pages of the hymnal I was using and fell out. I thought I saw something drop, but I couldn't find whatever it was. No wonder—I was standing on it."

"And you think this means . . ."

Bert gave a brisk nod. "Yup. I think one or the other of them did in the reverend's poor wife so the pair of them could be together."

Dear Reader,

I now have a lovely row of glass jars on my counter glittering with beautiful shades of ruby red and deep purple from my canned beets. I know that many of you are probably thinking—yuck, beets—but they will brighten our dinner plates all winter long. We try to live off our land as much as possible here on Love Blossom Farm, and beets are a crop we can always count on.

Bert was, as usual, a huge help. I don't know what I'd do without her. She's been in our lives for almost as long as I can remember. I have to admit, though, that I was incredibly shocked by that note she showed me. I am sure there must be an innocent explanation no matter what Bert thinks. Life here in Lovett can some-times be on the . . . quiet side . . . and it's tempting to imagine that innocent happenings are more exciting than they are.

I'm off to take Amelia to choir practice, and I'm sure the talk will be all about Prudence's murder. I hope the police solve the case soon so we can go back to the peaceful life we normally live here in Lovett.

"Amelia! Billy! We have to leave *now*," Shelby yelled up the stairs, resisting the urge to stamp her foot.

She heard feet thumping overhead, and Billy appeared at the top of the stairs.

"Do I have to go?"

"Yes. We have to take your sister to church for choir practice."

"Can't I stay here, Mom? I'm old enough."

Shelby hesitated. She was tempted, but with a killer on the loose . . . "No! Get your shoes on and let's get in the car."

Amelia came skulking down the stairs in a pair of cutoff denim shorts that made Shelby's breath catch in her throat.

"Amelia! What did you do with your shorts?"

Amelia gave her mother a sly look. "Nothing. They started to fray, so I trimmed them a bit. They weren't even, so I trimmed them some more and . . . well. . . ."

"You can't wear those to church."

Amelia rolled her eyes. "We'll be wearing our choir robes, Mom. It's going to be *fine*."

There was that word again. Shelby was coming to hate the word *fine*. But there was no time to argue or they would be late. Albert Long, the choir director, did not tolerate *tardiness*, as he always put it. Shelby sometimes wondered if half the choir wasn't habitually late because they had no idea what the word *tardy* meant.

This was one of those times when Shelby missed her late husband something fierce. She was convinced he would be able to handle Amelia much better than she was—didn't daughters look up to their fathers during this period of adolescence? Sometimes she wondered if she ought to give in to the temptation to begin dating so she could provide her children with a male role model. Both Matt Hudson and Jake Taylor had made it very clear they were just waiting for a signal from her.

Shelby finally hustled both children into the car and pulled out of the driveway. As soon as they were seated in the car, Amelia reached out and fiddled with the radio, changing to a station that was playing music that set Shelby's teeth on edge.

Amelia immediately began complaining about having to go to choir practice, but Shelby closed her ears to Amelia's complaints. Her daughter had a beautiful soprano voice that Shelby was ashamed to admit she envied. She herself could barely sing well enough to croak out "Happy Birthday" within the safe confines of a group of other people, and during hymns in church she generally just mouthed the words.

"What did you and Kaylee do today?" Shelby asked as she turned onto the main street that led into the small downtown area of Lovett.

"Oh, you know . . . stuff," Amelia mumbled.

"Stuff? Like what?"

"Just stuff, Mom, okay?" Amelia turned and glared at her mother.

Shelby felt the stirrings of alarm. She remembered the

sound of that boy's voice in the background on the telephone call and had to force herself to clamp her lips shut.

Billy, as the younger sibling, was relegated to the backseat whenever his sister was in the car. He leaned forward and held his index finger an inch from Amelia's shoulder.

"I'm not touching you," he said in a singsong voice.

Amelia ignored him.

"I'm not touching you," he said louder, his finger hovering closer but still not touching.

"Don't be such a *baby*." Amelia sneered.

"Billy, stop that or else," Shelby exploded, turning around to glare at Billy in the backseat. His expression was as innocent as that of the angel on top of the Christmas tree.

"Or else, what?" Amelia asked, momentarily looking up from her cell phone.

Shelby didn't have an answer for that, but she was saved by the fact that they were now pulling into the church parking lot. She was surprised by the number of cars already there. Choir practice during the summer was usually much less well attended. She suspected it was morbid curiosity that had brought everyone out tonight.

They were heading into the building when Billy began to tug on Shelby's arm.

"Mom, there's Zach. Can we go play?"

Shelby hesitated, then said okay. She would have a chance to talk to people and find out what was going on and if anyone knew anything—she at least wanted to find out if Prudence's funeral had been scheduled yet.

Billy and Zach ran inside with a gleeful shout and shot down the corridor toward the church meeting hall, where they would be able to run around and not disturb anyone.

Amelia bolted for the choir room and Shelby found herself standing alone.

"Excuse me," a woman behind her said.

Shelby spun around to find Grace Swanson with her arm linked through her husband's.

"I've persuaded Alan to join our little choir," Grace said with a smile, giving his arm a squeeze. "He has a wonderful baritone voice, and it's a waste to only use it in the shower."

Alan smiled at the joke. "Has there been any news about . . ."

Shelby shook her head. "Not that I know of. I was going to ask you."

"I wonder when the funeral is," Grace said with a frown.

"I don't know," Shelby said, making a mental note to see if Mrs. Willoughby was in her office.

"Poor Daniel," Grace said. "He must still be in shock. Perhaps he hasn't had a chance to make any plans yet."

Alan ran a hand over his chin. "It's possible the police haven't released the . . . body yet."

Shelby and Grace shuddered.

"I should think it was fairly obvious what killed her," Shelby said, flashing back to the scene in the mudroom.

Alan shrugged. "I imagine they still have to go through the motions."

Just then, Mr. Long, the choirmaster, stepped out of the choir room and looked up and down the hall, clearly checking for strays.

"We'd better go," Grace said.

She and Alan said good-bye and continued down the hall, their footsteps quickening as Mr. Long frowned at them.

Shelby mounted the old, creaking stairs to the second

floor. The carpet was worn to the threads in spots, and the original rich colors had faded over the years. The church offices were located on the upper level along with the nursery for the infants and toddlers. The place smelled of damp, causing Shelby to wonder how much money the potluck had brought in. She peeked into the nursery—it hadn't changed much since she used to drop Amelia and Billy off there on Sunday mornings—the same worn playpens and battered plastic toys bearing the teeth marks of several generations of children.

The smell of damp intensified as Shelby made her way down the hall and she noticed two large buckets lined up against the wall. It looked as if the roof was going to need repairing sooner rather than later.

Most of the doors on the second floor were closed, and the hall was quiet and dark except toward the far end, where light spilled out of one of the offices. The worn Oriental runner absorbed the sound of Shelby's footsteps as she continued down the hall toward the open door.

Shelby stood just outside the office and cleared her throat loudly, not wanting to startle anyone who might be inside. She didn't hear any papers rustling or computer keys tapping, so she stuck her head around the edge of the door. The room was empty.

The office chair was pushed away from the desk as if someone had recently gotten up, and the computer monitor hadn't yet gone dark but instead showed a collage of pictures of smiling children of various ages. Mrs. Willoughby must have very recently stepped out.

A door on the far wall led to Reverend Mather's office. It was firmly closed. Shelby wasn't surprised—she hadn't expected Daniel to be back on the job so soon.

Shelby glanced at the computer. Had Mrs. Willoughby already entered the time and date of Prudence's funeral on the church calendar?

Okay, Dear Reader, I know what you're thinking—that I'm more interested in checking the reverend's calendar than checking the date of Prudence's funeral. But I'm not quite ready to admit that to myself.

Shelby peered down the hall, but it was quiet and empty. She sidled closer to the desk and jiggled the computer mouse. The pictures of children faded, and the screen sprang to life. It was open to the church's e-mail program.

Shelby hesitated, listening for any sounds from the hallway, but there were none. She leaned over the desk, grasped the computer mouse, and clicked on the calendar icon. The page for the month of June filled the screen.

Shelby scanned the entries for the coming days. There weren't very many—summer was a quiet time on the church calendar. The earlier Sunday service would be canceled for July and August, and most of the church committees didn't meet again until the fall. Shelby didn't see any entries for Prudence's funeral, although there was the Mason–Stilton wedding scheduled for the coming Sunday. Perhaps plans hadn't been solidified for the funeral yet? Poor Daniel was probably still in shock.

But Shelby did see something interesting—in the square for Thursday at three p.m. was written the name *Isabel Stone.*

||||||||||||||||||||||||

Shelby pulled into the driveway of Love Blossom Farm just as Kelly was about to turn away from her front door. Kelly must have heard the car crunching over the gravel drive, because she stopped as she was about to step off the porch.

Amelia and Billy jumped out of the car, ran ahead, and in through the front door. Shelby hoped the police would release the mudroom soon—having to go in and out of the front of the house was tracking even more dirt than usual into the living room.

Shelby caught up with Kelly, who was waiting for her.

"Perfect timing." Shelby put her arm around Kelly as they walked up the porch steps.

Kelly wasn't looking like her usual cheerful self. There were dark circles under her eyes and lines of strain around her mouth. Even her normally buoyant curls looked deflated and limp.

"Called out late last night?" Shelby asked.

Kelly shook her head. "No, why?"

"No reason," Shelby said, taking in Kelly's worn jeans and a T-shirt advertising a rock concert that had taken place at least a decade ago. "You look a little tired."

Kelly let out a gusty sigh. "I am tired. I didn't sleep well. I kept thinking about Seth and that money in Prudence's purse."

"Let's go inside and pour ourselves a cold drink."

Shelby led the way through the living room and into the kitchen. Kelly perched on one of the kitchen stools with her elbows on the island and her chin in her hands while Shelby retrieved glasses from the cupboard and a pitcher of iced tea from the refrigerator.

"How's this?" Shelby waved the pitcher in Kelly's direction. "Or would you rather have something stronger? I have a bottle of white wine in the fridge."

Kelly rolled her eyes. "Bring on the wine. It's been that kind of day."

Shelby retrieved a wineglass from the cupboard, filled it, and placed it in front of Kelly. She filled a glass for herself and took the stool opposite Kelly across the island.

"You're not seriously worried that Seth had something to do with Prudence's murder, are you?"

"I know it sounds ridiculous, but I can't get it out of my mind. I thought we knew each other quite well, even though it has been something of a whirlwind courtship. Neither of us is getting any younger. . . ."

Shelby had known that Bill McDonald was the one for her almost from the first moment she set eyes on him. They were married three months after they officially started dating in a small ceremony at St. Andrews. Shelby had worn cowboy boots under her wedding gown and they'd celebrated with a large picnic of fried chicken and homemade potato salad on the front lawn of Love Blossom Farm.

Shelby leaned her chin in her hands, mirroring Kelly's pose. "I was hoping to have better news for you." She sighed.

Kelly looked up sharply. "What do you mean?"

"You know Isabel Stone? The woman with all the flowery perfume who is constantly batting her eyes at Daniel and generally throwing herself at him?"

Kelly choked slightly on her sip of wine. "I think everyone knows her by now. Not exactly subtle about her intentions, is she? My daddy always said it wasn't necessarily the fisherman with the flashiest lure who caught the biggest fish."

Shelby went on to explain about Bert finding the note from Daniel to Isabel stuck on the bottom of her shoe.

Kelly's face brightened immediately. "But that makes her the perfect suspect! She murdered Prudence so she could sink her well-manicured claws into Daniel."

"I hate to burst your bubble . . ." Shelby traced the base of her wineglass with her finger.

"But?" Kelly's look of elation turned to one of disappointment.

"I checked the agenda on Mrs. Willoughby's computer, and . . ." Shelby made a face. "The assignation is more like an appointment, since it's noted on the church calendar."

Kelly slumped in her seat. "You're supposed to be finding suspects, not eliminating them."

"I know. I'm sorry."

Kelly brightened slightly. "But that doesn't necessarily mean it wasn't an assignation. Perhaps Daniel had Mrs. Willoughby put it on the calendar to throw people off the scent."

Shelby groaned.

"Hey, no pun intended," Kelly assured her with a smirk.

Shelby paused with her glass halfway to her mouth. "But you know, you could be right—about Daniel attempting to fool people into thinking he's seeing Isabel for a legitimate reason."

"Yes, when it's really for an illegitimate affair."

Shelby stared at a spot on the opposite wall for a minute. "I still can't picture Daniel having an affair. It wouldn't be like him at all. He's a man of the cloth."

Kelly shrugged as she tossed back the last glug of her wine. "Okay, who's our murderer, then—if not Isabel Stone?" She laughed. "Besides Seth, of course. Who would want Prudence dead? What was there to gain? Anything? Maybe it was a random killing."

"What? A killer decided to buy a ticket to the St. Andrews potluck in the hopes of finding an accommodating victim?"

"Well, when you put it like that . . ." Kelly slid off her stool.

"What we need to do is find out more about Prudence. It's always possible that someone from one of Daniel's former churches nursed a grudge of some sort."

Kelly shivered. "It's still so hard to believe. Someone committing murder here in Lovett."

9

Dear Reader,

If you don't understand the term "getting up with the chickens," you certainly would after a few days on a farm! My Rhode Island Reds wake as soon as there's the merest glimmer of light in the sky and immediately begin scratching and squawking for their food. It doesn't matter if it's your birthday, Christmas morning, or the day after you stayed up all night with a colicky baby—they demand to be fed, and pronto. Fortunately I have to be up early anyway if I'm going to get everything done in the daily twenty-four hours allotted to us.

Last night I took the fresh yogurt I'd made and placed it in a sieve lined with multiple layers of cheesecloth. It had been sitting in a bowl in the refrigerator draining overnight. By this morning, all the whey had drained off (remember—save the whey for baking!), leaving the yogurt the consistency of cream cheese— but with much less fat! I will be adding fresh herbs to create a variety of yogurt cheeses. It's wonderful spread on crackers, bagels, toast, or even fresh vegetables.

It's so easy. You can start with commercial yogurt if you want. It's such a good feeling to create something fresh in your own kitchen.

Shelby spooned the drained yogurt into a bowl and put it back in the refrigerator. She grabbed a woven wicker basket from the counter, slipped on her gardening clogs, and headed out the front door. The morning air was still cool and damp. Light mist swirled above the wet ground—Shelby had woken up briefly during the night to hear rain pounding on the roof. She was always happy when Mother Nature watered her gardens for her.

Love Blossom Farm boasted an extensive herb garden with orderly rows of basil, rosemary, parsley, thyme, and more. Some of the plants were perennials and came back every year, while others had to be planted anew each season.

Shelby snipped some herbs, breathing deeply and enjoying the heavenly aroma that arose from their crushed stems. They would be delicious chopped and mixed in with the yogurt cheese.

Back in her kitchen, Shelby stripped off her gardening gloves, kicked off her clogs, sending them spinning in the direction of the blocked-off mudroom, and pulled her knife from the knife block. She sharpened it carefully and set it aside. First she had to wash and dry the herbs, pressing them carefully between several sheets of paper towels.

She was going to add the basil to one batch of cheese,

and the parsley and thyme to another. She made short work of chopping the herbs, splitting the yogurt cheese into two batches and carefully folding them in. You had to be gentle and couldn't stir the yogurt too vigorously or it would separate.

Once that step was completed, Shelby got out a batch of plastic containers she ordered regularly from a factory in northern Michigan and which she had pasted a Love Blossom Farm label on. She filled them carefully and placed them in the basket she'd used to collect the herbs. Now they were ready to be delivered to the Lovett General Store.

At the last minute, she dashed into the downstairs powder room—which doubled as a pantry with rough wooden shelves running along one wall, where Shelby kept some of her canned goods—and ran a powder puff across her nose, slicked on some lip gloss, and stared hopelessly at the tangle of dark curls she optimistically called a hairstyle.

She paused with her comb halfway through a hunk of hair. What had come over her? She rarely worried about her personal appearance. She knew she was attractive, but she had other, more important concerns—like running the farm and bringing up her children. More often than not, she had dirt on her face and under her fingernails.

The thought that seeing Matt Hudson might have something to do with this sudden interest in grooming stopped her in her tracks. She took a deep breath. She wasn't uninterested in dating again right now. She liked men—she just wasn't sure the time was right. The kids needed her, the farm was an enormous amount of work, and she still dreamed about her late husband almost every night.

No matter. She had to go and face Matt Hudson because he was waiting for his herbed yogurt cheese.

Shelby snuck into Billy's room—he was still sleeping soundly. She watched him for a moment—he looked so young and vulnerable with his worn stuffed teddy under his arm. Shelby planted a whisper of a kiss on his forehead.

Amelia was asleep as well—one arm slung over her head and the other tucked under her chin. Shelby shook her gently.

Amelia groaned softly and swished her legs back and forth restlessly.

Shelby shook her again.

"Whaaat?" Amelia said without opening her eyes.

"I'm going to the General Store to deliver some things. Will you keep an ear out for Billy?"

Amelia exhaled heavily. "Fine."

Shelby decided to take the car and backed it down the driveway—she had an old, barely functioning pickup truck as well for when she needed supplies that wouldn't fit in the trunk of a car—but her load was light today and she decided she didn't need it.

The mist that had hovered near the ground earlier had cleared as the sun rose higher in the sky and warmed the air. Shelby rolled down the windows and enjoyed the smell of freshly mown hay, wildflowers, and sunshine as she drove into downtown Lovett.

The Lovett General Store was located at the intersection of the two main roads in town, with the Lovett Feed Store right next door. Shelby pulled into the gravel parking lot that, despite all of Matt's plans, had yet to be paved and parked near the entrance.

She retrieved her basket from the backseat of the car and balanced it on her hip as she pushed open the door to the Lovett General Store. Grocery items were stacked at the front of the shop, seguing to a hardware area, a car parts section, a couple of gardening aisles, some sewing and craft supplies, and finally, at the very back, several racks of outerwear and rain gear. Two bright red kayaks hung from the peaked wooden ceiling.

Matt stood behind the counter, thumbing through a seed catalogue. He rushed to take the basket from Shelby. "What have you brought me?" He peered inside. "Great, some of your yogurt cheese. It's been a big hit. Even Liz Gardener stopped in for some the other day. She said her neighbor had told her about it, and she wanted some for a cocktail party they were throwing."

"I suppose I ought to be impressed that the very elegant Liz Gardener is serving *my* homemade spread at her party."

Matt laughed, and the crinkles around his eyes deepened. "You've really hit the big time, it looks like." He leaned on the counter. "Has there been any news from the police? About poor Prudence's murder?"

Shelby shook her head. "Not a word. I'm still waiting to get my mudroom back, although after what's happened I don't know if I ever want to go in there again." She shuddered.

"How about I give you a hand painting the room?" Matt offered. "If it looks different, it may take away some of the bad associations."

"That's a great idea. That's kind of you to offer."

Matt grinned. "My pleasure."

Shelby had been thinking about doing some redecorating—the house was pretty much as her parents had left it. It was time to put her own stamp on it. And what better place to start than the mudroom?

"Shall we go pick out some paint?" Matt pointed toward the back of the store.

Shelby was startled. Redecorating and painting were just pleasant things to think about—like when she couldn't fall asleep at night. But maybe Matt was right. Why not actually do it? And why not start now?

Matt led the way to the paint section, where the store carried a selection of brushes, rollers, and painter's tape and had a small display of stacked paint cans and a tiered shelving unit stocked with paint chips.

"What colors did you have in mind?" Matt's hand hovered over the paint chips. "Unless you want something basic like white or cream, I'll have to order it for you. We don't have room to stock much. Doesn't take long to get it in, though."

Shelby hesitated. Until now she hadn't given it much thought. Correction—she hadn't given it any thought. Suddenly she wondered how she could have let things slide for so long. No sense in beating herself up over it—the key was to start somewhere. "I do a lot of planting in the mudroom, so I'm thinking maybe something like a sage green?"

Matt turned to the wall of paint chips and selected several cards with glossy dabs of color on them. "Do any of these strike your fancy?"

"Any of these would look lovely." Shelby caught her bottom lip between her teeth. "I think I like this one best." She pointed toward a shade in the middle of the other two.

"How about a touch of terra-cotta as an accent?" Matt turned to the paint chips again, selected one, and handed it to Shelby.

"Oh! That's a wonderful idea." She studied the paint sample. "This is the shade of my flowerpots."

Shelby was so busy envisioning the changes to her mud-room that she nearly ran into a display of cream of mush-room soup on their way back to the checkout counter.

"Whoa," Matt said as he steadied the cans.

Shelby grinned. "I guess I'm excited about your idea."

"I'm glad." Matt slipped behind the register. "As soon as the paint comes in, I'll let you know, and we can get started."

We—the word took Shelby aback for a moment. It had been too long since she'd been part of a *we* with anybody. She had to admit, she rather liked the idea.

"Good morning," Matt called out to someone.

Shelby turned to see a customer had entered. It was a woman, and Shelby thought she remembered her from the potluck—she had a brace on one knee and walked with a slight limp because of it.

"Let me know if I can help you with anything," Matt said to the woman before turning back to Shelby, gestur-ing at the paint chips in her hand. "Hopefully we can turn your mudroom back into your sanctuary again and not a place where a . . . murder was committed." He frowned. "I still don't get it. Who on earth would have wanted to murder Prudence, and why?"

Shelby explained her theory about Isabel Stone. "Even though Daniel noted their appointment in the church cal-endar, that doesn't necessarily mean it wasn't for . . . other purposes." Shelby willed herself not to turn red. "There could still be something going on between them."

"And you think she might have killed Prudence to pave the way for her to become the second Mrs. Daniel Mather?"

The customer had filled her basket by now with a

number of canned goods, a bottle of laundry detergent, and two dozen finishing nails. She approached the counter.

Matt took the basket from her and began ringing up the items as he unloaded them.

Shelby was about to say good-bye when the woman turned to her.

"That was a lovely potluck, wasn't it? I'm sorry I had to leave before all the excitement." Her eyes twinkled. "I wouldn't have gone so early except I'd given a ride to my neighbor Isabel and the heat was affecting her and she wanted to leave. She was feeling a bit poorly. She's rather delicate—not like me." The woman laughed.

"Isabel?"

The woman nodded as she opened her purse and dug out her wallet. "Yes. Isabel Stone. She's a member of St. Andrews—she's the one who wears all those flouncy dresses and drowns herself in perfume?"

"So you left with Isabel before the police arrived?"

The woman nodded again. "Before Prudence was murdered. We said good-bye to her on our way to the car." She gave Shelby a shrewd look. "That's what they're saying— that Prudence was murdered. I heard it at the library yesterday afternoon. Is that even true, do you think?"

Shelby was at a loss for words. If Prudence was still alive when Isabel Stone left the potluck, then Isabel was now out of the running as a suspect.

10

Dear Reader,

I don't know why I hadn't thought about sprucing up the farmhouse before. I guess it takes someone from the outside to see the obvious. It is so kind of Matt to offer to help—I have to admit that I'm looking forward to doing the project with him.

Now that Isabel Stone has been eliminated as a suspect, I don't know where to turn. Daniel? It's hard to picture such a mild-mannered man resorting to something so drastic as murder. Besides, would he have asked me to go looking for Prudence if he was guilty? I suppose he might have done it to throw me off, but I can't picture his being so conniving.

I hope the children are up. I need their help weeding some of the gardens today. Instead I will probably find their breakfast dishes waiting on the counter for me, since it never occurs to either of them to put the dirty plates and silverware in the dishwasher. Bert thinks I let them get away with too much, and I suppose I do. I think I'm trying to make it up to them for the loss of their father. I don't imagine this is exactly the right way to go about it. I will have to learn to put my foot down before something goes wrong. Now that Amelia is approaching her teenage years, there are more dangers lurking than ever before. Sometimes I long for the days when it was so much simpler—my biggest concern was getting her to eat her vegetables. Now we have that whole subject of b-o-y-s to worry about.

Shelby spent the ride back to Love Blossom Farm envisioning her new—in her mind it would be new—mudroom. She realized she hadn't given a single thought to finding Prudence's body in the room—had that been Matt's intention? If so, it was working like a charm.

Bert's dusty and dented old van was parked in the driveway when Shelby arrived home. The vehicle was almost twenty years old and so much paint had rusted off that it was almost impossible to tell what color it had been, but Bert continued to nurse it along. She often joked that she planned to be buried in it.

Bert was in the kitchen when Shelby walked in. She had a basket on the counter filled to the brim with large brown eggs.

"Those Rhode Island Reds sure do know how to produce," Bert said, holding up one of the oversize eggs in her palm. "We've got a couple dozen beauties here." She shook the egg at Shelby. "The Krommendykes who have that farm back behind the Feed Store insisted on buying some exotic breed—Buttercups, I think they're called. Completely useless when it comes to egg laying. I told them so, but they wouldn't listen. Now, you take your Rhode Island Reds like you've got, or your Delawares, and you're going to get good egg production all year long—even in the winter." She made a face. "Except for that useless one you named Paris. I can't help thinking she'd be far more useful to you as Sunday dinner."

Shelby listened politely. Bert had an opinion on just about everything, and it did no good to argue with her.

Shelby laid the paint chips out on the counter and considered them again in the light from the kitchen window.

Bert pointed at the chips. "What's that you've got there?" she asked, her tone suspicious.

"I'm going to do some redecorating—starting with the mudroom. Matt helped me pick out these colors."

Bert peered at the chips, her eyebrows lowered, her mouth a thin, tight line. "I don't see what's wrong with things the way they are now." She threw her hands in the air. "Young people! Always wanting to change things." She shook a finger at Shelby. "This place was fine for your parents and your grandparents before them. No need to go messing with stuff. Leave things well enough alone." And she nodded once as if to say that *that was that*.

Shelby tucked the paint chips away in the kitchen drawer as Bert went back to her eggs. Once the room had been painted, she was quite sure Bert would like it. She certainly wasn't going to let Bert's opinion stop her.

Bert suddenly wheeled around to face Shelby again. "And look at St. Andrews," she said.

Shelby was hard-pressed to make a connection

between painting the mudroom and St. Andrews, so she waited with interest to hear what Bert had to say.

"Changing rectors on us, just like that." She snapped her fingers.

"They didn't do it on purpose," Shelby said. "Reverend Bostwick retired. He had a heart attack and his doctor told him he needed to rest. They had no choice but to find someone new."

"And who did they get?" Bert asked, raising her eyebrows. "A minister who's changed churches three times in three years. What's the matter with him—he have ants in his pants or something? Can't stay in one place long enough to get to know people?" She shook her finger at Shelby again. "Mind you, there's a reason those churches wouldn't have him anymore, and it will come out—don't you worry." With a final sniff, she went back to boxing up the eggs.

Shelby began helping Bert with the eggs. She doubted that there was anything sinister in Daniel Mather's past that led him to change churches three times in as many years. Most likely there was a completely innocent explanation.

A thought occurred to Shelby while she was working, and she nearly dropped the egg she was holding. What if the Mathers hadn't left those churches because of something Daniel had done? What if they had left because of something Prudence had done?

Shelby felt the stirrings of excitement—was she onto something? She'd need to find out what church Daniel had been at before coming to St. Andrews. She had a vague recollection of reading his bio on the St. Andrews Web site. She would check it as soon as she and Bert were finished.

"Have you seen Billy and Amelia?" Shelby asked as they put the last of the eggs in a carton stamped with LOVE BLOSSOM FARM.

Bert grunted. "Billy came down and got himself a bowl of cereal. When he was done, I sent him out to weed the back garden where you've got your green beans growing. Amelia had a piece of cold leftover pizza she found in the refrigerator and then took off, saying she was going to her friend Kaylee's house. I assumed that was okay with you."

"Yes," Shelby said, hoping Bert didn't seize on the slight hesitation in her voice. She had to stop being so suspicious of Amelia—it wasn't fair. Amelia had done nothing wrong, because even though it had alarmed Shelby, she had to admit that talking to a boy was hardly a crime.

||||||||||||||||||||||||||

As soon as Bert left, Shelby made herself a cup of tea and powered up her computer. She found the St. Andrews Web site easily enough and spent a minute or two watching the slide show of the impressive stained glass windows the church boasted. The roof might cave in before they could repair it, but at least the parishioners had their windows to brag about.

Shelby clicked on the tab for administration, and Daniel Mather's picture popped up. She thought the photo must have been taken quite a while ago—Daniel looked younger, with a fuller hairline, and much calmer and less harried than he had the last time she'd seen him.

Shelby read through the brief bio beneath Daniel's picture. There were the usual mentions of college and seminary, plus the names of family members. She found the information she was looking for near the end—Daniel had been the rector of Calvary Church in Cranberry Cove, a town on Lake Michigan that was not quite an hour's drive away.

Shelby briefly thought about all the things that needed to be done that day. And what excuse could she possibly give for showing up at a strange church asking questions about their former rector? She thought of pretending to be new to town and interested in joining the church, but she didn't think she could bring herself to lie like that. She'd be sure to be found out.

On impulse, Shelby brought up her favorite search engine, entered Calvary Church, and clicked on the link. She scrolled through Calvary Church's Web site. It was very similar to the one for St. Andrews. She was about to click off when something caught her eye. She leaned forward to read. VENDORS NEEDED FOR THE ANNUAL CALVARY CHURCH BAZAAR, the headline said. Shelby scanned the rest of the article quickly. A meeting was being held that very afternoon at two to discuss the upcoming bazaar, which, despite being labeled a Christmas bazaar, was actually held at the end of October. The last line read VENDORS WELCOME.

Shelby jumped up from her seat and began pacing the kitchen. What could she offer to sell? Perhaps some of her strawberry and blueberry preserves . . . and maybe some canned vegetables and fruits would be appreciated. She could prepare some cheese, too.

Shelby glanced at the clock. Hopefully Bert could come back and look out for Billy and Amelia when Amelia got home from Kaylee's house. Amelia had been spending an awful lot of time with Kaylee lately. Shelby would have to suggest that next time Amelia invite Kaylee to their house.

Shelby grabbed the phone and dialed Bert's number. Bert grumbled that she needn't have wasted the gas if she'd known Shelby was going to want her to come right back. Shelby smiled—Bert lived barely a mile away, so the trip had hardly drained her gas tank. She murmured copious apologies and hung up.

She needed to make herself presentable—no easy task, she thought, staring into the mirror in her bathroom. Her face was clean even if her hair was going every which way. She pulled it back into a ponytail and pinned it into a reasonable resemblance of a twist.

Shelby opened the drawer where she kept her little-used makeup. She was surprised it hadn't all dried up since the last time she used it. Bill had claimed he never noticed whether she wore makeup or not, which was fine with Shelby.

She glanced in the mirror again. A dash of powder and perhaps some mascara were in order. She was about to go whole hog and apply eye shadow when Billy called from downstairs.

"What's for lunch? I'm starved."

Shelby dropped the eye shadow back in the drawer and slammed it shut.

"Coming," she yelled down the stairs as she slipped out of her shorts and T-shirt and exchanged them for a clean pair of jeans and a white blouse. She looked down at her feet in dismay. She would have to wash them if she planned to wear her sandals. But meanwhile she had a hungry boy to feed.

||||||||||||||||||||||||

Shelby got under way slightly later than planned but hoped to make up the time en route to Calvary Church.

She enjoyed the ride—she was rarely alone in the car, as most of her time behind the wheel was spent ferrying Billy or Amelia to or from something.

Calvary Church was relatively easy to find—Cranberry Cove was a small town with one main street and only one traffic light. The parking lot, which was quite small, was filling up as Shelby pulled in. She followed a young woman in a blue-and-white gingham sundress, which made her look like Dorothy in the *Wizard of Oz,* around to the side of the building and through a door that led into the kitchen.

"Going to the bazaar meeting?" the woman asked as she held the door for Shelby.

"Yes. Do you know where it is?"

"Sure. Just follow me."

They ended up in what looked like an old-fashioned parlor with scratchy overstuffed furniture, dark gloomy wallpaper, and portraits of severe-looking men with varying degrees of facial hair on the walls.

All the armchairs and sofas were already taken, but someone had brought in a number of metal folding chairs and arranged them in a rough circle. Shelby perched on one of them and looked around her. The women were casually dressed, which was a relief. There were no Liz Gardener types in attendance, making everyone else feel worn and dowdy in comparison to her fancy clothes. A number of women were gathered together chatting, but others were sitting by themselves and appeared to be new to the group.

An older woman with sparse white hair came in pushing a walker. She parked it next to one of the folding chairs and maneuvered her way into the seat.

One of the women on the couch jumped to her feet.

She was middle-aged with graying hair and wire-rimmed bifocals.

"Velma," she called to the older woman, who had just sat down. "You come sit here." She patted the sofa cushion and bustled over to where Velma had perched on the folding chair.

She helped Velma to her feet, got her ensconced on the sofa, and then went back to sit next to Shelby.

"I couldn't see letting Velma sit on this hard chair," she confided in a whisper. "She had a hip replacement last year, and it's still painful for her. She's so thin, too—I've got a lot more padding than she has." She laughed and patted her ample hips.

Before Shelby could say anything, she continued. "Personally I don't think her surgeon did a good job. Not a good job at all. She should be healed by now and not still in pain. Dr. Franken, his name is. He did old Mr. Dykesterhouse's hip the year before last, and he's still using a walker. That shouldn't be, you know? I would consider a malpractice suit myself, but that's just me."

Shelby smiled to herself. She'd certainly landed next to the right person. She doubted it would take much prodding to get this woman talking.

"I'm Virginia, by the way." The woman turned toward Shelby and extended her hand. "You're not from around here, are you?"

Shelby squirmed in her seat a bit. "No, I'm from Lovett. It's about an hour away. Reverend Mather told me about your Christmas bazaar." Shelby crossed her fingers behind her back.

"Reverend Mather? He was our rector before the one we've got now."

"He seems like a very nice man."

"Oh, he is," Virginia gushed. "We were so sorry to see him leave."

"He wasn't here very long, was he?"

"No, but it wasn't his fault. It was because of Doris Buiten making such a stink about it."

Shelby hoped she looked interested—but not so interested that she scared Virginia off.

A woman seated in an armchair at the head of the rough circle of chairs began rustling papers and fishing her half glasses from her purse. Shelby hoped she'd hear the rest of Virginia's story before the meeting was called to order.

Shelby lowered her voice to a whisper. "What happened? Why was someone making a stink?"

"It was that wife of his," Virginia hissed back. "We weren't sorry to see the back of her—I can tell you that."

"Prudence? What did she do?" Shelby held her breath as the woman at the head cleared her throat experimentally, obviously preparing to open the meeting.

Fortunately Virginia ignored the attempts to call the meeting to order and continued with the story. "She accused Doris's husband, Boyd, of pocketing money from last year's bazaar." She folded her arms across her chest. "Can you imagine? And there wasn't a shred of truth to it."

"Really?"

Virginia nodded emphatically. "And she accused the sexton of helping himself to some of our church gardening equipment."

"I gather that wasn't true, either?"

"Not a word of it." Virginia's eyes gleamed. "The poor sexton—he's from some foreign country, but he's been here for years working for the church—didn't know what to do. But Doris certainly did. There's no stopping Doris Buiten when she's taken something on. You didn't falsely accuse her husband and get away with it." Virginia paused, lost in thought for a moment.

The woman seated at the head of the group had now started speaking. Conversation slowly died down as she welcomed everyone to the meeting.

"What did Doris do?" Shelby whispered.

"Went straight to the bishop." Virginia pounded one fist into the palm of her other hand. "And he sent the Mathers packing. Offered them a brand-new start somewhere else. It wasn't fair that Daniel had to move because of that wife of his, but what else could be done?"

The woman sitting alongside Shelby and Virginia swiveled around in her seat and gave them a stern look.

Shelby shot back what she hoped was a winning smile and sank lower in her chair. She missed much of what the meeting leader was saying as she thought over what Virginia had told her.

It looked as if the bishop had given Daniel and Prudence their brand-new start in Lovett. But did that necessarily mean Prudence had changed?

Dear Reader,

The drive out to Cranberry Cove was certainly worth it! It looks as if Prudence was the reason the Mathers have been assigned to three churches in three years and it wasn't because of Daniel at all. I've not only learned an interesting fact about Prudence, but I've also arranged to have a booth at Calvary's Christmas bazaar to showcase some of Love Blossom Farm's delicacies. I thought of making some wreaths from the many boxwood bushes planted around the farm, but the bazaar is too early in the season for that. Boxwood is notoriously slow growing, but the bushes here have had a hundred years or more to mature.

This afternoon is my knitting circle at the church. I am completely hopeless at knitting, but I'm desperate to learn. The click-clack of the needles is so soothing, and it's something you can do while watching television so that you don't feel as if you are being totally unproductive while catching up on your favorite shows. The lovely ladies of the church have taken me in hand and are showing me the ropes. So far I've created a scarf with irregularly placed holes that I am insisting are part of the design, although I'm quite sure I'm not fooling anyone but myself! I have no idea what I will do with my masterpiece when it's done—maybe Jenkins and Bitsy would like to have it to play with? Both of them love a good game of tug-of-war. The other ladies are all knitting hats, scarves, and gloves for a sister church in Guatemala, where I suspect it is too warm to need them, but I've never been, so I can't be sure. Perhaps the people living high up in the Andes will be able to use them.

Billy was in the living room watching a movie on the television when Shelby got back to Love Blossom Farm. She stopped and said hello, but he didn't take his eyes from the show. Gone were the days when he'd run to greet her, tackling her around the legs in a warm hug. The thought made her slightly sad—time was going by too quickly.

Shelby found Bert sitting at the kitchen table, reading the local paper when she walked into the room. It was an unaccustomed sight—Bert rarely sat for long. She was always on the move, performing some task or other. When she'd done everything that needed doing, she'd invariably grab the broom and start sweeping the kitchen floor.

Bert pointed to the front page of the paper. "The *Journal* is full of talk about the murder, although as far as I can tell, the reporters don't know much and as usual are making things up. According to this, the police are . . ." Bert paused and slipped on the glasses that hung from a chain around her neck. She traced a paragraph on the front page of the paper with her index finger, and then continued. "The police are pursuing a promising lead." She dropped the paper on the table and pulled off her glasses, letting them rest on her chest. "What do you suppose they mean by that? Do you think they've got their eye on someone?"

Shelby sighed. "I don't know." She thought of Seth and felt a moment of panic. Surely the police weren't pursuing *him*?

"Can't you pump your brother-in-law for info?" Bert folded up the newspaper and pushed it to one side.

Shelby chewed on a ragged edge of her thumbnail. "I'm sure he wouldn't tell me a thing." She'd never known Frank to talk about his work—even at family gatherings and even after a couple of ice-cold beers.

Shelby suddenly glanced at the clock. She'd forgotten all about the time. "Is Amelia home?" She looked toward the ceiling, half expecting to hear music coming from Amelia's bedroom.

"Nope. I haven't seen her since this morning."

Shelby bit her lip. Should she call Amelia and check up on her? That was her first instinct. But would that make her one of those helicopter parents people were always talking about? She decided a quick text was the perfect middle ground.

Shelby was drying her hands when her phone dinged, indicating a message. Amelia had returned her text and was asking if she could stay at Kaylee's for dinner. Shelby sighed. She had been hoping Amelia could stay with Billy while she went to her knitting group, but it didn't seem fair to constantly stick her with babysitting duties. *Fine*, she texted back, wondering if Amelia would catch the irony.

"Billy," Shelby yelled as she walked into the living room. "You're going to have to come with me. Please turn off the television and go wash your hands and face."

"Do I have to?" Billy answered in a wheedling tone.

"Yes, now go." Shelby gave him a push in the direction of the powder room.

Bert was folding up her paper. "I'd stay and keep an eye on him, but tonight's my poker night. It's at my house, so I have to go by the General Store and pick up some chips and pretzels."

"That's fine." Shelby held the front door for Bert. "Have fun tonight."

"I will if I win," Bert said with a wink as she walked toward her car.

"Billy," Shelby yelled. "Let's go."

Sometimes she felt as if all she did was yell. She opened the front door and gave a sharp whistle. Jenkins and Bitsy came bounding up the front steps, their tongues hanging. Jenkins must have been digging again, because his front paws were all muddy. "Inside, you two. I've got to go out."

Billy finally appeared. He'd missed a spot of dirt on the side of his nose. Shelby licked her thumb and rubbed at it. Billy tried to squirm away, but she persisted until it was gone.

"Do I have to go with you?" Billy whined from the back-seat of the car, where Shelby had made sure he was buckled in. "Zach's mom lets him stay home alone sometimes."

The phrase *If Zach jumped off a cliff, would you, too?*

sprang to Shelby's lips, but she squelched it. How many times had she heard her mother say that? And her grandmother, too?

Shelby decided no answer was the best answer and turned her attention to driving. She had to brake suddenly a mile from the church when a group of five wild turkeys decided to waddle slowly across the road. Soon she'd have to be on the lookout for deer. Shelby tapped the steering wheel impatiently. She didn't want to be late.

Billy was still sulking by the time they got to the church, but one of the other women had brought her son along and the two of them took off together to play.

Shelby hesitated leaving the boys to their own devices, but then Bojan, St. Andrews's sexton, came around the corner carrying a broom. He smiled at Shelby and gestured toward the two boys. "Don't worry. I'll keep an eye on them." He gave a wicked grin. "Maybe I'll put them to work, eh?"

The boys looked momentarily panic-stricken and Bojan threw his head back and laughed.

The knitting group was already assembled in the church parlor—a comfortable spot with ancient, overstuffed, chintz-covered sofas and chairs. The click, click, click of the needles punctuated the women's soft conversation. Knitted garments of all sorts dangled from their needles—a blue baby bootie for Coralynne, whose daughter was expecting her first baby in three months, a red scarf for Eleanor, and the very beginnings of a multicolored hat for Mrs. Kendrick.

Shelby was surprised to see Grace Swanson sitting at the end of the sofa. She'd joined the group in the beginning but hadn't been to the meetings in ages. She was working on a red sweater with elaborate cables on the front. She smiled when she saw Shelby and patted the sofa cushion next to her.

The springs on the old couch had given their all a long time ago, and Shelby felt herself drop nearly to the floor as the sofa cushions curved up and enveloped her on either side. Eleanor was on her left, her needles moving with lightning speed. Grace's lips moved silently as she counted stitches.

Shelby pulled her knitting from her bag with a sheepish expression. She'd done barely anything on it since the last time the group met, and what she had accomplished was full of holes and seriously askew. She held it up and regarded it balefully. She'd followed the instructions—what had she done wrong?

"Oh my, dear." Eleanor leaned toward Shelby, her face puckered in concern. "What do we have here?" She fingered the bit of knitting descending from Shelby's needles.

"A scarf?" Shelby said with a complete lack of conviction. She sighed. She was never, ever going to master this knitting thing, so why not stop now?

"Dear, you're dropping stitches." Eleanor pointed to the holes. She sounded like a disapproving schoolteacher.

"I seem to have trouble keeping my stitches on the needles," Shelby said apologetically.

"That's because you're not holding your needles right. Here, let me show you." Eleanor picked up her own knitting. "Like this." She held the needles toward Shelby. "Hold them like you would a pencil."

Coralynne stopped what she was doing and leaned

toward Shelby and Eleanor, her reading glasses swinging on their chain. "That's not how I hold mine," she said authoritatively, her face inches from Eleanor's.

"It's the way my grandmother taught me," Eleanor shot back, "and it's served me well all these years." She stared at Coralynne as if challenging her to a duel.

Shelby looked from one to the other of them, wondering how to defuse the situation before it escalated into full-blown war. She giggled hysterically at the vision she had of Eleanor piercing Coralynne with a knitting needle and Coralynne retaliating by putting Eleanor's eye out with one of hers.

Coralynne gave an exasperated sigh, her enormous bosom rising and falling like a bellows. "Dear." She put a hand on Shelby's arm. "Find a position that's comfortable for you. That's the important thing."

Dear Reader, Shelby thought, *I don't think that the way I'm holding my needles is the problem here. I think it is my complete and utter lack of skill and talent as it relates to knitting that's the problem.*

Eleanor began to open her mouth again, and Shelby knew she had to do something to stop this argument or there might be a very unseemly fight in the parlor of St. Andrews Church. She had another vision of the two older women rolling around on the worn Oriental rug, wrestling each other, and had to stifle a laugh.

"I heard something interesting today about Reverend Mather." Shelby looked around to make sure Daniel wasn't lurking nearby—tucked in a closet or hiding behind one of the overstuffed chairs.

The click-clack of knitting needles ceased all at once, and the silence in the room became nearly palpable.

"You know how the Mathers have been assigned to three different churches in the last three years?" Shelby asked, looking around.

The women nodded, all their attention now focused on Shelby.

"I couldn't imagine why, since Reverend Mather seems to be such a fine rector and certainly a very nice man," Shelby said.

A murmur of agreement went around the group, and several women nodded at each other.

"I think he does an excellent job," Eleanor said, her face taking on a look that dared anyone to disagree with her.

Clearly Coralynne was up for the challenge. She sniffed loudly. "I don't know about that—I do believe things ran more smoothly when Reverend Bostwick was in charge."

Shelby hastened to continue. "Well, I mistakenly assumed that Reverend Mather must have done something to upset or anger his congregations. Something serious that caused him to be removed from his posts."

"That's what we all thought," Eleanor said, her knitting forgotten in her lap, her eyes focused on Shelby.

"But it wasn't Reverend Mather who was causing the trouble." Shelby paused for breath and looked around the room. "It was his wife, Prudence."

"I have to say I'm not surprised," Coralynne said with relish, puffing out her rather ample chest.

"Nor am I," Eleanor said, for once in agreement with Coralynne.

They both leaned toward Shelby.

Mrs. Kendrick suddenly spoke up. "I agree that Prudence's personality could be a bit . . . annoying at times. All that hand wringing is terribly tedious, but that's hardly cause for dismissing her husband." She looked around as if seeking support.

"It seems that Prudence was given to accusing others of things they didn't actually do," Shelby said. "When they were at Calvary Church in Cranberry Cove, she accused one parishioner of siphoning money from the proceeds of the church's annual Christmas bazaar, and she blamed the sexton for some missing garden equipment."

"I wish I could say that surprises me, but it doesn't," Grace said suddenly, her lips thinned to a grim, straight line. "She accused Earl Bylsma of skimming from the collection plate here at St. Andrews. It upset the poor man so much he resigned his position as head usher."

So that was what had happened to Earl! Shelby had suspected there was more to it than what he'd admitted to her. Shelby didn't believe Prudence's accusations for a minute—Earl had been a pillar of the church for almost as long as Shelby had been going. But she could see how it could easily cause trouble for Earl—even if nothing was ever proven, the lie would linger and tarnish his reputation.

Eleanor picked up her knitting again. "I can see how Prudence's penchant for spreading rumors could cause trouble within Reverend Mather's parish. No wonder the poor man was asked to move on."

"And not just that," Coralynne said, pointing at Shelby and Eleanor with her knitting needle. "Imagine the secrets the wife of a minister is privy to!"

"You don't think Reverend Mather would—" Eleanor began, but Coralynne interrupted her.

"Pillow talk," she said smugly. "Besides, I doubt Reverend Mather could stand up to the sort of relentless urging Prudence was capable of to get him to reveal what went on behind his closed office door."

Eleanor sniffed. "Urging? Bullying is more like it."

Suddenly the church bells began to peal loudly.

The ladies all looked at one another.

"What on earth?" Eleanor put down her knitting and stood up. "Why are the bells ringing? It can't be six o'clock already."

Mrs. Kendrick looked at her watch. "It isn't. And there's no service in the church today that I know of."

They all looked up when they heard someone dashing past the open door of the parlor. It was the sexton, Bojan, with Mrs. Willoughby right behind him, her face flushed and her breath coming in huge gulps. Almost as one, the ladies abandoned their knitting to follow the two down the hall, out the door, and across the courtyard to the church itself. They certainly made a strange procession, Shelby thought as she brought up the rear.

The bells continued to peal, albeit to a strangely irregular rhythm. Who on earth could be ringing them? Shelby thought. The answer that came to mind nearly brought her up short, and she stumbled on the uneven edge of one of the pieces of slate that made up the path between the parish hall and the church itself.

Grace put out a hand and grasped Shelby's elbow. "Do be careful. These stones are treacherous."

Shelby's suspicions were confirmed when they trooped into the church to find Billy, rope in hand, energetically pulling it up and down, ringing the church bell with youthful vigor.

While her knitting group tut-tutted, Shelby dragged

Billy away from the bell and out the door. She was too furious to even speak as she marched him back to the parlor to retrieve her abandoned knitting. She nodded good-bye to the ladies. She knew her face was flaming red, both from anger and embarrassment.

Shelby stomped toward the car, where she wordlessly held open the car door and pointed inside.

Billy's expression was sulky, but he didn't protest.

"You know you're grounded for the rest of your life," was all Shelby said as they made the trip back to Love Blossom Farm.

Billy did not seem particularly distressed by her pronouncement, but he bolted from the car as soon as they pulled into the driveway and promptly disappeared around the back of the farmhouse.

Shelby was opening the front door when she heard a car bumping over the ruts in the driveway. She looked over her shoulder to see Frank getting out of his pickup truck. Once again he was casually dressed in jeans, a short-sleeved oxford shirt, and a baseball cap, and looked like anything but the razor-sharp detective he was.

Shelby waited for him on the front steps, watching as he approached. It was almost like seeing Bill walk toward her. She forced that thought from her mind.

Frank touched the brim of his hat briefly and smiled. "I hope I'm not interrupting anything."

"No, not at all. Come on in."

Shelby led him into the living room, where she had to chase Bitsy and Jenkins off the furniture. Frank took the chair recently vacated by Jenkins, and Shelby perched on the edge of the sofa. She couldn't imagine why Frank wanted to talk to her—maybe there was some news?

"I have some good news," Frank said, almost as if he'd been reading Shelby's mind.

Shelby raised her eyebrows. She could use some good news.

"We're finished with your mudroom, and you can take down the police tape. I hope it hasn't been too much of an inconvenience."

"Have you discovered anything?" Shelby asked with a bit of trepidation. She couldn't tell from the expression on Frank's face—he had a well-developed poker face, unlike his brother, Bill, who had been an open book.

Frank scowled. "Nothing, unfortunately. Despite all the hours we've been putting in. Nancy is complaining that I'm never home. We're still trying to find out why Prudence was carrying so much money around in her purse. Her husband said he had no idea what she was doing with it." Frank paused. "If he's to be believed. . . ." He put both hands flat on his thighs and stood up. "Then again, the money might have nothing to do with her murder at all."

Shelby gave a tight smile. She couldn't help thinking about Kelly and the possibility that Seth had paid Prudence off. "Didn't you find any fingerprints or anything like that?"

Frank shook his head. "No such luck. We think the killer may have used your gardening gloves. They were sitting out by the sink. We'll get them back to you as soon as we're finished with them."

Shelby thought a pair of her gloves had been missing. She hadn't realized the police had taken them as evidence. She shuddered to think that something of hers had played a part, no matter how small, in Prudence's murder. "Please throw them away when you're done with them. I don't want them back after . . ."

"Sure. I understand." Frank flashed a quick smile and put his arm around Shelby's shoulders. "Are you sure you're okay? This can't be easy for you."

They were at the front door, and Shelby opened it. "I'm okay." She put a hand on Frank's arm. "Say hello to Nancy for me."

A funny look came over Frank's face. "Sure," he said as he began walking back to his pickup.

Shelby closed the door behind him and leaned against it for a moment. She gave a sigh of relief, then headed toward the mudroom. She couldn't wait to rip down the yellow-and-black crime scene tape and begin to return the room to normal. If only their lives could be returned to normal that easily.

Shelby heard the front door open and stopped halfway through the kitchen. They never did lock their doors during the day. The one time her parents had taken her on a weekend trip to Mackinac Island, they had had to hunt for a key to the front door. Lovett was that sort of place, and it hadn't changed much over the years. Although now, with Prudence's murder, Shelby wasn't so sure anymore.

"Shelby?"

Shelby heard Kelly's voice coming from the living room, followed by her footsteps in the hall.

"You just missed Frank," Shelby said when her friend came into the room.

"I know. I saw his truck in your driveway and parked down the road until I saw him leave. I'm afraid he'll start asking me questions." She rolled her eyes. "Is there anything new?"

"Not really, but I can take down the crime scene tape and get my mudroom back."

"Wonderful. Want some help?"

"Sure."

They went out to the mudroom, where they started tearing down the black-and-yellow tape.

"This is surprisingly satisfying," Shelby said as she gathered the tape together and stuffed it into a garbage can.

"I'll be glad when this nightmare is over," Kelly said, plopping into the wicker rocking chair next to the door to the kitchen.

"Be careful," Shelby warned her. "The seat on that chair is starting to go. I keep meaning to get it fixed, but—"

"I'm thinking of calling off the wedding," Kelly blurted out. "Or at least postponing it."

"But why?" Shelby turned from her gardening table, where she had righted a toppled flowerpot and was sweeping up the spilled dirt. Had it been overturned in Prudence's struggle with her killer? Shelby shuddered. She couldn't wait till she and Matt transformed the room—perhaps the redecorating would help slay the ghosts that had taken possession of it.

"Seth refuses to tell me where he was during the potluck. I don't know why. If it was something innocent, why not just tell me, for goodness' sake?" Kelly picked at a loose piece of wicker on the edge of the chair.

"Are you still worried that he might have given Prudence that cash the police found in her purse?"

"Yes. No." Kelly wrung her hands. "I don't know." She buried her face in her hands. "He's hiding something, I know that." She looked at Shelby and there were tears in her eyes.

Shelby took a broom from the corner where it had been leaning, and began sweeping around the gardening table. "Maybe it's something he's embarrassed about?"

"Like what?"

"I don't know." In Shelby's experience it took an awful lot to embarrass a man unless it related in some way to his athletic prowess or anything else where competition was involved. Walking out of the men's room trailing a long strand of toilet paper wouldn't embarrass him—it would just make him laugh.

Kelly groaned and ran her hands through her long tangle of red hair, dislodging a couple of pieces of hay.

"I did find out something interesting," Shelby said as she swept the accumulation of soil, dust, and dried, curling leaves into a pile. She reached out with the broom and snagged the hay that Kelly must have brought in with her. "You know how we wondered why Daniel had been assigned to three different churches in three years?"

"Yes. It seemed . . . odd. He's doing a good job here at St. Andrews, or so everyone says."

Shelby leaned on her broom. "It turns out it wasn't Daniel's fault that things didn't work out in his other parishes." She paused dramatically. "It was Prudence's."

Kelly shot bolt upright in her chair, nearly upsetting it. "Prudence? Dear, sweet, butter-wouldn't-melt-in-her-mouth, hand-wringing Prudence?"

Shelby laughed. "Yes, that Prudence."

"What did she do? Have an affair with the choirmaster?"

This time Shelby roared. Kelly joined in. It was good to laugh. Even though it had only been a couple of days, it felt as if this murder had been hanging over their heads for ages.

Kelly wiped her eyes with the sleeve of her T-shirt. "Since the idea of an affair with the choirmaster seems too far-fetched, what do you think Prudence really did to get herself and her poor husband banished to Lovett?"

"According to the ladies in Cranberry Cove, their last parish, Prudence made a number of false accusations against members of the church. She claimed the sexton stole gardening equipment belonging to the church and that another member helped himself to some of the proceeds from their annual Christmas bazaar."

"And it wasn't true?"

"Apparently not. But she stirred up a lot and got the parishioners riled up to the point where Daniel could no longer do an effective job and the bishop made the decision to move him to another church."

Kelly shook her head. "Poor Reverend Mather."

"And there's more."

"Seriously?"

Shelby nodded. "Grace Swanson, who is in the St. Andrews knitting group, told me that Prudence accused Earl Bylsma of helping himself to money from the collection plate on Sundays."

Kelly whistled. "Is that why he quit ushering? I thought he was going to do that forever. He looked so proud every Sunday—giving that serious little bow before handing you the program and leading you to your seat."

"I know." Shelby swept the broom into the very corner of the mudroom.

Kelly stopped rocking abruptly. "But don't you think that gives him a motive for murder? He must have been furious with Prudence—his reputation ruined even though nothing was proven. I know if it were me, I'd certainly feel homicidal."

"But Earl? He's so mild-mannered and . . . and . . ."

"You see stories like it all the time in the paper." Kelly leaned forward eagerly and nearly catapulted out of the rocking chair. "The Casper Milquetoast who snaps and murders his nagging wife. Earl was here at the potluck—he had a motive and he found the means."

Shelby had a sudden flashback to the slow cooker cord around Prudence's neck.

"But who's to say it wasn't Daniel himself who snapped?" she said. "By all accounts, he was henpecked half to death."

"True," Kelly said.

"Although I can't see Daniel in the role of murderer." Shelby slumped against the broom handle. "Besides, how will we ever prove that either of them did it?"

12

Dear Reader,

I think it's going to be a late night. I promised to make my cottage cheese pies for Prudence's funeral luncheon tomorrow. Mrs. Willoughby is arranging everything for Daniel, and she asked me especially if I would mind making some. I don't mind at all—for some reason I feel responsible for Prudence's death, even though I know that's ridiculous. Just because she met her end in my mudroom doesn't mean I need to feel guilty about it.

Billy and I had a quick dinner of macaroni and cheese—not the kind from the box, of course, but homemade with real cheese and milk from Jake's cows. Billy is watching something on television—there's a lot of shooting but no swearing or naked women, so I suppose it's okay.

Amelia isn't home yet. She and Kaylee have obviously become very close—almost like sisters. I'm glad she has this relationship. So many girls her age are only interested in boys, boys, boys. And while I like boys plenty myself, it's your girlfriends who will see you through the hard times. Don't you agree, Dear Reader?

Shelby cleaned away the dinner dishes, scraping the hardened bits of macaroni off Billy's plate, rinsing them, and stacking them in the dishwasher. She glanced at the clock. It was seven o'clock. Surely Amelia was finished with dinner at Kaylee's house by now. They didn't keep New York hours in Lovett—dinner was usually on the table by five o'clock—six at the latest for those who worked in offices or in town and not in the fields. For Lovett residents, it was early to bed and early to rise, just like in the old proverb.

Shelby felt weariness threaten to melt her bones. She put the kettle on the stove and got out a tea bag. She'd make herself a good, strong cup of tea. While the water heated, she grabbed the telephone and dialed Amelia's cell phone. Shelby had been adamantly opposed to purchasing a cell phone for her daughter, but she was soon convinced of the usefulness of it and gave in. She'd already told Amelia that not answering her mother's phone calls would result in grounding plus the confiscation of said phone for possibly the rest of her life.

The phone rang once, twice, three times, four times. Soon the call would go to voice mail. Shelby felt a combination of irritation and worry. She picked at the ragged cuticle on her thumbnail while she waited. Finally Amelia's voice came over the line.

"Yeah?"

"Amelia, it's getting late. Do you need me to pick you up?" Shelby devoutly hoped not—she needed to get going on those pies if she was going to manage to eke out five hours of sleep before the chickens demanded to be fed.

"No, Kaylee's mom is bringing me home."

There was a muffled giggle in the background. The hair on the back of Shelby's neck stood up. It didn't sound like Kaylee. It sounded like a boy, but she wasn't sure. Besides, Amelia said Kaylee had a brother, so she was probably being paranoid again. "Okay, but make it soon."

"Fine."

Amelia disconnected.

Fine, Shelby muttered to herself. *Dear Reader, how is it that a simple word with four ordinary letters can be said in such a tone that it becomes fraught with so much meaning and emotion—irritation, annoyance, disdain . . . ?*

Shelby shook her head and got out a blue-and-white mixing bowl that was probably as old as Love Blossom Farm itself. It had been passed down from generation to generation and no one could quite remember when it had actually been purchased or by whom.

She measured out flour, butter, and ice water for her pastry crust. She had just finished fitting the dough into the first pie plate when she heard the front door open.

"Amelia?"

No answer.

There were footsteps on the stairs and the slam of a bedroom door. Shelby went into the living room, wiping her hands on her apron, and saw the glare of retreating headlights through the front windows.

She shrugged and went back to her pies, but she

couldn't shake the feeling of something being off. Amelia was definitely up to something. The question was what?

||||||||||||||||||||||||

The next morning Shelby was up and on her feet even before the chickens, which was no small feat. She pushed aside the curtain in her bedroom and looked out the window as she shrugged on her robe. It looked as if it was threatening to rain. It was suitable weather for a funeral—certainly more so than a bright sunny day would have been.

She quickly straightened the sheets and pulled up the comforter. The bed didn't get nearly as messy as it had when Bill was alive. Shelby pushed the thought from her mind and started down the stairs to the kitchen.

Her pies were completed and ready to be packed into the waiting boxes. She was also making several salads with her heirloom tomatoes and gourmet lettuce varieties. Other women from the church had signed up to bring various casseroles, vegetable platters, homemade bread, and fruit trays. If Prudence had been alive she would have been bringing her slow-cooker meatballs, Shelby thought somewhat irrationally. But of course Prudence was gone, and all of this was being prepared for her funeral.

Shelby scrambled herself some eggs and ate them out of the frying pan while standing over the sink. The sky was still black outside the kitchen window and the temptation to crawl back into bed was strong. Instead she mounted the stairs to her bedroom and quickly changed into a pair of jeans and a T-shirt.

Shelby fed the chickens, who seemed particularly

fidgety and demanding this morning—perhaps they sensed the storm that was brewing. Shelby glanced at the sky, where she could make out ugly dark clouds moving swiftly overhead. It was now light enough to pick some lettuce and tomatoes for her salads. She passed the patch of garden where the enormous leaves on the zucchini plants made her think of the old children's story *Jack and the Beanstalk*.

Billy was growing a zucchini especially for the county fair in September. They would leave it on the vine to let it grow as large as possible—Shelby crossed her fingers that the rabbits wouldn't go after it. The county fair had always been a favorite of the children's, and she and Bill had taken them every fall. Would Amelia even want to go this year? Shelby and Bill had gone while they were courting—Shelby remembered sneaking a kiss behind the barn, where the horses were stabled. The smell of manure still brought back the memory.

There would be hayrides, chickens, pigs, and cows raised by the kids in the local 4-H club, and Billy's favorite—the largest vegetable contest. Every year there were pumpkins weighing nearly as much as a small car and other gigantic produce that made you feel as if you had suddenly been transported to the land of the giants. Liz Gardener had won the last two years with her prize squash, but Billy was determined that this year his zucchini would be the largest. Shelby hoped he wouldn't be disappointed if he didn't win.

Shelby finished collecting the makings for her salad and headed back to the farmhouse, where she rinsed the lettuce and washed the tomatoes. After drying them, she began assembling her salads.

She was slicing tomatoes when Billy wandered into the kitchen, his eyes still puckered with sleep, his cowlick more pronounced than ever. She fixed him a bowl of oatmeal with cinnamon and sugar and then began wrapping up her pies.

Shelby hoped Amelia would be up soon, since she had to head to the church, but she knew that was wishful thinking. Several shouts up the stairs finally brought a sleepy and cranky Amelia to the landing.

"Watch your brother, okay? I have to deliver some things to the church."

"Fine."

Amelia flounced downstairs in her bare feet, dropped into a chair in the living room, and immediately began texting on her phone.

Shelby sighed and carried the first batch of pies out to the car. Two trips later, she was all loaded and ready to go. She was about half a mile from home when fat drops of rain began to splatter across her windshield, creating a blurry landscape of cornfields interspersed with farmhouses that were weather-beaten to pastel hues.

Shelby wasn't looking forward to making numerous trips between her car and the church, especially as the rain had intensified and was now a steady downpour. Mrs. Kendrick from her knitting group was getting out of her car as Shelby pulled into the space next to her in the church parking lot.

"Do you need some help?" she asked, turning to Shelby after beeping her car locked.

"That would be wonderful."

Shelby opened her trunk, where she'd stashed the pies

in individual boxes inside a large cardboard carton. Hopefully they hadn't shifted too much during the car ride.

With her hands full, Shelby couldn't hold an umbrella. Mrs. Kendrick had had the foresight to don one of those plastic rain hats they used to give out at savings banks— Shelby didn't know if they even made them anymore. Fortunately it didn't matter what happened to her hair, since she'd pulled it back and stuck it up on top of her head in a tenuous bun that wobbled as she walked.

Shelby had been determined to carry everything in one trip this time, and could barely see over the stack of boxes in her arms. She prayed fervently that she wouldn't trip and spew her hard work all over the slate path.

"What's that smell?" Mrs. Kendrick sniffed loudly. "Someone is smoking."

Shelby suddenly got a whiff of it, too. She looked around and spotted a young man squatting under the partial shelter of a tree, puffing on a cigarette. As they got closer, Shelby thought he looked nearer to thirty than twenty. His dark hair was long, and he had that small triangular patch of hair in the middle of his chin that seemed to be so popular with young men these days. He had a disreputable air about him, although Shelby couldn't put her finger on exactly what made her think that.

Mrs. Willoughby must have seen them coming, because she was standing at the entrance to the church kitchen, holding the door ajar. Shelby edged her way around Mrs. Willoughby's considerable bulk and into the room.

"Set the things on that table over there." Mrs. Willoughby pointed toward a long metal table that had an industrial-sized pot rack suspended over it.

Shelby gladly set down the boxes of pies and breathed a sigh of relief at their safe arrival. Mrs. Kendrick put the bowls of salad she had carried in for Shelby on the table and untied her rain hat.

"Is it absolutely frightful out there?" Mrs. Willoughby asked, adjusting the belt on her dress, which encircled her waist much like the equator circling the globe.

"The rain has picked up." Mrs. Kendrick shook out her rain hat, folded it back up, and slid it into its plastic pouch. "Perfect weather for a funeral, if you ask me."

A dreamy look came over Mrs. Willoughby's face, and she put her hand to her bosom. "*Be still, sad heart! And cease repining; behind the clouds is the sun still shining; thy fate is the common fate of all, into each life some rain must fall.*"

Shelby and Mrs. Kendrick stared at her openmouthed.

"Longfellow," Mrs. Willoughby said sheepishly. "I was an English literature major at Albion College until I met my Richard and left to get married."

Mrs. Willoughby shook herself as if shaking off the rain and her face resumed its usual businesslike expression. "What do we have here?" She inspected the boxes Shelby had set out on the table.

"Cottage cheese pies. Do you want me to take them out of the boxes?"

Mrs. Willoughby clapped her hands together. She inhaled deeply. "I remember your pies from the potluck. Absolutely heavenly! Did you make the cheese yourself?"

"Yes." Shelby nodded as she slid the last pie out of the box. "And the milk is fresh from Jake Taylor's cows."

"It doesn't get fresher than that." Mrs. Willoughby giggled.

Mrs. Kendrick peered at one of the pies, then turned to Mrs. Willoughby. "Who was that rather unsavory young man outside? He's crouched under that large elm tree near the door smoking a cigarette." She shuddered. "Nasty things. My late husband used to smoke. It took me a year and a half to get the smell out of the house after he died."

Mrs. Willoughby rolled her watery blue eyes heavenward, pursed her lips, and shook her head. "Him! They say the apple falls close to the tree, but obviously not in this case. Poor Prudence. I don't know how she could bear it." She raised her chin and sniffed. "I feel quite blessed that my son has a good job and a future ahead of him."

"But who is he?" Mrs. Kendrick asked with a querulous look on her face.

Mrs. Willoughby was known to go off on a tangent at the drop of a hat, and reining her back in again was not for the faint of heart.

Mrs. Willoughby lowered her voice to a near whisper, even though they were alone in the kitchen. "He's Prudence's son."

Mrs. Kendrick gave a gasp, and Shelby was hard-pressed to repress one herself.

"Her son!" Mrs. Kendrick exclaimed. "Well, I never!" She looked slightly affronted—as if this information had been withheld from her on purpose.

Mrs. Willoughby nodded again, setting her stiff gray curls quivering. "It seems Prudence was married before— before marrying Reverend Mather, that is."

"The son hasn't been around before, has he?" Shelby grabbed a paper towel from the roll on the counter and wiped off a bit of cottage cheese that had gotten onto her thumb as she was taking the pies out of their boxes. "I don't remember seeing him at church."

"He just showed up out of the blue," Mrs. Willoughby said. "Reverend Mather was quite put out, I can tell you that. It seems that Wallace—that's the young man's name—and Prudence had had a falling-out two years ago and hadn't seen each other since. What a fine thing showing up now that she's dead." Mrs. Willoughby's many chins quivered in indignation.

"Is he here for the funeral?" Mrs. Kendrick asked.

Mrs. Willoughby made a sound that was halfway between a laugh and a snort. "Hardly. He's come here to get some money; what else?"

"Really?"

Shelby must have sounded skeptical, because Mrs. Willoughby immediately continued. "He's already been after Reverend Mather for some cash. I heard them arguing about it. The door to the reverend's office was closed, but their voices were raised, and I could hardly help hearing every word."

Dear Reader, what do you think the odds are that Mrs. Willoughby had her ear pressed to the door?

"The poor reverend can hardly spare any money—he has holes in his shoes as it is." She shook her index finger at Shelby and Mrs. Kendrick. "What that young man needs is to put in an honest day's work and collect an honest wage. But I can tell by the looks of him that he'd rather get other people to pay his way."

"Did he think he was going to get money out of Prudence?" Mrs. Kendrick scowled. "The lot of a pastor's wife is not a rich one. Unless Prudence had means of her own."

"I shouldn't think so," Mrs. Willoughby said.

Shelby flashed back to the thousand dollars in Prudence's purse the day of the potluck. Where had that money come from? Was it from Seth, or, as Mrs. Kendrick had suggested, did Prudence have a bank account of her own?

13

Dear Reader,

Prudence's funeral was well attended. In a small town like Lovett, people pull together during times of crisis. The Women's Auxiliary has already arranged for meals to be delivered to Daniel for the next several weeks. The ladies of Lovett are all getting out their casserole recipes, determined to outdo each other. And every widow and divorcée in town is aflutter now that Daniel is a widower and will eventually be back on the market so to speak—the pool of marriageable middle-aged men being quite small here—minuscule, in fact. And Daniel's not the type of man to stay alone for long—he'd be lost without someone telling him what to do.

The service was lovely. Prudence would have enjoyed

the hymns—Alan Swanson sang "Nearer My God to
Thee" and Grace was right—he has a magnificent voice.
Once again my cottage cheese pies were a success.
In case you missed it, I'll post the link to the recipe again.

Shelby was on her way home when the thought struck
her—could Prudence's son, Wallace, possibly be the murderer? Mrs. Willoughby seemed to think he'd only arrived
in Lovett after Prudence's death, but was that true? It was
possible he'd arrived earlier—before Sunday—and Daniel simply hadn't thought to mention it. Perhaps Wallace
had gone to the church hoping to catch Prudence or Daniel there, but they had already left. If he saw the notices
for the potluck, it would have been easy enough for him
to put two and two together. Shelby didn't remember seeing him that afternoon, but there'd been so many people
milling around on the lawn of Love Blossom Farm that
it was possible she had just missed him.

Shelby was so engrossed in her thoughts that she
nearly went past her turn and had to slam on the brakes
at the last minute. She made a mental apology to the
driver of the car behind her as she made the turn—
practically taking it on two wheels.

Maybe Wallace approached Prudence at the potluck?
Or he could have already gone to her asking for money
and that was why Prudence had all that cash in her purse.
And then perhaps she'd changed her mind—or she'd dis-
cussed it with Daniel and he talked her out of giving
anything to Wallace. If he'd arrived at the potluck expecting to get money from Prudence, her refusal might have
made him mad enough to kill. Shelby had felt from the

beginning that the murder had been a spur-of-the-moment act driven by anger, desperation, or frustration.

Shelby felt stirrings of excitement as she pulled into her driveway. She had a feeling she was onto something. If Wallace had arrived in town earlier, he'd probably stayed at the rectory with Daniel and Prudence. Shelby bit her lip. She didn't want to ask Daniel about it while the poor man was in mourning, but perhaps there was someone else who would know. . . . Shelby mentally snapped her fingers. She remembered Coralynne from her knitting group once saying that she helped out at the rectory a couple of times a week running the sweeper, dusting, and cleaning the kitchen. Maybe she would know if Wallace had been there before Prudence was killed?

The rain had stopped and when Shelby opened her car door, she was assaulted by a wave of heavy, humid air that the rain had brought with it. Puddles filled the ruts in her driveway, and she had to be careful to step around them as she made her way to the front door.

Shelby had barely walked inside when Amelia came barreling down the stairs, nearly colliding with her mother. Amelia was wearing a tank top and cutoffs so short they made Shelby frown. "Where are you going in such a hurry?"

"Kaylee's mom is picking me up in a couple of minutes. Bert's here, so it's okay. She said she'd stay with Billy."

"Oh," was all Shelby managed to say.

She was heading toward the kitchen when she heard a horn honk outside.

"I'm going Mom, bye," Amelia said.

The front door slammed before Shelby had a chance to reply. On an impulse, she headed toward the foyer, walking as quickly as she could without actually breaking into a trot. Something was compelling her, although she couldn't say what it was. She yanked open the front door. She was in time to see a car backing down the driveway. And it wasn't Kaylee's mother at the wheel, but Jodi Walters. Amelia was in the backseat, looking very cozy with Jodi's son Ned.

Shelby was tempted to run after the car but realized just in time that that would only serve to make her look ridiculous. She pulled her cell phone from her purse and punched in Amelia's number. After a brief pause, the call went directly to voice mail. Shelby was tempted to throw the phone in frustration but managed to restrain herself.

She stomped into the kitchen, where Bert was preparing to make pickles. She had a basket of Persian cucumbers from Shelby's garden on the counter. Persian cukes are smaller, with a smoother skin and no seeds.

"I love these cucumbers," Bert said with her back to Shelby. "They fit perfectly in the canning jars so you can leave them whole." She turned around. "Jeez-o-pete, what's gotten into you? You look as riled up as a twister about to strike ground."

Shelby took a deep breath and tried to release the tension from her shoulders. She opened her clenched fists and shook out her hands. "Amelia . . ." She sputtered to a stop.

"What's she been up to now? Besides being a perfectly normal teenage girl. I had three of those myself—two at the same time with the twins. If I could survive that, you can survive this."

Bert turned on the tap and began to scrub the cucumbers under the running water.

Shelby opened the cupboard and got out a jar of dill seed, mustard seed, some black peppercorns, and a container of kosher salt. "All this time Amelia has been claiming she was at her friend Kaylee's house, when she's actually been hanging out with a boy. Ned Walters. Jodi's son."

"So?" Bert paused in her scrubbing.

"So she's not even thirteen yet, and he's already fourteen."

"That's about the time it starts." Bert lined up a set of pickling jars on the counter.

"What starts?" Shelby grabbed a towel and began drying the cucumbers.

"An interest in boys. I think there's a switch that gets turned on as they near their teenage years."

"I still think she's too young."

Bert carefully lowered the glass jars into the pot of water boiling vigorously on the stove. "Look at your pullets and heifers. They know when the time is right."

Shelby turned sharply toward Bert and stood with her hands on her hips. "My daughter is hardly a chicken or a cow."

Bert chuckled. "Of course not. But it's Mother Nature's way of making sure the species continues. You can't fight it."

"I'm afraid the species will have to continue without Amelia's help for quite a few more years."

Shelby could remember the moment the doctor had handed her the beautiful, red-faced squalling baby that was her daughter. Bill was by her side and they couldn't stop smiling at each other. They were a family. It was only a moment ago. And now Amelia was on the cusp of womanhood. Time should not be allowed to go that fast.

Shelby and Bert finished putting up the pickles and Bert left for home, taking a couple of jars with her. Shelby tidied up the kitchen and tried to decide what to do. Should she go to Jodi's house and confront Amelia? She tried Amelia's cell again, but the call went to voice mail as before. Shelby stamped her foot in frustration.

How could Jodi let Amelia fool her mother like that? But then maybe Jodi didn't know Amelia had said she was at her friend's. Jodi might think Shelby was perfectly okay with Amelia spending time with Ned. Which she most certainly wasn't.

||||||||||||||||||||||||||

Shelby was grateful to have her mudroom back, although she still found herself scurrying through the space, her eyes averted from the spot where Prudence's body had lain. She was looking forward to redecorating as Matt had suggested. The paint she'd ordered should be in any day now.

She opened the back door, stepped outside, and cupped her hands to her mouth. "Billy," she shouted. She put two fingers in her mouth and gave a long, drawn-out whistle. That brought Jenkins and Bitsy running. In their book, a whistle usually meant dinnertime. Shelby shooed them into the house and went back outside to wait for Billy.

"Billy," she shouted again through her cupped hands.

He appeared over the small rise, running lightly and easily toward Shelby, as if it took no effort at all. One of the straps on his overalls had come undone, and the knees were caked with dirt.

"Mom, Mom," he yelled excitedly as he got closer. "You've got to come see!"

"See what?" Shelby asked when he was within reach. She ruffled his hair—a gesture that made him scowl and duck away.

"The mouse that Patches killed. It's right outside the barn, and its head is missing. It's really cool."

Shelby shuddered. "How about you show me later, okay? It's time for your piano lesson."

"Aw, Ma, do I have to? Mrs. Van Buren is mean." He kicked at the dirt with the toe of his sneaker.

"She's not mean—she's strict. How else are you going to learn to play?"

"I don't want to play the piano," Billy whined. "I want to play the drums."

Shelby shuddered. "Come on." She gave him a gentle push toward the house. "You'll be glad you know how when you're older."

Billy continued to protest, but Shelby steered him toward the powder room to wash his face and hands. It was too late to send him to change, but she held him still long enough to reattach the undone strap on his overalls and brush the loose dirt off the knees.

Unlike Amelia's, Billy's bad moods were like a brief rain shower—within minutes the sun was out again.

"Mrs. Van Buren usually gives me a piece of candy when I come. I hope she has some Snickers today," Billy said as Shelby watched while he buckled himself into the backseat of the car.

She got behind the wheel, backed down the driveway, and headed toward the small development where Mrs. Van Buren lived.

"It sounds as if she isn't as bad as all that," Shelby said as they pulled into the piano teacher's driveway.

Billy shrugged and bounded out of the car and up the steps to Mrs. Van Buren's modest ranch-style house. Shelby waited until the door opened and then backed out of the driveway.

She'd taken a dozen of her homemade potato dough

rolls from the freezer and collected a basket of Love Blossom Farm preserves and canned fruit before leaving the house. She had no idea if she would find Coralynne at the rectory today, but if not, she at least had an excuse for calling on the pastor.

The rectory had been built in the late 1800s in the Gothic Revival style common in religious structures of the day. It was a sturdy house of redbrick with a peaked roof in the center and fanciful white gingerbread trim that was at odds with the serious and slightly gloomy look of the rest of the home.

An early-model Ford Focus was in the driveway. Shelby hoped that meant that today was one of Coralynne's days for cleaning.

She hooked the basket over her arm, grabbed the package of rolls with her other hand, and pushed the car door shut with her hip. She climbed the steps under the portico, set down her basket, and rang the bell.

Shelby was relieved when Coralynne opened the door. She had an apron tied over an old-fashioned-looking silk dress and was wearing a strand of pearls and low-heeled black pumps.

"Shelby, dear, come in," she said, standing back from the door.

"I've brought some things for Reverend Mather." Shelby gestured with her chin toward the basket and the bag of rolls.

"How lovely of you," she said. "Let's put these in the kitchen."

Shelby glanced into the parlor as they went past. The furniture looked as if it had come with the house—stiff, high-backed chairs and a rather stern and forbidding-looking sofa. Shelby couldn't imagine anyone kicking off their shoes and getting comfortable in there. Perhaps there was another room—a den or family room—that was more hospitable.

Coralynne led the way into the kitchen, where she opened the freezer door and pointed to the contents. It was stuffed with casserole dishes labeled in small, neat handwriting—chicken tetrazzini; tuna noodle; broccoli, chicken, and rice. "We're keeping the poor, dear man well fed, as you can see." She shook her head. "Not that he has much of an appetite these days. But I suppose that's normal under the circumstances."

Shelby handed over the rolls. Coralynne peeked inside the bag. "I'll just keep these out for his dinner, shall I? They'll go quite nicely with the chicken and dumplings Eleanor brought."

Coralynne placed the bag on the counter and turned to Shelby. "Would you like a cup of tea?"

"I don't want to interrupt. . . ."

"Not at all. Today isn't my day for cleaning, but Reverend Mather asked if I could come because people might be stopping by. I made a batch of friendship bread and some shortbread cookies in case there were visitors. That way he doesn't have to cope on his own." She sighed. "Prudence was always the one to handle the social aspects of being rector of a church. Reverend Mather is rather shy and easily overwhelmed by it all."

Coralynne opened a cupboard, took out a kettle, and began to fill it. She was putting it on the stove to boil when the doorbell rang.

"I'm certainly getting my exercise with the doorbell ringing constantly," Coralynne said with a smile. "I'll be right back."

Shelby heard another feminine voice coming from the hallway, and Coralynne ushered Grace into the room. She was carrying a covered casserole dish.

"I've brought the reverend some chicken divan for his dinner." She put the dish down on the counter.

"We're all set for his dinner," Coralynne said, getting cups and saucers out of the cupboard. "But I'll label it and put it in the freezer for later. Now." She turned to face Grace with her hands on her hips. "Would you like to join us in a cup of tea?" Coralynne turned back toward the cupboard, her hand hovering over a third teacup.

"Why not?" Grace dropped into a kitchen chair. "Alan is away on business, so I'm all by my lonesome."

"What does Alan do exactly?" Coralynne asked as she poured out the tea and put sugar and creamer on the table.

"He's an insurance salesman," Grace said. "It's a good job, and I'm not complaining, but it does take him out of town for half the week." She looked at Coralynne and Shelby from under her lashes. "We've only been married three months, so we're honeymooners still, and I hate him having to be gone so much."

"Don't worry," Coralynne said, settling into one of the chairs. "You'll come to appreciate it after a while. My Roger is retired now and just between you and me, having him around all the time is very difficult. He always wants to talk when I'm involved in something."

Shelby had a sudden thought—would she ever be able to adjust to married life again? She'd been on her own for quite a while now, answering to no one and doing things her way.

"I wonder if Reverend Mather will marry again," Grace said.

"I should imagine so," Coralynne said. "It wouldn't be seemly to have a bachelor as a rector. Best if he chooses someone and settles down as quickly as possible."

There were footsteps in the hall and for a moment Shelby panicked, thinking it was Daniel and that he might have heard what they were saying about him. A person appeared in the doorway—it was Wallace. He stuck his head into the room.

"Got anything to eat?"

Coralynne stiffened, her mouth set in disapproving lines. "Some shortbread cookies and some friendship bread."

Wallace made a face. "No, thanks." He headed back down the hall, whistling as he went.

Coralynne gave a loud harrumph.

"Rather unsavory young man, isn't he?" Grace said after Wallace had retreated down the hallway. She sniffed. "Hard to believe he's Prudence's son."

"I was quite surprised to hear about him," Shelby said, glad that Grace had brought up the topic for her. "I didn't realize Prudence had been married before. Has he been here in Lovett long?"

Coralynne harrumphed again. "Long enough. He got here the day before the murder. He wasn't here even twenty-four hours before I heard him and Prudence arguing."

"Do you think he might be responsible for Prudence's death?" Shelby asked, trying to look as innocent as possible.

"I never thought of that." Grace took a sip of her tea.

"Did either of you see him at the potluck?" Shelby asked.

Grace looked up, as if she would find inspiration in the ceiling tiles. She tapped her chin with her index finger.

"There were so many people, of course. And I was quite busy introducing Alan to everyone." Her face glowed with possessive pride.

"I couldn't say," Coralynne said, her brow furrowed in concentration. "I was occupied with helping the Women's Auxiliary get everything set up, and afterward I found a shady spot under a tree where I could enjoy my meal. It was excellent, I must say, although Mrs. Kendrick will insist on putting too much mustard in her potato salad. One wants only a hint of the flavor, and not to be hit between the eyes with it." She puffed out her chest.

Grace turned toward Shelby, her eyes sparkling and eager. "I think I do remember seeing Wallace at some point. Or at least, there was a rather sordid-looking dark-haired young man lurking about. I remember he kept picking bits of food off the platters—an olive here, a crust of cheese there. Very unsavory, I must say." She shivered.

"So it's quite possible Wallace was at the potluck, and he did kill Prudence," Shelby said.

Grace frowned. "But I still wonder about Earl—the usher at St. Andrews." She looked at them over the rim of her teacup. "He was furious with Prudence for accusing him of stealing that collection money. I heard them arguing and he definitely sounded mad enough to kill."

14

Dear Reader,

I certainly have a lot to think about! It looks as if Wallace as the murderer is logistically possible—if not really probable. But how could someone kill their own mother? Grace brought up a good point about Earl. Certainly being wrongly accused would make someone very angry—angry enough to kill, perhaps. Especially if they pride themselves on their honor and trustworthiness. Of course the question remains—was Earl wrongly accused? That is something I still have to figure out. Maybe he really did dip his hand into the collection plate?

And then there's Amelia and this boy she's seeing on the sly. Ned. I've heard he's a nice boy—his mother seems to think so, but then she would, wouldn't she?

I don't look forward to confronting her about her lying. This is one of those moments when I wish Bill were still here so we could face this together. I know he would have some wise and clever solution.

Meanwhile, I need to get back to Love Blossom Farm and check on my lettuce to see how that potion I put on it—the canola oil, water, and dash of liquid dishwashing detergent—is working to stem the mildew.

Shelby smelled cigarette smoke as she was leaving the rectory. Wallace must be smoking somewhere outside again.

She found him near the rosebushes at the end of the drive, a lit cigarette in his hand. Shelby braved the miasma surrounding him and approached him. "Wallace?"

He nodded, his glance shifting away from Shelby's as he looked down at his feet. He was wearing a pair of expensive but very worn athletic shoes. Shelby suspected he might have purchased them secondhand.

"I'm very sorry for your loss." Shelby uttered the pat phrase even as she realized how trite it sounded.

Wallace looked at Shelby briefly and grunted.

"I'm glad you had the chance to see Prudence before she . . . she died."

Wallace nodded, turned his head to the side and blew out a long stream of cigarette smoke.

"I hope you enjoyed the potluck." Shelby tried again. Wallace certainly wasn't much of a conversationalist. "Prudence put a lot of effort into it."

"Wasn't there," Wallace mumbled with his mouth around the cigarette.

"That's a shame. I'm sorry you missed it."

Wallace shrugged. "Not my thing—all those church people."

Shelby had no idea what to say to that, so she said good-bye and walked to her car.

Shelby drove to Mrs. Van Buren's, where Billy was waiting. His earlier bad humor had evaporated, and he was happily enjoying the sucker his piano teacher had given him. Shelby was relieved—she didn't think she could deal with it if Billy started whining and complaining again on the way home. She had too much on her mind as it was.

But things seemed to have gone well. Mrs. Van Buren said he was making progress on his scales and she praised him for having practiced them during the week.

Dear Reader,

I had to bite my tongue when Mrs. Van Buren said that about Billy practicing because Billy has been no closer to the piano than was required to change the channel on the television. What was it that Abe Lincoln said? Something about you can fool some of the people all of the time? That's Billy for you. If all you need to succeed in life is charm and a little blarney, he's got it made.

Shelby heard noises coming from the kitchen when they got home and was startled when Amelia suddenly came around the corner. Shelby thought she'd have a bit more time before having to confront her daughter. Her thoughts were still in a jumble, and she wasn't nearly ready.

Billy bolted past Shelby and out the door before she could say a word. She supposed it was because of pent-up energy from having to sit still for an hour at the piano.

"I didn't expect you to be home," Shelby said to Amelia. Her eyes were on her daughter's face.

"Kaylee had to go to the dentist," Amelia said, her eyes sliding to the right of Shelby's.

"Let's sit down," Shelby said, pointing toward the living room.

She took a seat on the couch and Amelia perched on the edge of the armchair opposite. She looked wary and plucked at a loose thread on the throw draped over the arm.

"You weren't really at Kaylee's house this afternoon, were you?"

Amelia looked momentarily shocked, but then a mulish look came over her face. "I was, too." She crossed her arms over her chest. "I don't see why you won't believe me. You keep thinking I'm with some boy."

Shelby gave the ghost of a smile. "Some boy named Ned Walters? I saw his mother pick you up this afternoon."

Amelia's jaw dropped and her eyes turned as round as pennies. "You were spying on me?"

"Hardly. I happened to walk outside as Mrs. Walters was pulling out of the driveway."

Amelia's face took on an even more mulish look. "If you weren't so old-fashioned and would let me date, I wouldn't have to go behind your back," she shot back.

Shelby sighed. "Twelve is too young to date."

"I'm almost thirteen."

"Thirteen is also too young. I wouldn't mind if you went to a school event with a boy, but real dating will have to wait until you're a little older."

"I'll be ancient by then, and I'll never get a boyfriend." Amelia burst into tears and stomped up the stairs to her room.

Dear Reader, well, that went well—don't you think? Maybe it's hormones?

||||||||||||||||||||||||||

The skies had clouded over again while Shelby was cooking dinner for Amelia and Billy. *Dear Reader, please don't judge me, but I made macaroni and cheese from a box for them, and had toast and a cup of tea myself. I am worn-out! Soon I'll share my recipe for macaroni made with three cheeses and a homemade cream sauce. Promise.*

By the time Shelby had finished cleaning up the kitchen and was settled in the living room with a book, trying to ignore the sitcom Billy had blaring from the television set, rain was pelting the windows. It sounded like handfuls of pebbles being flung at the glass. The dogs were restless—howling at the far-off thunder and pacing back and forth until the sound of their nails on the wooden floor threatened to make Shelby scream.

At ten o'clock she made Billy turn off the television and get ready for bed. It was hard getting him to sleep any earlier, since it wouldn't be completely dark for at least another half hour. Since Lovett was on the westernmost edge of the eastern time zone, summer days were long in west Michigan. Amelia had disappeared upstairs right after supper—during which she hadn't said a word but had stared at her plate the entire time—and Shelby presumed she was texting all her friends to tell them what a dinosaur her mother was and how unfair it was that she wasn't going to be allowed to date for a few more years. Shelby tried not to let it bother her, but she had to admit Amelia made her feel like an ogre—and worse, that she wasn't in touch with what was going on.

Shelby let Bitsy and Jenkins out for one last time, waiting at the door until they came bounding back inside, shaking the rain from their fur. They followed her upstairs and made themselves comfortable on the bed while she washed up and changed into her nightgown.

She'd planned to read in bed for a bit but found her eyes closing after the first page. She turned out the light, fluffed up her pillow, and drifted off to sleep.

It was just after midnight when the dogs woke Shelby. At first they did nothing more than emit a deep, low growl—the kind they made when they weren't sure if something was friend or foe—but then they progressed to outright frantic barking. Jenkins ran for the stairs and Bitsy, heavier and clumsier, was right behind him, sliding on the throw rug and then regaining her footing and giving chase.

They both threw themselves at the front door, their barking reaching a frenzied pitch. Shelby padded down the stairs in her bare feet. She glanced over her shoulder, expecting to see Amelia and Billy following her. Neither of them appeared and she sent up a silent prayer that the commotion hadn't woken them.

She couldn't imagine what had gotten the dogs so riled up. A coyote venturing too close to the house perhaps? Or something smaller and more benign like a possum or, heaven forbid, a skunk? Both dogs had been skunked on more than one occasion—not something Shelby wanted to repeat, especially not at this time of night.

She was hesitant to open the door, but she was afraid their incessant barking would eventually wake the children. Besides, if it was a harmless possum, Jenkins and Bitsy would soon send it packing.

The rain had stopped, although dark clouds still moved swiftly across the sky. It looked as if the next downpour could happen at any moment. Shelby peered into the darkness but didn't see anything. Bitsy and Jenkins pushed past her, running in circles, their noses to the floor.

Shelby stepped out onto the front porch. The boards were wet from the rain, which had settled in small puddles on the uneven wooden floor. She scanned the driveway and the yard, but all she could see was the suggestion of a retreating headlight in the far distance and even that might have been her imagination.

"Come on, Bitsy," Shelby said in her most authoritative voice, which she feared sounded more whiny than firm. "Come on, Jenkins."

She held the door wide, trying to entice them back into the house. Bitsy, who was the more easily tired of the two, took the bait and lumbered into the foyer, where she stood panting and dropping huge gobs of drool onto the floor. Jenkins, however, was not as easily corralled. He continued sniffing in an ever-widening circle.

Shelby thought it was strange that neither of them had left the porch. The scent that intrigued them so was clearly not out in the yard. The thought momentarily made her shiver. Had someone strange been standing on her doorstep?

Shelby called Jenkins again, but he still refused to heed the command to come. Shelby sighed. That was a terrier for you—they were quite convinced that they ruled the world and your job was simply to make life easier for them.

"Jenkins, that's enough. I want to go back to bed." Shelby yawned.

Jenkins was too busy sniffing around the railing that enclosed the porch to pay attention. Shelby sighed again and began to walk toward him, ready to grab his collar and drag him in if necessary.

She was halfway there when something smacked her in the face. She screamed but then quickly stifled it. She looked up. Something was hanging from the hook in the ceiling where she had hung a planter with flowers. Shelby looked around and found the planter itself had been taken down and placed on the floor.

Shelby grabbed for the object that continued to swing back and forth from a long piece of cord. It was too dark to see exactly what it was, but it was cool and smooth in her hands. She ran into the kitchen, flicking on lights as she went, and grabbed a pair of kitchen shears from the pot on the counter before heading back outside.

Shelby felt her way across the porch, sweeping her arms in front of her until she felt the rough cord brush against her hand. She grabbed it and sliced through it easily enough with the scissors. She tucked the object under her arm and gave a sharp whistle. "Come on, Jenkins."

Jenkins hesitated, unwilling to abandon his quest for the unknown scent on their porch, but Shelby grabbed him by the collar and dragged him inside.

Bitsy and Jenkins followed her down the darkened hallway to the kitchen, where she'd left the light on.

Finally Shelby could see the object that had been hanging from the ceiling of the front porch. It was a butternut squash with a length of cord wrapped around its neck like a noose.

Shelby screamed and dropped it on the floor.

15

Dear Reader,

People think life in the country is dull, but I can assure
you that life in Lovett in general and at Love Blossom
Farm in particular has been anything but lately. There
was Prudence's murder, and now it seems as if someone is trying to scare me to keep me from investigating.
Why else would they hang a squash with a noose
around its neck to the ceiling of my front porch? Not
that I'm going around quizzing people like one of those
detectives on television—it's more a matter of keeping
my eyes and ears open. And it seems I've touched a
nerve—but whose?

Shelby finally crawled back into bed, but she spent an
uneasy night alert to every sound. Bitsy and Jenkins—her

early warning signals—slept soundly, so the noises she thought she heard were probably a product of her over-worked and heightened imagination.

She woke before the alarm, slipped into her clothes, and went downstairs. She thought about breakfast but decided she would feed the chickens first. They seemed surprised to see her so early. They pranced around flapping their wings, as if she'd woken them.

Shelby scattered the feed and put the bucket back in the barn. She kept looking over her shoulder and jumping at every rustle and creak in the old building. If the person who had hung the squash was intent on scaring her, it was working admirably.

As soon as the chickens were fed, and a pot of coffee was brewing, Shelby picked up the phone and dialed the Lovett Police Station. They assured her that Detective McDonald would be there shortly.

Shelby was in the garden checking on the pole beans—she'd had a great crop this year—when she heard the sound of a car in the distance. She stripped off her gardening gloves and headed around toward the front of the house.

Frank got out of his pickup, which was no longer dusty but instead was now spattered with mud. He walked toward Shelby, scrubbing a hand over his face. When he got closer, Shelby could see the fatigue in his eyes and the tight set to his jaw.

"You look like you could use a cup of coffee," she said.

"That bad, huh?"

Shelby laughed. "Come on inside. I have a pot ready and waiting."

Frank followed her into the house. Bitsy and Jenkins

were out on their morning romp, but they must have sensed the presence of a visitor, because all of a sudden, Jenkins was pressing his nose to the screen door to the mudroom and making a racket.

Shelby opened the door and let them in. Frank staggered back a step as Bitsy put her paws on his shoulders and began to lick his face. Jenkins sniffed every inch of Frank that he could reach as if performing some sort of canine identity check. Shelby often thought Jenkins could get work in security at the airport.

Frank accepted his mug of coffee, declined cream and sugar, and took a sip.

"Ahhh," he sighed before putting the mug down on the table. He turned to Shelby, who had sat down opposite him with her own cup in her hands. "Dispatch told me you found a squash hanging from the ceiling of your front porch. Unless Ashley's hearing is going? Because that would be a shame, since she's only twenty-nine."

Shelby explained about the dogs barking and her middle-of-the-night find.

"Do you still have the squash?" Frank asked, a look of concern settling on his face.

Shelby got up and went to the counter next to the refrigerator. "Here it is. Someone had taken down my planter and used the hook in the ceiling to hang this."

Frank pulled a handkerchief from his pocket, opened it, and held it toward Shelby. "I don't suppose we'll get any useful prints off here, but you never know."

His eyes narrowed as he examined the butternut squash and the rough cord that was wrapped several times around its neck. "It does look something like a noose," he said, holding it up. The squash swung back and forth.

"Especially with the knot tied here in the back." Frank twisted it around so Shelby could see.

She glanced at it quickly and then turned away.

"Can you show me where you found this?" Frank got up from his chair, coffee mug in hand.

Shelby led him back through the living room and out the front door to the porch. Bitsy and Jenkins were right on their heels. They ran circles around Frank for a minute or two, sniffing furiously at his clothes, and then retreated to the far corner of the porch, their pink tongues hanging.

Shelby stood under the spot where the squash had been hanging and pointed to the ceiling. "There's the hook."

Frank came to stand next to her, squinting as he looked up to where she was pointing.

"They must have needed a ladder to get it up there," Shelby said.

Frank looked around the porch. "Not necessarily. They might have dragged one of those chairs over." He pointed to the wrought-iron chairs that surrounded a small table, where, on cooler nights, Shelby and the children sometimes ate their dinner.

Frank bent over and examined the floor, squatting down to take a closer look. "Looks like there are some tracks in the dust."

Shelby stiffened. "It's impossible to keep the dust and dirt off this floor. Even sweeping every day—"

Frank laughed, interrupting her. "I'm not here to award you the Good Housekeeping Seal of Approval, you know." He motioned for Shelby to come closer. He pointed at the floor. "Look. There's a slight scratch here." He glanced over toward the table. "It could easily be from one of those chairs." He straightened up with a grunt. "Then again, maybe not. Who knows?" He took a glug of his coffee. "Do you suppose it could be a prank? Some kids wanting to play a trick on you?"

Shelby wrapped her hands around her warm mug—they'd suddenly turned cold despite the summer temperature. "I suppose it's possible. It just seems too coincidental—Prudence was strangled with the cord of her slow cooker—the squash has a cord wrapped around its neck. I think someone is trying to tell me something."

Frank gave a small smile. "Why would that be?"

Shelby bit her lip and looked around the porch as if for salvation. "I suppose I've been asking some questions. Questions the murderer might not want asked."

Frank heaved a gigantic sigh and rolled his eyes heavenward. "How about this? You stop asking questions. Leave that to me, okay?" He squeezed Shelby's arm. "I promised Bill I would look after you," he said with a slight catch in his voice.

Shelby nodded. "Okay."

Dear Reader, I really did mean it at the time. Honest.

"Have there been any developments in the case?" Shelby finished the last of her coffee and put the mug down on the small wooden table beside one of the rockers. It wobbled slightly. She kept meaning to even up the legs but somehow never got around to it.

Frank hesitated. Shelby could tell he was trying to decide what to tell her—if anything.

"Let's just say we're following up some leads, okay?"

Shelby strongly suspected that was code for *we don't have a clue*.

Frank drained his cup and put it next to Shelby's. "That

was just what I needed. Thanks." He reached into his shirt pocket and pulled out a small plastic bag. He held it out to Shelby. "Do you recognize this?"

Shelby took the bag and peered at what was inside. It appeared to be a length of red yarn, maybe two inches long.

Frank tapped the package with his finger. "We found that when we searched your mudroom. Since everything is potential evidence, one of the men bagged it up. Of course it's probably nothing at all."

"It's a piece of yarn, obviously. It may have come from the scarf I'm knitting—or trying to knit. I think the wool is the same color."

Frank sighed. "I figured something like that. But we can't ignore anything."

"Do you want this back?" Shelby held the bag toward Frank.

"Yes. Thanks. It's logged in as evidence, so we have to keep it for the time being even if it does turn out to be worthless."

Shelby smiled. "Don't worry. I don't think I'll need it back."

Frank stuffed the plastic bag back into his pocket. "Mind if I take this with me?" He held the squash toward Shelby, dangling it from the cord.

She shuddered. "No, not at all." She couldn't wait to get that thing out of her house, and if she never saw it again, that would be fine with her. She was hardly going to cook it up for dinner.

Frank started down the porch steps, then stopped and turned around. "Be careful, okay? If you see or hear or suspect anything out of the ordinary, give me a call. I don't care what it is or when it is. I would never forgive myself if something happened to you."

‖‖‖‖‖‖‖‖‖‖‖‖‖‖‖‖‖‖‖‖

Shelby did some weeding in her herb garden while the sun was still low in the sky, and the air pleasantly cool. The ground was damp from the rain, making the chore much easier than usual. The rich smell of dark earth mixing with the pungent notes of basil, thyme, and rosemary helped to soothe her still-frazzled nerves as she pulled out clumps of weeds and shook the dirt off. She didn't always bother with gardening gloves—she mostly used them for tasks that could be rough on her hands like raking or hoeing and trimming the rosebushes. She never minded getting dirt under her fingernails.

An hour later, Shelby stood up and brushed the dirt and bits of grass from her knees. Bitsy and Jenkins were due at Kelly's veterinary clinic for their annual shots. Amelia could babysit Billy, since she was grounded for the rest of her life—if not longer.

She gave a loud whistle and both dogs came running. Jenkins had dirt on his snout and front paws. He'd no doubt been digging for buried treasure again. Shelby was forever finding small holes all over the farm. Bitsy had pieces of tree bark and leaves in her fur. Shelby looked at her watch. She didn't have time to give the dogs a bath—she wanted to stop by St. Andrews to pick up her salad bowls from Prudence's funeral lunch—but she could at least wipe Jenkins's paws and face and run a brush through Bitsy's fur. Then she'd have to scrub her

NO FARM, NO FOUL   161

own hands and nails, change out of her dirty clothes, and drag a comb through her hair.

Blessedly both dogs were very cooperative. Shelby gave them each a treat then led them to the car. Both Jenkins and Bitsy enjoyed riding in the car. Shelby had once had a dog that got carsick just backing down the driveway, so she was grateful that the two were good passengers.

Jenkins always rode shotgun, sticking his head out the window to sniff the air rushing past. Bitsy stretched out on the backseat, panting happily.

They both got excited when Shelby pulled into the church parking lot. She snapped on their leashes and let them out of the car. Jenkins sniffed every inch of the path between the car and the door to the church, and it took Shelby almost five minutes to get them both inside.

She had no idea where Mrs. Willoughby had stored the dishes left over from the funeral luncheon, so she headed toward her office, hoping she would be in. The dogs pulled her up the stairs and down the hall, their noses working overtime.

The light was on at the end of the corridor, and Shelby hoped that meant that Mrs. Willoughby was in. The dogs burst into the office ahead of Shelby, and she heard a high-pitched squeal as she went through the door.

Mrs. Willoughby was backed up against her desk, trying to distance herself as much as possible from Bitsy. Bitsy, meanwhile, was leaning against Mrs. Willoughby, hoping in vain for a back scratch.

"I'm so sorry," Shelby said, yanking on both dogs' leashes and reining them in. "I'm afraid they got away from me."

"It's not . . . not vicious, is it?" Mrs. Willoughby said,

pointing at Bitsy, who was hardly behaving like an attack dog. But Shelby could understand how someone might be frightened by her sheer size.

"No, she's extremely friendly," Shelby said.

"It's just that they surprised me," Mrs. Willoughby said, trying to gather up the remains of her dignity.

She had a pair of half glasses pushed up onto her forehead and another pair dangling from a chain around her neck. Her computer was on, and there was a brightly colored picture on her monitor. Shelby got a glimpse of it before the screen went into sleep mode, and she thought it looked as if it was taken at the recent potluck.

"I'm working on the church newsletter." Mrs. Willoughby sighed. "It was so much easier in the old days when all I had to do was type it up and print it out. Trying to work with this computerized newsletter program is making me a nervous wreck." She gave a short bark of laughter. "I guess you really can't teach an old dog new tricks."

She jiggled her computer mouse, and the monitor sprang to life again. "People have sent me some lovely pictures of our potluck, and I'd like to include them in the newsletter." She settled her half glasses in place and sat down at her desk. "You might like seeing some of these yourself."

The first picture was taken from a distance and showed the tent on the lawn of Love Blossom Farm and all the people milling about the tables of food. Shelby had to admit—everything looked quite lovely.

Mrs. Willoughby clicked to another shot—this one of the children playing. Shelby noticed Billy in the picture—his shirt was untucked, and she could see that his face was dirty. Hopefully Mrs. Willoughby wouldn't pick that one for the newsletter. The next shot was a very nice one of Grace Swanson and her husband, Alan. They were standing arm in arm and smiling at the camera.

Mrs. Willoughby clicked on the next photograph. It was rather blurry, as if the photographer had failed to focus the camera properly.

"Well, I certainly can't use that one." Mrs. Willoughby hit the delete key. "Here's a nice one," she said as another shot popped up on the screen.

It was a group picture. Shelby recognized Liz Gardener, Jodi Walters, and a few other people. Mrs. Willoughby was about to click to the next picture when Shelby stopped her.

"Wait!" She leaned forward to get a better look at the picture.

There was a young man standing apart from the crowd, partially turning away. Shelby stared at the photo.

Shelby tapped the screen with her index finger. "That's him. That's Wallace, Prudence's son. He lied to me. He was at the potluck after all."

iiiiiiiiiiiiiiiiiiiiiiiiiiiii

Kelly held her clinic once a week in a trailer just outside town. She'd set it up in the parking lot of an abandoned building that had once housed a Chinese restaurant. The large red sign out front still read CHINA CITY, but everyone in town knew this was where Kelly's practice was located.

There was one other car in the lot when Shelby pulled in. Both dogs spilled out of the car as soon as Shelby opened the doors. She managed to corral them and snap their leashes back on. Jenkins immediately tried to pull her toward the lone car and its enticing tires—he lifted his leg on anything and everything.

The trailer had a small waiting area, and if Kelly was running late, it wasn't unusual to find owners and their pets waiting outside. Today the single occupant—a woman in pink shorts and a tank top—sat with a ring-tailed cat in her lap. She clutched the cat to her chest when Bitsy and Jenkins burst into the room.

Shelby reassured her that both dogs were not only friendly but used to cats, but the woman seemed far from convinced. Fortunately Kelly popped her head out of the examining room just then, and the woman and her cat jumped up, obviously glad of the chance to escape.

Shelby grabbed one of the tattered magazines scattered across the coffee table, but she found it didn't hold her attention. She kept reliving the moment when she'd walked into the hanging butternut squash. Was someone really out to warn her off?

Before she could think about it any longer, the door to the exam room opened and the woman and her cat came out. Kelly nodded at Shelby. She grabbed the dogs' leashes. "Come on, guys, it's our turn."

Shelby followed Kelly into the exam room. Bitsy and Jenkins seemed to have had a sudden recollection of their last visit to the vet, and Shelby had to drag them in after her. Jenkins was immediately intrigued by the incredible quantity of smells in the room and was busy sniffing his way around the perimeter.

"I guess you're first, then," Kelly said, scratching Bitsy behind the ears.

Together, she and Shelby got Bitsy onto the examining table.

"You're looking tired," Shelby said, glancing at her friend's face. "Another middle-of-the-night delivery?"

Kelly shook her head. "No, it's been rather quiet lately."

"What is it, then?" Shelby knew Kelly well enough to know that something was wrong.

"I know it sounds ridiculous, but I'm still worried about Seth—I can't help it. I keep thinking, what if he gave that money to Prudence to keep her quiet and protect my reputation? And maybe she accepted the money but then told him it wasn't enough—she was going to tell everyone about the mistake I'd made anyway."

Kelly turned away from Shelby and got two vials of vaccine from a locked cabinet. "Then they argued, he got angry, and he killed her."

When Kelly turned around, Shelby noticed there were tears in her eyes.

"You don't really believe that, do you?" Shelby asked.

"I don't know. Why won't Seth tell me where he was during the potluck?"

"I'm sure he has a good reason, and he will tell you soon enough. Maybe he's planning some kind of surprise for you?"

Kelly scowled. "Seth? I doubt it. That's not his style."

"I don't think you have anything to worry about," Shelby reassured her. "I think I know where the money came from."

Kelly put down the syringe she was filling. "You do?"

"Yes. I think the money was Prudence's, and she planned to give it to her son."

"Son?" Kelly blurted out.

"Yes. Prudence was married before and had a son,

Wallace. He's around thirty, I'd say, unkempt and rather rough-looking." Shelby gave an exaggerated shiver. "He apparently came here looking for money from Prudence."

Kelly filled the syringe and paused with it in the air. "Do you think he killed Prudence?"

"Yes."

"But why?" Kelly asked as she stuck the needle in the unsuspecting Bitsy.

Bitsy obviously didn't notice, because she turned her head and tried to lick Kelly's face. After removing the needle, Kelly gave her a dog biscuit, and Bitsy jumped off the examining table.

"He wanted money," Shelby said.

"But Prudence had money in her purse, so she must have been planning on giving it to him. Why else would she be walking around with so much cash?" Kelly asked.

"I think she did plan on giving it to Wallace but then changed her mind. Maybe she talked to Daniel and he told her it was a bad idea. I don't know. But I think her refusal enraged Wallace, and in a fit of anger, he killed her."

Kelly shuddered. "That's so . . . so cold-blooded. He must be a wretched young man."

"He certainly didn't seem particularly distressed that his mother was dead."

"And in such a horrible way. . . ."

Kelly lifted Jenkins onto the examining table. He wasn't as content to be still as Bitsy and walked to the very edge and peered over it, as if he was assessing how high the jump was. Kelly clamped a hand on his collar while she reached for the second syringe.

"When I talked to Wallace, he denied having been at the potluck. But Mrs. Willoughby was showing me some photographs from the event, and Wallace was in one of them, skulking around the edges of the crowd. I don't remember seeing him, but there were so many people, not to mention so many things that needed to be done."

"I was oblivious, I'm afraid. I was on the lookout for Seth." Kelly gave Jenkins his shot, and he whipped his head around, eyes fierce, to see what had stung him. "But I really think you may be onto something."

16

Dear Reader,

Every Thursday, Lovett has a farmers' market in what
passes for downtown in our small community. St.
Andrews Church and the Catholic church, St. Mary Mag-
dalene, are clustered together, just down the road from
each other. Baptists and Methodists have to go further
afield for their Sunday services—all the way to Allenvale,
the next town over. Sandwiched between the churches
are the Lovett General Store, which I've already told you
about, the Lovett Feed Store, which also carries lawn
mowers and snowblowers because in Lovett, as soon as
you finish with one, you're going to need the other—
spring and fall are short around here. Just a ways down
the road, past our one streetlight, is the Lovett Diner,
where locals grab a cup of coffee in the mornings along

with a helping of town gossip, or stop for lunch after shopping at the General Store, or go to celebrate anniversaries, birthdays, and graduations.

The farmers' market is held on the empty field just before you get to the diner. Everyone brings their own table and a canopy to put over it—some more makeshift than others. I've already picked and packed the produce I'm selling—bunches of fresh-smelling herbs, delicate lettuces still wet with dew, the few vegetables I don't plan on canning for the winter, and some of my homemade cheese spreads.

Shelby pulled her faded red pickup onto the rough lane that ran alongside the field where the farmers' market was being held. She bumped over the ruts and hillocks until she came to the spot that had been allotted to her. Love Blossom Farm had been assigned that same location for several decades now. Shelby put the truck in reverse, swiveled around in her seat, and backed up to the area where she would be unloading.

She jumped down from the driver's side of the truck and went around to the back to let down the tailgate. The truck was old, and the pins holding the tailgate in place were often stubborn. Shelby made a mental note to put some lubricant on them. She leaned against the tailgate so it wouldn't fly open and managed to yank the pins out.

The back of the pickup truck was filled with crates. Shelby had stacked a long folding table on top of them so it would clear the wheel wells on the inside of the truck. By the time she got the table out and set up, she had worked up quite a sweat. She could feel the hairs at the nape of her neck plastered to her skin. There was no need to join a gym if you were a farmer—you got plenty of exercise doing your daily chores.

By now any clouds left in the sky had scattered, and the sun shone down unimpeded. Shelby wrestled the purple-and-white canopy with LOVE BLOSSOM FARM written on the front from the bed of the truck. It was relatively easy to set up, but nevertheless one of the other farmers ambled over to help her.

He hooked his thumbs under the straps of his worn overalls. "Need a hand with that?"

Dear Reader, I am perfectly capable of putting up the canopy all by myself, but if I refuse I'll be in danger of being labeled "one of them feminists" by the other farmers here.

"Don't want your lily white skin getting burned?" he asked as he helped her drive the stakes into the ground. He jerked his head in the direction of his own booth, which stood in full sun.

Shelby was used to being ribbed by the other farmers. She was one of the few women who came to the market by herself and didn't have a man to help. She merely nodded, thanked him, and went about her business.

With the table and canopy set up, it was time to unpack the crates. Shelby set out her wares, fussing a little with the arrangement. She wanted her booth to look inviting to customers. She had lined a basket with a red-and-white-checked napkin and poured in a box of crackers. She would offer them to people so they could sample her herbed cheese spreads. She'd found that after tasting the cheeses, customers generally bought at least one container.

Shelby was putting the finishing touches on her booth when Liz Gardener ambled over. She had a large blue-

and-white tote over her arm that Shelby strongly suspected was a genuine Coach bag.

Dear Reader, I did learn a few things when I lived in Chicago.

Liz wore a short white tennis skirt with a pale blue polo shirt festooned with the emblem of a country club that Shelby had heard of but never been to. The pompom on her short white socks matched her top perfectly.

"Shelby," she gushed as she looked over the display. "You always have such beautiful things." She pointed to the pyramid of containers stacked in the middle of the table. "Are those your famous cheese spreads?"

"Yes, would you like to try some?" Shelby handed Liz the basket of crackers and an open container of spread.

"Mmm, this is heavenly," Liz said, nibbling delicately on the cracker. "Thyme?"

"Yes. And a dash of lemon."

"I tried the recipe from your blog for chicken potpies, and my husband is still raving. He didn't think I could cook, and frankly neither did I." Liz laughed. "Your recipe was so easy to follow that even I managed to pull it off, despite being all thumbs in the kitchen," she said as she put two containers of the cheese spread in her tote and handed Shelby the money. "We're having a big cocktail party on Saturday night." She wrinkled her nose. "Mostly my husband's colleagues from the hospital. This cheese spread is just what I needed to round things out."

She waggled her fingers at Shelby as she moved on to the next booth.

Shelby looked around the market. Customers buzzed about the booths, filling their totes or the reusable grocery bags with farms' names on them that some of the farmers handed out.

Shelby turned back to her booth to see a woman approaching her. She was older, with tightly permed white hair and blue eyes surrounded by a web of wrinkles. She was wearing apricot-colored capri pants and a coordinating T-shirt. Shelby recognized her from church but didn't know her name.

The woman smiled when she got to Shelby's booth. "You go to St. Andrews, don't you?"

"Yes."

"I thought I recognized you." She stuck out her hand. "I'm Deirdre Fitch."

Shelby introduced herself in turn. "What can I help you with?"

"I'm making some wax bean soup. I grow my own beans," Deirdre said almost apologetically, "but my dill didn't take this year. Do you have any?"

"Certainly." Shelby pulled out a bunch of dill tied with a string. "You made that soup for Prudence Mather's funeral lunch, didn't you? It was delicious."

Deirdre beamed. "Why, thank you. The recipe was my grandmother's." She pulled her wallet from the large handbag hanging from her arm. "Poor Prudence. Have you heard anything about the police investigation? Have they discovered anything?"

"Not that I know of," Shelby said as she placed the herbs in a bag. "It's hard to imagine someone as meek and mild as Prudence stirring anyone to murder."

Deirdre gave a snort. "Prudence made plenty of enemies, even in the short time she was here. You know she accused Earl Bylsma, our former head usher, of stealing from the collection plate? Herb—he's my husband—is the treasurer of St. Andrews, and he said Prudence went to him on more than one occasion accusing the poor man of stealing."

"Really?"

This wasn't news to Shelby, but it was confirmation of what Grace had already told her.

"Earl was absolutely furious with Prudence. He could hardly stand to be in the same room with her after that. He quit ushering even though Herb tried to persuade him to keep the position." Deirdre stuffed her wallet back in her purse. "And here's the ironic part." She leaned closer to Shelby. "After Earl quit, Herb was still short when he double-checked the cash before readying the bank deposit."

"Seriously?"

"Absolutely. The Sunday Prudence was murdered, nearly a thousand dollars went missing from the collection."

⸻

Shelby could hardly wait to call Kelly to tell her what she'd learned from Deirdre. The market was beginning to wind down, and she'd sold all of her cheese spread and most of her herbs, lettuces, and vegetables. She looked around, pulled her cell phone from her pocket, and began to dial Kelly's number.

"Excuse me. How much are the cucumbers?"

Shelby ended the call abruptly and turned to her customer. Why hadn't she seen her coming?

After a bit of haggling over the price, the woman bought all of Shelby's cucumbers, several heads of lettuce, and the remainder of the herbs. Shelby packaged everything up and handed the bag to the woman with a smile.

She checked again, but no one was approaching her booth. She pulled out her cell phone once more and quickly dialed.

"Can you meet me at the diner in half an hour?" she asked when Kelly answered.

"Sure. I'm finished with my last patient—a very obstreperous miniature poodle who tried to take a bite out of my thumb when I took his temperature. Not that I blame him. I wouldn't like it much, either. I have to close up, but that won't take long."

"Great. See you in about half an hour. I should be able to get everything back in the truck by then."

"Don't rush. I'll get us a booth."

Shelby began carrying the crates back to the truck. It was a lot easier now that they were almost all empty. It was still hot, though, and she paused for a minute to take a drink from her water bottle. A nice cold pop was going to taste really good.

Shelby recognized Kelly's car when she pulled into the parking lot of the diner. The macadam was lifting up in places and crumbling in others, making for a rather bumpy ride. Shelby backed the truck into a spot and got out.

Scrubby grass grew alongside the walk that led to the diner's red-and-white front door. A rotating sign on the roof read OPEN 6 A.M. TO MIDNIGHT. Farmers got up early and went to bed early, but the diner also catered to long-distance truckers passing through.

Several of the aluminum letters spelling out the name on the front of the diner were missing so that it had become LOVE DIN R. The general feeling was that if you didn't already know it was the Lovett Diner, then you had no business being there. The truckers were tolerated because they arrived after all the locals had gone home and were fast asleep in bed and the two never had to meet.

Kelly was tucked into a corner booth when Shelby walked in. She was still wearing the blue scrubs she'd had on earlier that morning, but they were considerably dirtier and more stained now. Her hair was yanked back in an elastic with half of it escaping and curling around her face. Even from a distance, Shelby could see she looked even more tired than she had earlier—tired and still worried.

Shelby sat down opposite her friend. The top of the table was worn and scarred from years of use, and someone had carved the initials F & P in the corner. The tableside jukeboxes were mostly broken now, although a few still played the tunes that only went as far as the late 1960s.

"I hope it's good news," Kelly said as soon as Shelby sat down. She took a long pull on the straw in her glass of pop.

"I think it is," Shelby began but stopped when the waitress swooped by their table, her pad and pencil at the ready.

Shelby ordered a pop and a plate of fries.

"What?" She looked at Kelly. "I'm hungry. I've been hauling crates around all day."

Kelly laughed. "I didn't say anything. It's your guilty conscience talking, not me."

"You're probably right."

Almost immediately the waitress was back with Shelby's pop and fries. She put the plate down on the table between them.

"Looks like you have to share," Kelly said, snatching a fry from the pile.

Shelby peeled the wrapper off her straw, plunged it into her drink, and took a long sip.

"So, what is this great news? Don't keep me in suspense." Kelly grabbed another fry.

"It's about Prudence and the money missing from the collection at church."

"The money she claims Earl stole?"

Shelby nodded, her mouth full of fries. "Deirdre Fitch came by my booth at the farmers' market today. Her husband, Herb, is the treasurer at St. Andrews."

Kelly stopped chewing and raised her eyebrows.

"She says . . ." Shelby paused to take a drink.

"Go on," Kelly urged.

"She says that money went missing after Earl stopped ushering. The Sunday of Prudence's murder, as a matter of fact."

"So either two thieves are at work at St. Andrews, or Earl isn't guilty."

"Exactly. And get this . . ." Shelby picked up a fry.

"Don't keep stopping like that," Kelly grumbled. "The suspense is killing me."

Shelby grinned.

Kelly pointed a french fry at her. "You're doing it on purpose. To tease me."

"Sorry. I couldn't resist. Anyway, Deirdre told me that the Sunday morning Prudence was murdered, nearly a thousand dollars was missing from the collection."

"A thousand dollars!" Kelly put down the fry she was about to eat. "But that's how much was found in Prudence's purse."

"Exactly," Shelby said with satisfaction.

"You don't think . . ."

"What else?" Shelby took a sip of her pop. "It's logical, isn't it? A thousand dollars is missing from the church. Prudence has a thousand dollars in her purse."

"Therefore Prudence is the one who stole the money," Kelly finished for her. She nibbled the end of her french fry. "Prudence had some nerve accusing Earl of stealing when she was the one with her hand in the cookie jar."

"Well, we don't know for sure that Prudence—"

"It's too much of a coincidence to be anything but true," Kelly insisted. "I don't blame Earl for being so mad. I would have felt like killing Prudence myself." She looked at Shelby. "You do think Earl did it, don't you?"

17

Dear Reader,

The farmers' market was a success. I sold most of the produce and cheese I brought with me. Living on a farm means keeping a tight rein on your spending and praying you'll have enough to keep body and soul together.

My cell phone is still the old flip-top kind. Amelia's is much fancier and cost a fortune. Fortunately her paternal grandparents gave it to her for Christmas. The elder McDonalds are living in Florida now. They up and moved when Grandpa McDonald sold his plumbing business to his younger partner.

I haven't quite taken to cutting my own hair yet— there's a salon over in Allenvale that's quite reasonable— but I certainly don't go as often as I'd like. Fortunately

my blog has started to bring in some money, much to
my surprise, since Armor Cookware approached me
about advertising on my site.

As Shelby drove out of the parking lot, she thought over
what she'd learned. It was hard to imagine Prudence stealing from the church, but maybe there had been something
wrong with her? Shelby had read of cases like that—where
a brain tumor caused a person to act completely out of the
norm. She supposed that would have shown up when they
had done the autopsy. The thought made her shiver.

She hadn't ruled out Wallace as a suspect yet, but Earl
was the front-runner as far as she was concerned. He
certainly didn't seem the type, but then, look at Prudence—
she wasn't at all what she'd seemed, either.

Shelby pulled into the parking lot of the Lovett Feed
Store. She needed to buy a couple of bags of chicken feed.
The Lovett Feed Store was actually Van Enks Feed Store,
but people had been referring to it as the Lovett Feed
Store for so long that the Van Enks eventually gave up
and changed the name. The same family had been running the place since the early 1900s, and Harland van
Enk had been behind the counter since Shelby was a
little girl—his hair growing steadily whiter and his pos-
ture more stooped as the years went on.

The feed store itself was little more than a gussied-up
barn with exposed joists and rough flooring. Large bags
of feed were stacked against the wall and smaller ones
were on plain metal shelving. Shelby found the brand she
wanted and looked around the store.

A boy—most likely one of the younger generation of
Van Enks—rushed over with a cart. He hefted the bag

onto the cart as easily as if it didn't weigh a thing and wheeled it to the checkout counter for Shelby.

The man in line in front of Shelby looked vaguely familiar, and when he turned around she realized it was Earl. She felt strangely embarrassed, as if the fact that she'd been talking about him was apparent on her face.

"Oh, hi," he said. He looked startled—as if Shelby was the last person he expected to see.

"Another hot day, isn't it?" He jiggled the change in his pocket and motioned toward the counter with a tip of his head. "Harland's gone into the back to get me some dog food that just came in. Sorry to be holding you up."

"That's okay. It feels good to slow down every once in a while."

They were quiet for a moment.

"Say," Earl blurted out, "your brother-in-law works for the police, doesn't he?"

Shelby was slightly surprised by the question. "Yes, he's a detective."

"Has he said anything about . . . you know . . . the murder?" He jingled the change in his pocket faster and faster.

"Not really." Shelby was thinking fast—how to introduce the subject of Prudence and her accusations?

"It's not like old Prudence had a lot of enemies." Earl laughed, but there was nothing humorous about the sound.

"I gather she *did* have enemies. I understand you were pretty mad at her when she accused you of stealing."

Earl jumped. "Who told you that?"

"I don't remember," Shelby lied with her fingers crossed behind her back.

"It's not true. I didn't steal the money, and I told her so."

"I know. Mrs. Fitch told me that money was missing even after you left. But it still must have made you pretty angry." Shelby didn't want to push too hard.

A red flush rose from Earl's neck to his forehead. The tips of his ears were crimson. "Are you accusing me of murder?"

Dear Reader, I think it's time I backed down. As a matter of fact, I may have gone entirely too far. . . .

"Oh no, nothing like that," Shelby reassured him.

"Because if that's what you think, I can prove I didn't have nothing to do with it." Earl jammed both hands in his pockets.

Dear Reader, now, this is getting interesting. . . .

"I certainly didn't mean to imply—"

"I was with Matt Hudson the whole time. You can ask him. He needed some help carrying the empty crates back to his truck. We spoke to Prudence before we started—to let her know Matt was beginning to pack up—and we were together until we heard you come running out of the house yelling to call nine-one-one."

iiiiiiiiiiiiiiiiiiiiiiii

Shelby felt strangely guilty as she drove away from the feed store. She certainly hadn't meant to upset Earl. On the other hand, she had gotten some interesting information. She wondered if what Earl had said was true.

Shelby pulled into the driveway at Love Blossom Farm and was surprised when a truck pulled in right behind her. She could see LOVETT GENERAL STORE written on the side through her rearview mirror.

She got out of the pickup just as Matt Hudson was getting out of his.

"Perfect timing," Shelby said as she let down the tailgate. "I could use some help with this bag."

"At your service, ma'am." Matt tipped an imaginary hat. He pulled the bag out of the pickup and slung it over his shoulder. "Where to?"

Shelby led him back to the old barn. She threw open the doors to let in some light. "Mind the cat. Patches likes to wind around people's ankles."

"I know what you mean. My Whiskey does the same. He tripped me once, and I hurled an entire plate of food at the wall. It would have been funny if I hadn't been so hungry." Matt walked over to the far corner. "This okay?"

"Perfect."

He put the bag down and leaned it against the wall. "I've brought the paint for your mudroom. It came in this afternoon."

"That was fast."

Matt gave a mock bow. "We aim to please, ma'am."

Shelby laughed and led the way back to the house. She went inside while Matt went out to his truck to grab the paint cans.

She was surprised to find Bert in the kitchen, sitting in the old rocker that had been in the corner at least since Shelby's grandparents had owned the place. She had a ball of wool in her lap and was knitting a pair of mittens. She held them up. "Hard to believe we'll be needing these any time soon, but winter will be here before you know it."

"Let's not rush it," Shelby said. Winters were long and hard on the farm.

"I brought back that mending I promised I'd take care of for you," Bert said, her knitting needles making a ticktock sound as she flew through the row of stitches. "I put it in the laundry room. Didn't know if it needed washing or not."

"Thanks, Bert. You're a saint. I don't know what we'd do without you."

"Don't go getting all sentimental. You'll embarrass me."

Shelby laughed. "Is Amelia upstairs?"

Bert shook her head. "She's gone out. Said she was off to Kaylee's house. I told her I didn't mind sticking around until you got back."

Shelby froze. Kaylee's house? Not very likely.

"I hope that's okay?" Bert asked, a frown creasing the skin between her eyebrows.

"Sure." Shelby smiled brightly. It was kind enough of Bert to babysit. She didn't want to make her feel as if she'd somehow been negligent.

"Billy's outside playing," Bert said with a smile. "So like his father. You can't bottle them up inside—they won't have it."

Shelby smiled—a genuine smile this time. Bert was right. Billy was so much like his father, and the resemblance was more than merely physical.

The front door opened and Matt's voice rang out. "Here's your paint." He came in carrying two cans.

Bert's mouth puckered in disapproval.

"Shall I take them out to the mudroom?"

"Yes. Good idea."

Bert followed them. "Are those the colors?" she asked, pointing to the sample paint swipes on the tops of the cans.

Shelby nodded. "I think they're going to look great," she said, almost defiantly.

Bert looked around the room and ran a hand through her short gray hair. "You're right. It's about time this place got a face-lift. Besides, it's yours now. Time to put your stamp on it, I suppose. I don't know what your grandmother would say, but she's not here, is she?" She turned to Shelby.

Shelby hid a smile. She knew Bert would come around eventually.

Bert gestured toward the paint cans. "Let me know if you need any help. I'm pretty good with a paintbrush if I haven't lost my touch." She looked at the two of them with a bemused expression on her face. "I'm going to go throw those tops I mended for you into the washing machine."

Shelby and Matt were silent as they watched Bert walk through the kitchen and down the hall.

Matt opened his mouth, then closed it again. He appeared to have reconsidered what he was about to say. Finally, after a brief pause, he said, "I take it there's still no news about Prudence's murder? Your brother-in-law is the detective on the case, isn't he?"

"Yes, although the last time we spoke, he didn't have much of anything to tell me. At least not anything he was able to share." Shelby hesitated for a second. "I did have an interesting conversation with Earl—he's the church usher who quit when Prudence accused him of stealing from the Sunday collection."

"I know Earl. He's a good guy. I hope no one believed Prudence."

Shelby shrugged. "You know how those things are— no one wants to believe the story, but it gets repeated over and over until it becomes fact. People always seem to be quicker to believe something bad about a person than something good."

Matt grunted. "Human nature, I guess."

"And now people are saying . . . that Earl might have had something to do with Prudence's death," Shelby continued.

Dear Reader, I know I was the one thinking that Earl might have had something to do with Prudence's death, but I can hardly tell Matt that, can I?

"That's ridiculous." The words nearly exploded out of Matt.

"Obviously that's what Earl said. He also told me he was with you at the time of the murder."

Matt frowned. "You're right. He was with me. He asked me if I needed any help loading the empty crates and coolers back into the truck. We went to tell Prudence we were going to start packing up, and Earl was still with me when we heard you screaming for someone to call nine-one-one."

Looks like that successfully rules Earl out as a suspect, Shelby thought.

"I'd better be going," Matt said. "But I'll call you and we can fix up a time to do the painting." He gestured toward the walls of the mudroom.

Shelby showed him to the door and when she turned around Bert was standing behind her with a sly smile on her face.

"What?" Shelby asked.

Bert laughed. "Nothing. It's just that I think you have an admirer there." She gestured toward the closed door.

"Matt? I know."

"So?"

"So what?"

"So are you going to go out with him?"

"He hasn't asked me yet."

Shelby thought of the moment when Matt had opened his mouth and then quickly closed it again. Had he been about to ask her out but then changed his mind? She was glad he hadn't. She wasn't ready to say yes yet.

⁞⁞⁞⁞⁞⁞⁞⁞⁞⁞⁞⁞⁞⁞⁞⁞⁞⁞⁞⁞⁞⁞⁞

Shelby and Bert spent what remained of the afternoon testing a new recipe Shelby had created for a layered vegetable tart that made good use of the tomatoes, zucchini, and eggplant from her garden.

Amelia had already come skulking back—this time she'd really been to Kaylee's house. As soon as Shelby had heard the car in the driveway, she'd run out to check. That didn't change the fact that Amelia knew she was grounded but had gone out anyway. Shelby would have to decide how to deal with that later. If Bill were there, he'd know what to do. Although Shelby wondered if Amelia's sudden streak of obstreperousness wasn't a delayed response to her father's death.

They had just gotten the tart in the oven when Shelby looked at her watch and then turned to Bert. "I'm going to call Billy to come and start washing up. Depending on how dirty he's gotten, he may need a bath before dinner."

Shelby opened the screen door to the mudroom, cupped her hands around her mouth, and yelled, "Billy! Come get ready for dinner."

She waited, but there was no response. She scanned the horizon, waiting for Billy to appear. When he didn't, she put her fingers in her mouth and let out a loud whistle.

"Billy," she yelled again.

This time Bitsy and Jenkins came running. They'd

learned that when she called Billy to come in, dinner was probably not far off, and both of them were shameless beggars. It worked—rarely a night went by when they didn't get at least a couple of morsels of leftovers.

Shelby was beginning to get annoyed. Billy knew that if he didn't come home straightaway when she called him, he would be limited to playing on the front lawn or in the back where she could easily see him.

She yelled again and waited. A tingling sense of unease was making its way up her spine to the back of her neck and prickling over her scalp in a way that made her shiver. She thought about the squash that she had found hanging from her porch ceiling. Was someone trying to tell her something again?

The thought that they might have done something to Billy made her frantic. She screamed again, panic nearly blocking her throat.

"What's wrong?" Bert had come running out of the house to stand next to Shelby.

"It's Billy. He's not coming. He always comes when he hears me call."

Bert put a hand on Shelby's arm. "It's not like you to get so worked up like this."

Shelby thought of the squash and opened her mouth to explain but then shut it again. Talking about it would make it too real. Besides, she didn't want to worry Bert for no reason.

"The boy's probably just wandered out of earshot. Come on." Bert hooked her arm through Shelby's. "Let's go find him."

Shelby let Bert lead her past the kitchen garden, past

the herb and lettuce gardens, and back to where a handful of fruit trees grew. Shelby continued to call Billy at
regular intervals.

Shelby stopped and cupped her hands around her
mouth. "Billy. Come home this instant."

She and Bert listened intently.

"Did you hear that?" Shelby turned to Bert. "I thought
I heard something."

"I'm afraid you couldn't prove it by me. The hearing
isn't what it used to be."

There was another faint cry, and this time they both
heard it.

"It's coming from over there." Shelby pointed toward
a cluster of apple trees.

They headed in that direction. As they got closer, the
voice became louder.

"Mom, Mom, help!"

"Oh my goodness, I wonder what's happened." Shelby
quickened her pace. "Billy, where are you?" she called back.

Had he fallen down a hole? Was there an old well on the
property no one knew about? The thought gave Shelby chills.

"Can you see him?" Shelby asked Bert.

Bert shook her head. "No, but his voice sounds
strong—not like he's hurt."

Shelby clutched a hand to her heart. "I hope you're right."

As they got closer, Billy's voice became louder, but
they still couldn't see him. His voice sounded much
closer—almost as if he was standing next to them—so
where on earth was he?

"Up here, Mom. I'm stuck."

Shelby looked up into the branches of the apple tree
and was shocked to see Billy clinging to a branch.

"Billy, get down from there," she said, although she knew that was an irrational thing to say. Obviously if he could get down, he would have done so by now.

"I can't. I'm afraid."

"Then how did you get up there in the first place?"

"I don't know."

"I used to be a whiz at tree climbing, but not anymore," Bert said ruefully.

"Me, too, but I don't think I can reach up there." Shelby stared into the tree. She couldn't imagine how Billy had gotten himself so far up into the branches.

Shelby and Bert both whirled around when they heard someone clearing their throat.

"Sorry, ladies. Didn't mean to startle you," Jake said. "I couldn't help hearing you calling for Billy, and it sounded like you might be having some kind of trouble."

Shelby glanced at Bert, and she had that sly smile again.

"Do we need a ladder?" Shelby asked as Jake stared up at the tree branches. "I can't imagine how Billy reached that first branch." She pointed toward the lowest-hanging one, which was still well over Billy's head.

Jake laughed and gestured toward an overturned crate on the far side of the tree. "I'm guessing he stood on that."

"Oh! You're right." Shelby hadn't noticed the crate.

"Billy," Jake called into the tree. "Hang on. I'm coming to get you."

And with that, Jake jumped up and grabbed a branch. He pulled himself up until he was sitting on it.

Bert poked Shelby with her elbow. "He's strong," she said admiringly. "Good-looking, too. If I were younger . . ."

Jake made his way up the tree until he reached the

branch where Billy was stuck. He grabbed Billy around the waist and began to make his way back down, holding the boy firmly. When he got to the lowest branch, he held Billy out, and Shelby reached up and grabbed him. Jake jumped down himself, landing next to Shelby with a soft thud.

"Thank you so much," Shelby said, although she felt the words were inadequate even as she said them. She hugged Billy fiercely until he finally managed to squirm away with a scowl.

Jake shook his head. "No problem. Glad I could help. One of my heifers managed to get her head stuck in the fence, so I was on this side of the pasture, and I heard you yelling. If you ever need my help again, just call, okay?"

"Sure."

"I'll see you later, then." He nodded at Bert.

Shelby and Bert stood and watched his retreating back. Billy was kicking fallen apples against the tree.

Bert turned to Shelby. "Looks like you've got not one, but two men interested in you. I think you're going to have to think about dating again sooner rather than later."

18

Dear Reader,

Billy certainly gave me a scare today. I'm sure Bert and I would have figured something out, but it was nice to be rescued for once. There, I said it. I pride myself on my independence, but it's certainly nice to have someone working side by side with you or doing something that's easier for them than it would be for you.

Bert keeps after me to start dating. She's forgetting one important fact—no one has asked me yet. I'm pretty sure I could easily remedy that, but I'm still a little hesitant to leave the safety of the starting gate.

The vegetable tart was a big success. Even Billy had seconds, and he's not overly fond of vegetables—although he loves watching them grow in the garden. He is so proud of his on-its-way-to-being-gigantic

zucchini. I will be sharing the recipe for the tart with
you shortly—I have an idea for one more tweak before
I consider it perfect.

Shelby had insisted that Bert stay for dinner so she
could weigh in on the vegetable tart. It was her idea to
add a pinch of nutmeg to the mixture, and Shelby was
looking forward to trying that next time.

They were sitting around the table enjoying a cup of
coffee. Amelia was rinsing and stacking the dishes in the
dishwasher—reluctantly, which was obvious by the way
she was banging the plates and silverware around. Shelby
was turning a deaf ear—she would have felt sorrier for
Amelia, but she was still fuming that she'd disobeyed the
order that she was grounded.

Billy had been quiet during dinner. His face had been
as white as flour when Jake rescued him from that tree, and
he was still not back to his usual boisterous self. The house
seemed strangely quiet without his normal noise-making.

Shelby and Bert were finishing up their coffee when
Billy burst into the kitchen.

"Can I go check on my zucchini? Can I? Can I?" He
hopped from one foot to the other impatiently.

Shelby took a deep breath. Part of her never wanted
to let him out of her sight again. "I don't know. . . ."

"Oh, Mom, please. I just know it's gotten bigger. I
haven't checked it since before Sunday, so it's bound to
have grown a ton. It has to have so I can win the competition at the county fair. Kenny Gardener said he's going
to win, but he's just saying that. I saw his zucchini and it
wasn't half as big as mine."

Shelby looked at Bert.

Bert raised her eyebrows. "You can't wrap him in cotton wool," she said.

"Okay." Shelby sighed. "But you're not to go any farther than the vegetable garden, do you hear me? And absolutely no climbing trees."

"Sure," Billy, who was already halfway to the door to the mudroom, called over his shoulder.

Shelby sighed again.

Bert put her hand over Shelby's. "You can't protect him from everything."

"I know. But what if we hadn't found him this afternoon, and what if he'd tried to get down from that tree and fallen, and what if he'd lain there with a broken—"

"Whoa!" Bert put out a hand. "That's an awful lot of what-ifs, don't you think? Besides, nothing happened. Other than that we got to see your extremely hot neighbor in action." She grinned.

"Bert!"

"What? There may be wrinkles around my eyes, but they aren't interfering with my vision. I can still see and appreciate, you know."

Shelby laughed. "I guess you're right."

"I know I am."

They had just begun to clean up the coffee cups and saucers when they heard the screen door to the mudroom slam, and Billy burst into the room.

"So, how big is your zucchini now?" Shelby asked as she put the cups in the dishwasher.

"It's not." Billy's face was red with fury. "It's gone!"

"Gone? How can that be?" Shelby exchanged a glance with Bert. Had some hungry animal come along and eaten it?

"It's not there. It's gone." Billy's lip trembled, and Shelby could tell he was trying hard not to cry.

"Maybe you just missed it? The leaves on that plant are huge, and your zucchini might be tucked underneath one of them."

"I don't know. . . ." Billy's face started to brighten slightly. "Do you think so?"

Shelby nodded as she untied her apron. "I'm sure of it. Let's go find your zucchini." She mentally crossed her fingers. She wasn't at all sure they'd find it, and he would be heartbroken if they didn't.

They made a sad-looking parade as they trooped out to the garden—Shelby biting her lip, Bert with a frown between her eyebrows, and Billy hunching his shoulders against possible disappointment.

At this time of the evening, the sun was on its way down, and the garden was in shadow. The air was cooler than it had been all day and felt good against Shelby's warm face. She waded into the space between the rows of zucchini plants, feeling the leaves brushing against her bare legs.

"Where exactly was your zucchini?" Shelby asked. She'd lived in fear of accidentally picking it and had finally come up with the solution of tying a piece of twine around the stem to remind her not to.

"Here." Billy knelt in the dirt and separated the leaves. "It was right here."

"Maybe some of the plants have grown up around it?" Bert said as she stooped over with a hand to her back. She pushed back leaf after leaf.

Shelby did the same. It was undeniable. The zucchini was gone. Plenty more still clung to the vines but none nearly as big as the one Billy had been nurturing all month.

"Look," Bert said suddenly, parting two of the giant leaves.

A broken stem with a piece of twine around it was clearly visible, but it was obvious that the zucchini itself was gone.

"I told you," Billy said, rubbing his eyes in an effort not to cry. "Someone stole it. It was right there." He pointed to the stem.

Bert straightened up. "Who would do something like that?"

"I can't imagine. Do you suppose some animal ate it?"

Bert shook her head. "You can see the squash was twisted right off the stem. If an animal had taken it, the break wouldn't be so clean. And if they'd eaten it, there'd at least be a few remnants on the ground—some seeds or some peel or something."

"That's true." Shelby looked at Bert, her eyes wide in disbelief. "It really does look as if it was stolen."

<hr/>

Billy was inconsolable. Shelby finally bundled him into the car to take him for an ice-cream cone. She tried to convince Amelia to come along, but it was obvious she didn't want to be seen with her mother and younger brother. There was a soft-serve ice-cream shop on the road that led out of town. Shelby knew high school kids congregated there during the summer, and she supposed Amelia thought it would be uncool to be seen there with her family.

Or maybe she was afraid Ned would be there, and Shelby would embarrass her in front of him. Shelby could remember feeling the exact same way when she was

Amelia's age, so perhaps being embarrassed by your family was some sort of teenage rite of passage.

A double chocolate-dipped cone topped with sprinkles put Billy in fairly good humor again. Shelby treated herself to a small vanilla cone, and she and Billy shared one side of a picnic table with a father and his two daughters on the other side.

By the time they got back home, Billy was sleepy, dirty, and sticky. Shelby sent him off to take a bath and went into the kitchen to pour herself a glass of water. Amelia was sitting at the kitchen table, texting furiously on her phone. Shelby pushed the small cup of vanilla ice cream she'd brought home toward her daughter.

Amelia barely lifted her eyes from her phone as she peeled the paper off the flat wooden spoon that came with the ice cream.

"I know who took Billy's zucchini," Amelia said without raising her eyes from her texting.

Shelby stopped with her glass under the stream of water from the faucet. "What did you say?"

"I told you," Amelia said with an exasperated sigh. "I know who stole Billy's zucchini."

Water was now spilling over the side of Shelby's glass. She shut the faucet off quickly and turned to stare at Amelia. "Well, who?"

"Mrs. Gardener," Amelia said smugly. "Ned and I saw her take it during the potluck."

"Liz Gardener? What on earth would she want with Billy's zucchini?" And what on earth was Amelia doing in the back garden with Ned, where they were obviously hidden from view?

"I don't know." Amelia took a bite of her ice cream.

"Maybe she was afraid Billy would win the county fair contest this year instead of her son."

"Why didn't you say anything?"

Shelby watched in exasperation as Amelia shrugged and rolled her eyes.

"You know how much winning that contest means to your brother!"

Amelia gave Shelby a look that nearly froze her to the spot.

"You don't care, do you?" Shelby said to her daughter, realization dawning. Amelia was resentful—of her brother!

Shelby was shocked when Amelia brushed at her eyes. They were glistening with tears.

Amelia pushed away from the table, her chair making a loud discordant scraping noise against the floor. "It's always about Billy, isn't it?"

"Amelia. What on earth do you mean?"

"Ever since Billy was born, it's been all about him. Billy this . . . Billy that . . . ," she mimicked with a sneer in her voice. "Suddenly Dad had the son he'd always wanted, and I wasn't his girl anymore."

Shelby put her arms around her daughter. "Is that what this is all about?" She could feel Amelia struggle, but she didn't let go—just hugged her tighter. "Your father adored you. You were Daddy's girl, and Billy coming along didn't change that. Nothing could change that."

Amelia gave a loud sniff, and Shelby noticed she'd stopped struggling. "But Billy and Daddy did everything together—hunting, fishing, hiking."

"You and your dad did some of those things together, too," Shelby said, leaning her cheek against the top of her daughter's head. Her hair smelled like strawberry shampoo.

"Yeah, but then Billy started horning in."

"I know your father loved you both very much."

Amelia gave a loud sniff.

"And I love you." Shelby put a finger under Amelia's chin and tilted her face up. "I love having a daughter I can do things with."

This time Amelia did pull away. "Well, I don't want you. I want Dad."

She ran out of the kitchen, stomped up the stairs, and slammed her bedroom door.

Shelby stood stock-still for several long moments. She knew Amelia didn't mean what she'd said, but that didn't stop the tears from pricking the back of her eyelids.

The kids didn't understand that she wanted Bill back as much as they did. And hopefully they would never have to know what that kind of loss was like.

19

Dear Reader,

I know you probably think it's extreme that someone would steal a zucchini just so their son could win the largest vegetable prize at the county fair, but we take these things seriously around here. The kids pride themselves on their skills, whether it's growing vegetables or raising chickens, pigs, or rabbits, and the county fair is their chance to show off what they've been doing.

Not that they don't love technology and the latest gadgets like kids all over (case in point—Amelia and her cell phone), but farm life is full of so many things to do and so many things to learn that they tend to spend their time—in the warmer months at least—outdoors. Of course in the winter, there's sledding and ice-skating, so it's a rare day that they spend it all inside.

Shelby didn't look forward to talking to Liz Gardener about the zucchini she'd stolen from Love Blossom Farm's garden. But she couldn't just let it go, either. Besides, it was possible that Liz might have seen something while she was in Shelby's garden. The back door to the mudroom was plainly visible from the zucchini patch.

It was just unfortunate that Shelby had to be at the farmers' market right after her visit to Liz's, and that meant taking the pickup truck. Shelby tried to rise above the embarrassment of rattling down Liz's fancy street with the truck sounding as if it was losing parts of itself with every inch it traveled.

Liz's development was outside Lovett and offered a completely different sort of lifestyle. The houses were enormous brick Tudors, Georgians, and Colonials with vast and perfectly manicured front lawns and meticulously designed gardens. It was home to the professionals who supplied the local hospital with doctors and the local courts with lawyers.

Shelby couldn't imagine living in a place like this. This was the sort of place where, in order to keep up with the neighbors, you had to have your hair done, your nails done, your wardrobe up to date. Shelby couldn't remember the last time she'd had her nails done, was months overdue for a haircut, and spent most of her time in jeans or cutoffs.

She felt herself shrinking inside as she made her way farther down the street, on the lookout for Liz's number. She found it attached to a stately Georgian with a circular drive. She pulled the pickup to the front door, cringing at the noise the brakes made when she applied them.

Shelby smoothed down her shirt and patted her hair as she waited for Liz to answer the doorbell.

The door was flung open, and Liz looked astonished to find Shelby on her doorstep. A frigid blast of air wafted from the house, making Shelby even more conscious of the perspiration on her upper lip and the back of her neck. The truck's air-conditioning didn't work. *Dear Reader. Correction. The truck never had air-conditioning in the first place.*

Liz was wearing a pair of white jeans and a pale pink cashmere T-shirt. Shelby didn't even know that T-shirts came in cashmere. Liz's black patent leather thong sandals had a large gold horse bit on the top strap, and her toes were done in the French manicure style.

Shelby scrunched up her own toes inside her white sneakers, which were still a bit green around the edges from the last time she'd worn them to cut the grass.

"Shelby, what a lovely surprise," Liz said, managing to make it sound as if it was anything but. "Won't you come in?"

What Shelby really wanted to do was turn tail and run, but she dutifully followed Liz into the house and down the hall to the kitchen. The kitchen was state-of-the-art, and Shelby found herself nearly drooling over the double ovens, a stainless refrigerator that was the size of a small car, and the six-burner cooktop.

"Can I pour you a cold drink? Some iced tea?" Liz asked with her hand on the refrigerator door handle.

"Yes. Thank you."

Perhaps something to drink would help unstick Shelby's tongue from the roof of her mouth, where it seemed to have lodged itself the moment she stepped inside Liz's house.

Liz handed Shelby the glass of iced tea. "Shall we go into the living room?"

She led Shelby into a vast room that ran from the front of the house to the back. All the furniture was upholstered in varying shades of white and cream. Shelby devoutly hoped the seat of her shorts was clean. The pickup was way overdue for a good wash, both inside and out.

She tried as discreetly as possible to brush off her cut-offs before perching on the edge of one of the white sofas.

Liz sat in one of the chairs and leaned back, one leg crossed over the other, her sandal dangling from her perfectly painted toes.

"Now, what was it you wanted to see me about?" Liz looked at Shelby over the rim of her glass as she took a sip of her tea.

Shelby cleared her throat. This was it. *In for a penny, in for a pound,* as her grandmother used to say. "Billy's prize zucchini is missing—the one he was growing for the county fair."

Liz's eyes widened slightly, but other than that, she didn't move a muscle. "I'm very sorry to hear that, but I don't see what that has to do with me. . . ."

Shelby cleared her throat again—she must sound as if she was coming down with something. "Amelia—my daughter—saw you in the garden. She saw you steal Billy's zucchini."

Liz looked as if someone had dumped an entire bucket of ice water on her. She gasped and both hands flew to her cheeks, which were slowly turning the color of ripe beets.

"She's . . . she's . . . lying," Liz sputtered.

"I don't think so. Besides, someone else saw you as well."

No need to tell Liz that Amelia was in the backyard with a boy.

"Oh, all right," Liz snapped. "I did take it. Kenny needs to win that competition."

"What about Billy? He had his heart set on entering that contest."

Liz waved a hand as if that was completely inconsequential. "Kenny needs to develop a taste for winning. He won't get ahead otherwise. And right now he's too . . . too easygoing. He has to develop a lust for victory."

Shelby didn't know what to say.

"Anyway, I'm sure you understand." Liz took another sip of her tea.

Shelby decided that the better part of valor was to accept Liz's explanation. Especially since she had another agenda in talking to Liz.

Shelby couldn't quite bring herself to say she understood, so she contented herself with giving a brisk nod, which Liz fortunately seemed to take for acquiescence.

Shelby took a sip of her iced tea and tried to cultivate a cozy, conspiratorial tone. "Did you happen to see anyone while you were in the garden? You can see the mudroom from there, and it's just possible you saw something that might be important to the police."

"Do you think so?" Liz preened herself. "I did see someone go into the mudroom while Prudence was in there. Of course at the time, I didn't think anything of it."

Shelby felt her heartbeat speed up. Liz had actually seen someone, and it seemed quite likely that that person was the murderer.

"Did you happen to see who it was?" Shelby asked as if the answer was of no interest to her whatsoever.

Liz looked at Shelby over the rim of her glass, a coy look on her face. "It was a woman," she said breathlessly.

Shelby was momentarily startled. That wasn't the answer she had been expecting. She'd been ready to put her money on Wallace. And Wallace was most certainly not a woman. "Are you sure? Could it have been a man perhaps? With longish hair?"

Liz frowned. "I don't think so. You know how you can tell a man from a woman even from a distance, and even when you can't see them clearly? They walk differently, carry themselves differently."

"Did you see who it was?"

Liz gave a practiced pout. "I didn't. I'm afraid I'm a bit vain. Dr. Strong has prescribed glasses for me, but I never wear them."

"So maybe it was a man after all?" Shelby said, clutching at the proverbial straw.

Liz shook her head vehemently. "No. I'm quite sure it was a woman. Dark hair. I couldn't tell how tall from that distance, but definitely a woman."

IIIIIIIIIIIIIIIIIIIIIIIIII

Shelby was more relieved to leave Liz's house than she normally was leaving the dentist's office. Vendors were just beginning to set up for the farmers' market when Shelby backed the truck into her usual space. She had a bumper crop of fresh-from-the-vine tomatoes along with radishes, summer squash, and heads of butter lettuce to sell.

Shelby had just finished serving her first customer when she thought she saw a familiar figure in the distance ambling toward her.

"Hey," Kelly said when she came abreast of Shelby's booth.

She carried with her the unmistakable odor of manure. Shelby wrinkled her nose.

Kelly tilted her head to one side. "Do I smell?"

"Yes. Like you might have stepped in something."

Kelly put a hand on the booth for balance and, lifting up one foot, stared at the bottom of her shoe.

"I think you're right. I was over at Jake Taylor's farm checking on one of his cows. He suspected milk fever, and he was right. Hopefully the intravenous calcium I administered will cure it. I've had a high success rate with it so far."

"You've lost me, I'm afraid."

Kelly picked up a ripe tomato and sniffed it. "That's okay. But I obviously stepped in something while I was there. I'm beginning to smell it myself." She handed Shelby the tomato. "I'll take this tomato and some of your lettuce."

Shelby selected a head of butter lettuce and held it out. "Will this do?"

Kelly nodded.

"Is this a special occasion? I'm more accustomed to seeing you feasting on a granola bar than on a real meal."

"Seth is coming for dinner. I plan to wine and dine him and then pry out of him where he went to when he was supposed to be at the potluck."

"Are you sure you want to know?"

Kelly lifted her shoulders and let them drop. "Yes. I don't know. All I know is it's driving me crazy."

"You can breathe a sigh of relief on one account at least. He didn't have anything to do with Prudence's murder."

Kelly looked up sharply.

"Apparently Liz Gardener saw a woman go into the mudroom shortly before Prudence was murdered."

A slow smile spread across Kelly's face. "But that's wonderful."

"I know. The only downside is it rules out Prudence's son as the murderer. Earl's already been eliminated, so we're back to square one."

Kelly shrugged. "As long as Seth is out of the hot seat, I say let your brother-in-law do the investigating."

"Amen," Shelby said, although as soon as the word left her mouth she realized she didn't mean it. She'd been bitten by the investigative bug and wasn't willing to let go yet.

Before she could think about it any further, a woman approached her booth. She was wearing a denim skirt and a loose-fitting plaid shirt.

"Do you have any parsnips?" She began fingering Shelby's tomatoes.

"Not yet. The parsnips will be a lot sweeter after the first frost, so I won't be harvesting them until then."

The woman put down the tomato she'd been looking at. "Thanks." And she walked off.

Shelby shrugged. You couldn't please all the people all the time.

She was rearranging the heads of lettuce when she noticed Mrs. Willoughby approaching. She was wearing a cotton dress and had a handkerchief pressed to her forehead, which glistened with perspiration.

"Hello, dear," she said when she arrived at Shelby's booth. "Hot enough for you?" She tucked the handkerchief into the purse that hung from the crook of her arm.

"I've got some water bottles if you'd like one?" Shelby began to turn away.

"That would be just what the doctor ordered. But I don't want to take your last one."

"You're not." Shelby smiled and held up two bottles. "See?" She handed one to Mrs. Willoughby and twisted the cap off the other one for herself.

"Hello, ladies." The voice came from over Mrs. Willoughby's shoulder.

"Grace," Mrs. Willoughby exclaimed. She put her hand on the other woman's arm. "Have you met Shelby?" She tilted her head toward Shelby.

"Yes," Grace said in her deep voice. "At the church potluck, and we're both in the knitting group at St. Andrews."

Grace was wearing the same plaid shorts she'd worn to the potluck but with a red top this time.

"Do you have any beets?" Grace scanned the produce in the baskets on Shelby's table.

"I do." Shelby reached underneath the table and pulled out a crate filled with the ruby red vegetable.

"I'm trying that recipe I saw on your blog—the cold beet salad with leeks and goat cheese."

Mrs. Willoughby laughed and her double chin wobbled playfully. "My, you're ambitious. But I suppose being in the first blush of married life, you still want to impress your new husband."

"Well, we are newlyweds." Grace smiled coyly. "And you're right. I still enjoy making him nice dinners. I thought the beet salad would go nicely with the porterhouse I bought to do on the grill."

For some reason, the thought of the deep red beet salad reminded Shelby of the stain on Grace's husband Alan's white shirt, and she thought Grace ought to tell her husband to be careful. Beet stains were almost impossible to get out.

Mrs. Willoughby took a sip of her water and fanned herself with her hand. "Have you heard anything new about poor Prudence's murder? There's been nothing in the paper—nothing at all. You'd think they'd keep us informed," she said waspishly.

"No, not really." Shelby dropped several beets into a bag for Grace.

"I thought maybe with your brother-in-law being on the force and all . . ." Mrs. Willoughby absentmindedly picked up one of Shelby's tomatoes and began to rub it as if it were a worry stone. "I still think that useless son of hers had something to do with it."

Shelby shook her head. "I don't think Wallace could have done it. I just found out from . . . someone . . . that a woman was seen going into the mudroom while Prudence was in there, so it seems very likely that the murderer was female."

"You don't say?" Mrs. Willoughby put the tomato back in the basket. "Of course, Prudence set a lot of people's teeth on edge—I know the members of the Women's Auxiliary found her exasperating. But to hate her enough to kill her . . ." Mrs. Willoughby shrugged.

"Now that I think of it, there is someone who might have hated her enough," Grace said, looking around and lowering her voice.

Shelby had been organizing the cash in her cashbox while the women were talking, but she stopped abruptly. "Really? Who?"

"Jodi Walker."

"What on earth did Jodi have against Prudence? I didn't think they even knew each other all that well."

"They don't," Grace said, leaning closer. "But do you remember the time vandals hung toilet paper on all the trees around the rectory?"

"Of course." Mrs. Willoughby folded her arms across her chest. "Prudence was beyond furious."

"I do remember that." Shelby shut the lid on the cash-box. "I thought it was simply some kids being kids."

Grace shook her head. "Not to Prudence. You know how she was. She took it as a personal affront—said she was mortified."

Shelby couldn't see what this had to do with Jodi. "Surely Jodi wasn't the one who pulled the stunt? I can't imagine a grown woman—"

Grace held up her hand. "No, not Jodi, of course—her son Ned."

Ned. The boy Amelia had been sneaking around with, Shelby thought in panic.

"Prudence accused Ned Walker of doing the deed. She even called the principal of the high school and got the boy suspended."

"The nerve," Mrs. Willoughby exclaimed. "Why involve the school? Why not let the parents deal with it?"

"Do you really think that would make Jodi mad enough to kill?" Shelby couldn't imagine it herself.

"It wasn't only that," Grace confided, leaning toward Shelby. "Ned was removed from the soccer team. Apparently he was a very promising player, but being suspended was against the code the coach played by. And get this." She looked around her and lowered her voice even further. "Someone heard Jodi say that Prudence had ruined her son's life."

20

Dear Reader,

It looks as if Amelia's crush, Ned, is a "bad boy," if you know what I mean. There are some women who just can't help falling for them, and in this case, I guess she takes after me. Wild Bill McDonald wasn't called "Wild Bill" for nothing. And I fell for him hook, line, and sinker.

Not that toilet-papering the rectory is all that bad really. There are a lot worse things going on in the world today. But obviously Ned is the sort who doesn't always play by the rules. I hate to admit it, but there's a small part of me that's proud of Amelia.

Shelby stared at Grace. "Surely you don't think that Jodi murdered Prudence because Prudence got her son suspended?"

"Well, obviously I don't know for sure," Grace said. "All I know is that Jodi was quite furious with Prudence. It seems to me that that gives her as good a motive as any." She turned to Mrs. Willoughby. "What do you think?"

Mrs. Willoughby looked flustered. "I . . . I don't know."

Grace touched Shelby's arm. "I must be going. I'll see you in church on Sunday."

Shelby and Mrs. Willoughby watched Grace walk away.

Mrs. Willoughby turned to Shelby. "Grace certainly seems much happier these days."

"Was she unhappy before? I've only just met her."

Mrs. Willoughby frowned. "Not exactly unhappy perhaps. But not content, either." She gave Shelby a conspiratorial look. "Her first husband left her for a much younger woman. Someone who worked in his office, I think. Grace has been determined to find a second husband ever since."

She certainly didn't feel that way herself, Shelby thought. But then, she hadn't been dumped the way Grace had.

"Snagging Alan seems to have boosted Grace's confidence." Mrs. Willoughby shifted her purse to her other arm. "There was an element of desperation in the way she was going after men. She set more than one tongue wagging at St. Andrews with her behavior. I'm glad she's finally found someone and is settling down." She looked around Shelby's booth. "Now, what was it I wanted?"

She opened her purse and scrabbled inside, finally pulling out a piece of scratch paper. "Yes. Now I remember. I need a head of lettuce, some tomatoes—two would be fine—and do you have any parsley?"

"Certainly." Shelby filled a bag with Mrs. Willoughby's produce. "There you go."

"Thank you, dear. See you Sunday." Mrs. Willoughby waved and turned away.

Shelby waved back and then turned her attention to her booth. She'd sold most of her produce—it was time to pack up. She thought about the conversation she'd just had as she hefted crates and baskets back into her truck. She couldn't picture Jodi as a murderer, no matter how hard she tried. Grace must be mistaken.

⁙⁙⁙⁙⁙⁙⁙⁙⁙⁙⁙⁙

By the time Shelby got back to the farm, she was tired, dusty, and thirsty. A long, hot soak in the farmhouse's old claw-foot tub with her homemade salt scrub sounded fantastic, but it would have to wait until later that evening. Eggs needed to be collected, and some of her root vegetables needed harvesting and some beds needed weeding.

Shelby heard the sound of running water as she opened the door to the mudroom. Was Amelia doing the breakfast dishes? Shelby had left in too much of a hurry to wash out the pan she'd used for the scrambled eggs and had left the dirty dishes stacked on the counter because the dishwasher needed emptying.

She hurried through the mudroom, quickly glancing away from the spot where Prudence's body had lain. Perhaps she would rearrange the room after she and Matt had painted it.

She walked into the kitchen, her mouth open, ready to lavish praise on Amelia for helping out, but stopped dead in her tracks when she saw Bert at the sink. Her mouth snapped shut as quickly as a frog's when reeling in an unwary fly.

"I came to pull up some of your carrots," Bert said,

placing a dripping wet dish in the drying rack. I'm going to make our poor rector something for dinner. I'm doing my mother's famous chicken and rice casserole. It's always a hit at potlucks."

Bert reached for another dirty dish and plunged it into the soapy water in the sink.

Dear Reader, does feeling guilty and relieved at the same time that Bert is doing my dishes make me schizophrenic?

"I thought it was Amelia doing the dishes." Shelby pulled out a kitchen chair and sat down. "You don't have to do that."

"God gave me two hands to make me useful, didn't he?" Bert added another plate to the ones drying in the rack. "I saw the dishes, and I know how hard you work. I couldn't just leave them here."

Shelby smiled. "You're the best, Bert."

"I know," Bert shot back, plunging her hands into the soapy water again.

"Where's Amelia?"

"She was here when I got here." Bert used her arm to wipe some soap bubbles off her chin that had floated up from the sink. "She was on that cell phone of hers, gabbing away."

Shelby felt dread growing in the pit of her stomach.

"But as soon as I walked in, she was off, out the door faster than a Thoroughbred out of the gate at the Belmont Stakes."

Shelby suppressed a frisson of irritation. Bert knew she didn't want Amelia going off like that. Of course, Bert meant well, but she must have forgotten how stressful raising a teenager could be. Or, an almost teenager, Shelby corrected herself. Amelia was still only twelve years and eleven months.

Of course Amelia had gone to Ned's. Even though she was forbidden to. Even though she was perfectly aware of the fact that she was still grounded. And Shelby knew from her conversation with Jodi that Jodi saw nothing wrong in the two of them being together.

Anger built up inside Shelby. She was going over there right now and bringing Amelia home. And while she was at it, she'd feel Jodi out about the toilet-papering incident. Jodi seemed to take a rather lax attitude toward parenting— had it really bothered her as much as Grace had said it did?

Shelby jumped up from her chair, suddenly frantic to leave. "I've got to go. Leave the rest of the dishes, and I'll take care of them when I come home."

"Not on your life, young lady," Bert said as she took a clean dish towel from the cupboard. "I'll just get these dried and put away. You have enough on your hands as it is. And then I'll go help myself to some carrots."

"Save the tops," Shelby called over her shoulder. "There're wonderful in soups and stocks."

Bert stopped with her hand halfway to one of the dishes in the dish rack. "My grandma swore that they're poisonous."

"That's an old wives' tale," Shelby said as she stopped to fish in her purse for the keys to the truck. "They're actually loaded with vitamins. Some people eat the tops in salads or sauté them in butter, but they're a bit bitter for my taste."

"Well, I never," Bert said as she began drying a dish. "I'll have to give it a try. And here I grew up on a farm long before you were even a gleam in your parents' eye."

She scraped at a spot on the dish with her fingernail. "I reckon I can use all the vitamins I can get at my age."

Shelby stopped abruptly halfway through the mud-room. "Bert, I'm so sorry. I didn't even ask—can you stay with Billy till I get back? I won't be long."

"You take your time," Bert called out to her. "I'm not in any rush to leave. There's no one waiting for me at home."

Shelby smiled. "You need a pet."

"Maybe I'll get one of them birds that can talk. Just so long as it doesn't start arguing with me. That's one of the benefits of being alone—no one to disagree with you."

Shelby laughed as she let the back door close behind her. Bert was quite a character. Once again, Shelby realized she didn't know what she'd do without her.

Jodi's house was only a few minutes away, just off the main road that ran past St. Andrews and the Lovett General Store. The edge had begun to wear off Shelby's anger, although she was still plenty mad. She'd have to compose herself if she was going to have a mature, adult conversation with Jodi when what she really wanted to do was shake some sense into the woman.

Shelby pulled her pickup into the driveway of Jodi's small ranch-style house. It was surrounded by neatly trimmed bushes bordered with a small flower garden. The paint was fresh, and the lawn was well tended. Shelby felt a grudging admiration for the woman—how on earth did Jodi find the time to work, care for her children, and still maintain her home?

Shelby heard children's voices coming from the back-yard as soon as she opened her truck door. She peered around the edge of the house. A group of children was playing on an old metal swing set, and a large black dog was running back and forth between the swings and the slide, barking joyfully. It must have sensed Shelby's presence, because it turned and began to lope toward her.

"Don't worry. He won't hurt you," a towheaded toddler called to Shelby.

"I'm not afraid of dogs," Shelby reassured him as she crouched down to greet the Lab, who poked her hand encouragingly with its wet nose. Shelby looked toward the boy who had called out to her. "Is your mom home?"

"Sure. Just go on in." He pointed toward the back door.

"Thanks. I'll go around front and ring the bell."

The young boy shrugged as if to say *please yourself.*

Shelby went to the front door and rang the bell. Her breathing had returned to near normal—perhaps petting the dog had calmed her.

Jodi yanked open the door. "Yes? Oh, Shelby, it's you." She opened the door wider. "Come in."

"Where's my daughter? Is Amelia here?" Shelby tried to get control of her voice. Becoming adversarial wasn't going to get her anywhere. She could feel her chin jutting aggressively and tried to rearrange her face into a more neutral expression.

"Is that what this is about?" Jodi closed the front door. "Why don't we go into the kitchen?"

Shelby was in no mood for small talk, but she followed Jodi into a small kitchen, where a Formica table was crammed into one corner. A newspaper, its edges neatly aligned, was placed at one end.

"Would you like a glass of ice water?" Jodi gestured toward the avocado green refrigerator that appeared to be original to the house.

Shelby shook her head. "No, thank you. I'd just like to take my daughter home. She knows she's not supposed to visit boys at their homes, and she knows she's still grounded."

Jodi sat down at the kitchen table and motioned Shelby to one of the chairs. She was silent for a moment.

"Amelia doesn't want to go home," she said finally.

Shelby willed herself not to shout or jump up from the table. "What do you mean?" she said in as normal a voice as she could muster.

Jodi sighed. "According to Amelia the two of you haven't been getting along. As a matter of fact, she said you've been at each other's throats for months now."

"That's not true!"

"She wanted to get away," Jodi continued as if she hadn't heard. "And she called me to ask if she could come here."

"But that's ridiculous." Shelby's voice got louder in spite of herself. "We have our disagreements for sure, but at each other's throats? No way."

"That's what she told me," Jodi said matter-of-factly.

"Then she's lying. Like I said—we've had our disagreements, but I wouldn't even call them fights." Shelby sighed. She felt deflated. What was wrong with Amelia and why was she acting this way?

Jodi put a hand on Shelby's arm. "I know how you feel. Being the parent of a teenager is probably the hardest thing I've ever done. But Ned is a good boy, and I do keep a watch that nothing happens. . . ." She smiled tentatively at Shelby. "I know Ned likes Amelia . . . a lot . . . but right now I think he's comfortable being more friend than boyfriend."

Dear Reader, I know girls mature faster than boys. Is

Ned viewing this as a friendship while Amelia is imagining it as the romance of the century? I have a terrible feeling this is not going to end well.

"You're right," Shelby said. "I'm probably blowing things out of proportion. I'm sure Ned is a nice boy. . . . I can hardly blame someone for a spot of TPing, especially since . . ." Shelby trailed off. No need to admit to all her past transgressions.

"Toilet-papering?" Jodi asked. Her voice got higher and became shrill. "Ned would never do anything of the kind."

Shelby tried to settle her most conciliatory look on her face. She put up a hand in a gesture of surrender. "All kids do something like that sooner or later—"

"No." Jodi shook her head fiercely. "Who told you that? They're lying!"

"Prudence Mather told Grace Swanson."

"And you believed it?" Jodi asked with the hint of a sneer in her voice. "You're certainly quick to believe the worst." She shook her finger in Shelby's face.

Heat began to build up inside Shelby. She wasn't normally quick to anger, but she was tired, hot, and her nerves were frazzled—not a good combination.

"Fine," she said. The irony wasn't lost on her that she was using Amelia's favorite word. "I think I'll be taking my daughter home now." She put her hands to her mouth. "Amelia. Amelia, it's time to go home."

Footsteps clomped on the wooden stairs from the basement-level rec room and Amelia appeared around the corner, with Ned right behind her. So much for Jodi keeping an eye on them, Shelby thought.

"I'm not going." Amelia stuck out her chin in a gesture Shelby recognized as one Bill had used frequently.

"I'm afraid you'll have to." Shelby grabbed her purse, took Amelia by the arm, and all but frog-marched her to the front door.

"I'll call you," Amelia yelled over her shoulder to Ned, who stood looking shell-shocked.

Neither of them said a word on the way home. Amelia was plugged into the music on her phone, and Shelby didn't trust herself to speak calmly and rationally when she actually felt like screaming.

Amelia scrambled ahead of Shelby through the mudroom and the back door. She stopped halfway across the kitchen and turned to face Shelby. "Now look what you've done. You've ruined everything. I hate you," she ended on a sob before running up the stairs and slamming the door to her room.

21

Dear Reader,

Raising children isn't easy, is it? Especially teenagers. Especially teenage girls. I take heart in the fact that while Billy did his very best to prove the truth of the saying terrible twos, at least he will never be a teenage girl.

And a teenage girl in love is even worse. When Amelia was little, all it took to pull her out of a funk was a trip to the ice-cream parlor. I fear it's going to take a lot more than that now that's she's older.

"She doesn't mean it," Bert said, walking into the kitchen holding a stack of folded laundry.

Shelby slumped into a kitchen chair. "I know. It still hurts, though." She wiped the back of her hand across her eyes.

"Of course it does." Bert held out the bundle of laundry. "Where do you want these?"

Shelby waved a hand. "Put them on the kitchen table. I'll put them away later."

"There's one consolation, though," Bert said.

Shelby frowned. "I doubt that." She picked at a bit of food that was stuck to the table. She must have missed it with her sponge.

"Someday she'll have kids of her own, and one of them will say *I hate you* to her."

Bert dumped the pile of clean clothes on the table, and the scent of fabric softener wafted over toward Shelby. "Then she'll know how it feels."

Shelby folded her arms across her chest. Bert was right—as usual. Shelby remembered saying the same thing to her mother the time her mother wouldn't let her ride to school in a car with Bill, since he'd only gotten his license the day before. "Do you think I should go after her? See if she's okay."

"She's fine. Probably having a good cry. She'll get over it."

"Jodi Walker seems to think the attraction is all on Amelia's side." Shelby got up, took a pan from the cupboard, and filled it with water. "She practically made it sound as if Amelia was out to seduce her precious son." She turned the burner on under the pan and retrieved a box of tea bags from the cabinet.

Bert snorted. "I'm sure the young man is perfectly safe, if not perfectly innocent."

Shelby turned around and leaned against the counter. "Prudence accused Ned of TPing the rectory. Jodi insisted it wasn't true."

"She'd hardly admit it in any case, would she?" Bert plucked her purse from the hook by the back door.

"So maybe Prudence wasn't lying about that." Shelby drummed her fingers on the table. "But even so, it would have made Jodi furious when Prudence reported it to the school and Ned was suspended from the soccer team."

"Mad enough to kill?" Bert paused in the doorway, her purse swinging from the crook of her arm.

Shelby shrugged. "I don't know. Maybe."

⁜⁜⁜⁜⁜⁜⁜⁜⁜⁜⁜⁜⁜

Bert left and Shelby rummaged around in the refrigerator. Suddenly she was starving. Bert had given Billy the last of the hot dogs and had opened a can of beans. Shelby found the remainder of the beans, got a fork from the drawer, and began forking them up. *Dear Reader, what would you think of me if you could see me now? I blog about homemade foods, vegetables fresh from the garden, and pies made with organic fruit, and here I am, eating beans out of a can. Please don't judge me.*

Shelby felt a momentary pang of guilt. She really should see if Amelia wanted anything to eat. Maybe she'd already eaten at Ned's? At any rate, if Amelia was capable of sneaking around with a boy, she was more than old enough to make herself a sandwich.

Shelby finished the beans, rinsed out the tin, and tossed it in the recycling bin.

Bitsy and Jenkins came to the back door barking furiously, their black noses poking at the worn screen, which Shelby had painstakingly mended time and time again.

"What is it?" she asked as she opened the door to let them in.

By now Shelby spoke their language. She could recognize their barks for *I'm hungry, I need to go out—stat, let's play,* and *someone's at the door.* This was their *someone's at the door* bark.

As if on cue, Shelby heard someone rap on the wooden frame of the screen door at the front of the house. It was in marginally better repair than the one at the back, since they didn't use it nearly as much.

"Matt!" Shelby said when she saw his figure through the screen. She threw open the door while simultaneously sticking out a leg in an attempt to keep the dogs from knocking Matt to the ground.

"Don't worry. I love dogs," he said as Bitsy jumped up and put her paws on his shoulders.

"Sorry to barge in on you like this, but I had some time this afternoon and wondered if you'd like to get started on painting the mudroom." He gestured toward the door. "I've got some old clothes and my painting stuff in the car."

"Oh," Shelby said, feeling weariness wash over her.

Before she could say anything further, Matt put a hand on her shoulder. "You're tired. I can see it on your face. We can do it another time."

Shelby couldn't help smiling. How perceptive Matt was.

"Won't you come in, though? I'm making some iced tea."

Matt wiped a hand across the back of his neck. "Sounds great. It's another scorcher today."

Shelby led him out to the kitchen. She looked around the room quickly—too bad she'd told Bert to leave the clean laundry on the table, but at least there was nothing too embarrassing in the pile.

Matt didn't seem to notice as he took a seat and stretched out his legs.

Shelby poured the brewed tea over ice in two tall glasses and brought them to the table.

"This looks great." Matt took a big gulp before setting his glass back down on the table. "Lovett is still buzzing over Prudence's murder. Almost every customer who comes in the store has something to say about it."

"What are they saying?" Shelby eased her shoes off under the table. Her feet were probably dirty, but somehow she didn't think Matt would care.

"Everyone has their own opinion—Daniel did it because he was tired of being henpecked, someone at church was responsible because Prudence had made their life miserable, it was a neighbor who Prudence had offended, and so on and so forth." He sighed.

"Hopefully the police will solve the case soon, and this will all be over."

"I hope so." Matt ran his finger down the condensation on his glass, leaving a watery trail. "It might have been someone who wasn't at the potluck initially."

"What do you mean?" Shelby stopped with her glass halfway to her mouth.

Matt let out a puff of air. "I remember hearing Prudence on her cell phone. I don't know who she was talking to, but it was a woman. I could hear the voice of the party on the other end quite clearly, even though I couldn't distinguish the words. And she was furious about something—whether it was at Prudence or not, I'm afraid I can't say."

"That's interesting."

Shelby had a flashback to the potluck. She remembered Prudence pulling her cell phone from her pocket and walking off. There was something else, but at the moment it escaped her, which was unfortunate, because she had the feeling it was important.

There were stomping noises overhead and both Shelby and Matt looked up. Amelia, Shelby thought, voicing her displeasure. She made a concerted effort to ignore the noise.

Matt finished his iced tea. "Guess I'd better get going." He stood up.

"I'll be up for painting soon, I promise. It's been a rough couple of days—dealing with Prudence's death, some mildew on my lettuce"—Shelby pointed toward the ceiling—"and my daughter."

"No problem. Let me know when you're ready." Matt lingered for a moment at the front door, before putting a hand on Shelby's arm. "Be careful, okay?"

Shelby watched as Matt got into his car and backed down the driveway.

||||||||||||||||||||||||||

Shelby spent the rest of the afternoon in the garden weeding. The feel of the earth between her fingers usually soothed her, but today she was having trouble relaxing and letting go of the stress of the day. She kept glancing back toward the house to see if Amelia might have appeared. How long would she hold a grudge? Shelby feared this would not be over any time soon.

As she pulled weeds, she began to doubt herself. Had she done the right thing in bringing Amelia home from Ned's house? Was there really anything wrong in the two being together—especially if Jodi was right, and Ned was more interested in friendship than a romance?

She was still thinking about it when Bitsy and Jenkins

came zooming past her, headed for the front of the house. As usual, Jenkins was in the lead despite his shorter legs. If there was mischief to be had, Jenkins was the one who would find it and bring Bitsy along for the ride.

Shelby got up from where she'd been kneeling in the dirt. Her knees gave a bit of a creak and she wondered, was she getting old and rickety already? She hoped not—she still had many years to go before Billy and Amelia were ready to be released into the world on their own. She had this vision of a mother bird pushing its babies out of the nest and wondered how the bird managed to get up the courage. She'd keep her children wrapped in cotton wool until they were thirty if that was possible.

Jenkins and Bitsy kept up their barking. It was definitely their *someone's here* barking. Shelby wiped her hands on her cutoffs as she made her way around to the front of the house. She was surprised to see Frank's pickup truck in the driveway. He must have washed it, because the splatters of mud and dried dirt were gone and while it didn't quite shine, the paint having dulled with age, it was looking a lot more shipshape than previously.

Frank was headed toward the front steps when Shelby called to him. He spun around and a crooked smile lit up his face. Once again, Shelby was struck by how much he looked like Bill, and for a brief second her instinct was to run to him.

Frank walked over to where Shelby was standing. He took his hands out of his pockets and pushed his cap back on his forehead.

He jerked a thumb toward the road. "I was passing and thought I'd look in and make sure you were okay."

His face flushed, as if he was embarrassed, and Shelby was momentarily taken aback.

He grinned. "I guess you're just fine."

Shelby wanted to wail that she wasn't fine—not at all. She didn't know what to do with Amelia, finding that butternut squash hanging on her porch still gave her the shivers, and she was bone tired from trying to make a go of things all by herself. But she didn't. She invited Frank in for a cold drink instead.

He didn't hesitate but followed Shelby around to the back of the house.

"Has there been any progress on . . . the case?" Shelby asked as they walked through the mudroom.

Frank let out a gusty sigh and scratched the back of his neck. "Not much, no. There were so many people around and the scene was heavily trampled before we got here."

Shelby retrieved the pitcher of iced tea she'd put in the refrigerator after Matt left and poured them each a glass.

They sat across the table from each other in silence for several minutes. Shelby had the sense there was something she needed to ask Frank—something to do with the case— but she couldn't put her finger on it. Was it related to what Matt had told her? She thought back to their conversation and within seconds the answer came to her. She jerked abruptly and nearly knocked over her glass. Frank looked at her quizzically. She would have to word this carefully so as not to alert him to the fact that she was snooping.

"Do you happen to know if a cell phone was found on Prudence's body after she was . . . killed?"

Frank looked momentarily surprised by the question. He frowned and pinched the bridge of his nose. "Yes," he said finally. "We did. We traced the calls, but none of the people she phoned that day were at the potluck."

"Do you still have the phone?"

Frank shook his head. "There was no need to keep it and Reverend Mather needed it—he didn't have one of his own—he and Prudence shared it. Along with a land-line, of course. I guess clergymen aren't paid any better than civil servants." He tilted his chair back. "Why?"

Shelby played with a loose thread on the hem of her T-shirt, winding it around and around her finger. "No reason. Just wondering."

Frank didn't look convinced, and Shelby was relieved when he didn't ask any further questions.

"How's Nancy?" Shelby said to change the subject.

Frank frowned. "Don't know. She's gone to visit her mother in Ohio." He fiddled with a bright blue LEGO piece Billy had left on the table.

Shelby looked him in the eye. "Are you two having trouble?"

Frank's shoulders slumped. He wiped a hand over his face. Shelby could hear the scratchy sound as he ran his palm over his two-day growth of beard. She remembered the feeling of Bill's cheek against hers when he'd gone a day or two without a shave and had to close her eyes for a moment at the stab of unexpected pain.

When she opened them, Frank was looking down at the table, seemingly intent on Billy's LEGO piece. "She wants a trial separation," he mumbled.

Shelby couldn't believe it. Bill had been best man in their wedding and Amelia the flower girl. It seemed like yesterday.

Frank turned the LEGO piece over and over without

looking at Shelby. "I guess she knew I'd always really been in love with someone else."

Shelby sat in stunned silence while Frank drained his iced tea and pushed back his chair. It made a screech as it scraped across the linoleum floor.

"I think I'd better be going."

Shelby let him out the front door, closed it, and leaned against it. Frank couldn't be . . . it wasn't possible, Shelby thought, her mind whirling. Had she led him on in any way? His resemblance to Bill nearly always caught her unawares—maybe he'd picked up on a signal she hadn't meant to send.

Shelby looked into the living room at her sagging couch. She had to fight the urge to fling herself down on it, kick her feet, and howl.

22

Dear Reader,

When you live, work, and depend on a farm for your livelihood, you also become dependent on Mother Nature. She can be fickle at times—giving you endless days of sunny weather when the ground is already dry and cracking from lack of water. Or rain for days on end, when your crops nearly drown from the abundance of water, and mold and mildew become problems. Any early or late frost can kill delicate seedlings or bring the growing season to an abrupt end.

Shelby took a basket from the kitchen cupboard and went out to the garden. Clouds were rolling in and it looked as if it would rain—although whether it would be a mere shower or a real storm, she couldn't tell. The one predictable thing about the weather so close to the lake was that it was unpredictable.

She made her way along a row of bell pepper plants. There were still a lot of green ones, but a good many of them had already ripened to a brilliant red. Shelby picked several and placed them in her basket. The herb garden was next. She scanned the row of basil plants—the one on the end looked near to flowering, which meant she needed to cut it back right away. She snipped off the top, savoring the sweet and spicy scent, and added the sprigs to her basket.

Jake had brought her a container of cream that morning, and she planned on baking the peppers in some of the cream and then sprinkling them with strips of basil. *Dear Reader, don't worry—I'll be sharing the recipe on my blog . . . soon.*

Shelby's cell phone dinged with a message as she was setting her basket down on the table. She pulled it from her pocket and glanced at the screen. The message made no sense—at least to her. She glanced at the number but didn't recognize it. Someone had misdialed. Did you call it misdialing when you were sending a text? Shelby wondered. If not, then what?

Thinking about phones brought Prudence's cell phone to mind. Matt had said it sounded as if the person on the other end was angry. At Prudence? At something Prudence said? Shelby closed her eyes for a moment, thinking back to the potluck. She remembered Prudence pulling her cell phone from her pocket, but there was something else— something that had seemed odd at the time.

She was slicing the peppers for dinner when she remembered the rest of that scene. Shelby and Prudence had been talking when they were approached by Grace Swanson. Grace was with her new husband, Alan, and had started to introduce him. Shelby had said hello, but Prudence had murmured her apologies before taking off, pulling her cell phone from the pocket of her capris as she walked. Even at the time, Shelby had found it odd—Prudence was normally almost excessively polite, especially with members of St. Andrews.

Shelby sharpened her knife, light flashing off the blade as she swooshed it up and down the long metal sharpener. She began to cut the basil into thin ribbons, or what was known as a chiffonade. She would sprinkle these on top of the peppers.

Half her mind was on her cooking, but half was still focused on the murder. She wondered who it was Prudence had called right before she was murdered. Wallace? But Matt had said the voice was female, so that wasn't possible. If only she could find out. It might be completely irrelevant, but then it might hold the key to the solution.

Shelby arranged the peppers in the baking dish—she'd already peeled off their skins by blistering them over an open flame and then encasing the peppers in a plastic bag for ten minutes. When she removed the peppers, the skins slipped right off.

Shelby placed the last pepper in the casserole dish, poured the heavy cream over the top, and sprinkled it all with the strips of basil. She was opening the oven door when she stopped abruptly. Frank had told her that Prudence's cell phone had been returned to Daniel. Would it be possible to find out from the record on the phone who it was that Prudence had dialed the afternoon of the potluck?

Shelby felt stirrings of excitement. She had a strong

feeling she was on her way to solving the case. She put the peppers in the oven and checked the temperature.

What excuse could she use for dropping in on Daniel? And what story could she tell him about wanting to see Prudence's phone? She could tell him the truth, of course. It might backfire, but she would have to take her chances.

Shelby paced back and forth in front of her stove. She could take Daniel some food—although his freezer was already stuffed with enough casseroles to last for several months. Flowers? He probably already had enough of those after the funeral.

She would have to show up on his doorstep and bluntly tell him what she was after. She was certain Daniel was as anxious as anyone else to find the murderer.

Shelby rushed through dinner—hardly saying anything when Billy did little more than dash his hands under running water before sitting down. Amelia, unsurprisingly, continued to give Shelby the cold shoulder, but she barely noticed— which she suspected was frustrating Amelia to no end.

She even let them have ice cream for dessert with no arguments. Billy gave a huge whoop and immediately grabbed the container from the freezer as if he was afraid Shelby would change her mind. Amelia gave her a strange look but other than that did not respond—although she did help herself to two scoops.

Amelia picked up her bowl and was about to leave the room when Shelby called out to her, "Look after Billy for me, would you? I have to run a quick errand."

Dear Reader, I fear it's going to be more of an inquisition than an errand.

"Fine," Amelia said, then gave Shelby a look as if Shelby had somehow tricked her into talking.

Shelby grabbed her purse, ruffled Billy's hair, and dashed out the back door.

The rain started as she was backing out of the driveway. As a farmer she always welcomed rain—it was nature's watering system. The downpour grew heavier as she neared the rectory. Her wipers were going at full speed and still she had to strain to see through the rivers of water cascading down her windshield.

There was a car in the rectory's driveway. Shelby hoped she wasn't intruding on someone's counseling session. The rain hadn't abated at all and was pinging off the roof and hood of Shelby's car. She glanced in the backseat and then remembered the last time she'd used her umbrella, she had forgotten to put it back in the car. She'd have to make a run for it.

It was only a short distance to the front door of the rectory, but by the time Shelby reached the protection of the portico, she could feel the rain soaking through her thin T-shirt and splashing against her bare legs.

She paused for a moment and was shaking some water from her hair when she smelled an unpleasant odor. It smelled like smoke—cigarette smoke. Had Wallace been standing out here earlier, having a cigarette?

Shelby tried to pat her hair into some semblance of a hairstyle but suspected she had failed miserably. She stuck her hand in the pocket of her shorts and was relieved to find a hair elastic. She pulled her wayward strands into a loose ponytail and then finally rang the bell.

She half expected Coralynne to answer, but then remembered that Coralynne drove a Focus and the car in the driveway was a Kia. Instead it was Daniel who came to the door.

His shirt was rumpled and he was wearing a pair of worn corduroy bedroom slippers. His clerical collar was fastened around his neck and there was a smudge of something along the very edge. Shelby's first thought was that if Prudence were still alive, she would never let him go around looking so unkempt, let alone answer the door in his slippers.

"Shelby." He looked surprised, but his voice was flat and emotionless.

He motioned Shelby inside, and she followed him into the parlor of the old house. There was an odd musty smell in the air, almost as if the place hadn't been dusted in years, although Shelby knew Coralynne came regularly to help with the cleaning.

Shelby found the sofa was no more comfortable than it looked, the rough fabric scratching the back of her bare legs. She suddenly became conscious of the fact that she was wearing a pair of cutoffs that were frayed on the edges and a white T-shirt that had been through the wash a few times too many and had lost whatever shape it had originally had.

Daniel took a seat in an armchair perpendicular to the couch and scrubbed a hand over his face. "I don't imagine you have any news," he said before Shelby could say anything.

"I'm afraid not."

Daniel scowled. "I can't help thinking that Wallace had something to do with it. He came here looking for money from his mother—Prudence had inherited a small sum from a maiden aunt, and I insisted she keep the money for herself. But she found it hard to refuse her son. Right before the potluck she went to the bank and withdrew some cash. She planned to give it to him that afternoon. I had a talk with her and managed to change her mind." He sighed. "I think she finally realized she needed to stop supporting him in his idleness. After all, how long would it be before he came back for more?

"I suppose I shouldn't think ill of him. I've tried hard to like him. After all, as it is written in John 15:12, *This is my commandment, that you love one another as I have loved you.* Wallace just has a way of trying one's patience, I'm afraid." Daniel gave a sad smile.

No wonder Wallace had lied about being at the pot-luck, Shelby thought. She imagined he and Prudence must have argued about the money. She couldn't imagine Wallace giving up without a fight. And if anyone had heard them, it would have made Wallace a prime suspect. But if he had killed her, he would certainly have taken the money that had been found in her purse. She didn't have the heart to tell Daniel the money hadn't come from Prudence's account but from the church collection plate.

"I don't think Wallace had anything to do with it," Shelby said. "At the potluck, Grace Swanson was introducing Prudence and me to her new husband. Suddenly Prudence excused herself, pulled her cell phone from her pocket, and walked off." Shelby fiddled with a thread hanging from the hem of her shorts. "Matt Hudson said he heard Prudence speaking to someone on the phone— someone who sounded very angry."

Daniel's eyebrows rose to the middle of his forehead. "At Prudence?"

Shelby dipped her head. "We don't know. But we . . . I . . . am wondering if the call had anything to do with Prudence's . . . murder." The word stuck in her mouth.

Daniel ran a finger around his clerical collar as if it had suddenly become too tight. "Is there a way to find out, do you suppose?"

"Do you have Prudence's cell phone?" Shelby asked.

"Yes," Daniel said eagerly. "Do you think it will tell us something?"

"Possibly," Shelby said, sounding far more sure than she felt. "Can I see it? I'd like to take a look at the numbers she dialed before she . . . the day of the potluck," she amended hastily.

Daniel nearly sprang from his chair, showing more energy than he had since Shelby had arrived. "I'll be right back."

He disappeared in the direction of the kitchen and returned with the cell phone in his palm, holding it out to Shelby as if it were a rare, precious jewel.

It was an old-style flip phone—the same kind Shelby had herself. She powered it on and began pressing buttons, her lower lip caught between her teeth. The cell sprang to life and the front panel lit up.

Daniel stood over Shelby as she pushed the buttons. He was gripping one hand with the other and wringing them both as if he were squeezing out a wet washcloth. Shelby tried to ignore him as she fiddled with Prudence's phone.

She found the call list and began scrolling through it. The potluck had been on June 21, and she quickly found the list of calls for that day. The early-morning ones she ignored, looking instead for the ones that were made during the hours of the potluck. She couldn't remember exactly when it was that she saw Prudence pull out her cell phone, but she had a general idea.

Shelby soon found several possibilities. She rummaged

in her purse, but in her haste, she had managed to forget about bringing paper and a pen. She looked at Daniel with a pained expression on her face.

He backed away from her immediately. "I'll nip into my study and get a pad and something to write with, shall I?"

He reappeared moments later with a scratch pad with *Morgan's Plumbing* written at the top and a ballpoint pen.

Shelby quickly copied down the few telephone numbers that fell within the correct time frame. She tore off the sheet of paper and handed the pen and pad back to Daniel.

She was stuffing the notes she'd made into her purse when she heard footsteps coming down the hall. Wallace? Shelby looked up to see Grace Swanson standing at the entrance to the living room, her purse hanging from the crook of her arm.

"I've put the pot pie in the oven." She looked at her watch. "It probably needs another ten minutes to warm it. Dessert is in the refrigerator—chocolate pudding." Grace smiled.

"You're very kind," Daniel said, fussing with his clerical collar.

"Hello, Shelby," Grace said. "I didn't expect to see you here." Her expression was quizzical. "Have you brought the reverend some food?"

Shelby shook her head and felt her ponytail swish against the back of her neck. "No, I had . . . had something to discuss with him."

Grace turned to Daniel and cocked her head to one side. "Will you be all right now?"

"Yes. I'll be perfectly fine," Daniel said with uncharacteristic firmness.

Grace's smile grew somewhat forced as she said good-bye.

Daniel turned to Shelby. "Thank you for *not* bringing me something to eat. Everyone seems to think I need feeding, and frankly I don't have much of an appetite to speak of." He held up Prudence's cell phone. "You'll be sure to let me know if you find out anything. . . ."

"I certainly will." Shelby stood up and began to move toward the foyer.

Daniel let her out and shut the door behind her. Shelby breathed a sigh of relief. The smell of cigarette smoke was even stronger now than it had been before. She looked around, but there was no sign of Wallace. She wondered how long he was going to stay in Lovett and whether or not he even had someplace else to go.

‖‖‖‖‖‖‖‖‖‖‖‖‖‖‖‖‖

Shelby waited until Billy was in bed—she'd had to nearly drag him into the tub for a bath—before getting out the list of phone numbers she'd retrieved from Prudence's cell. Amelia was already in her bedroom, continuing to sulk. She had her own television in her room—something Shelby was beginning to regret—and there was little chance she would decide to come downstairs and join her mother in the living room.

Shelby held her phone in her hand for several minutes, rehearsing what she was going to say. No matter what words she came up with, it was going to be awkward. The fact that the people she was calling might hang up on her occurred to her as well. But she'd have to try.

Shelby's hands were slightly damp as she dialed the first number. No answer. She was partly relieved and partly frustrated. There were a total of three numbers on her list—she tried the next one wondering whether this was going to lead to anything. Maybe Prudence's phone call had had nothing to do with her murder.

The phone rang for the fifth time and Shelby was about to hang up when the call was picked up. She heard fumbling noises and finally a woman's feeble voice came over the line.

"Hello? Who is this?"

"This is Shelby McDonald. I was a friend . . . " Shelby hesitated over the use of that word. ". . . of Prudence Mather's."

"That poor thing. Terrible, isn't it? What's the world coming to? We didn't have things like that happening in Lovett back in my day. It was a good community with decent people."

Shelby wondered how she could break into the conversation and gently lead the woman around to the point of her call. Fortunately she eventually ran out of steam if not breath. "You were one of the last people Prudence called before she . . . before she died."

Shelby couldn't imagine how the woman on the other end of the phone could have anything to do with Prudence's murder. The whole idea suddenly seemed ridiculous to her.

"Yes, dear, she did call me. I had no idea it would be the last time we spoke."

"Do you remember what the conversation was about?" Shelby hoped the woman's memory was stronger than her voice.

"It was about the altar cloth I'm embroidering for St. Andrews. She called me with the measurements. This will be the fifth cloth I've made for our church, but I misplaced the piece of paper with the dimensions on it."

Shelby was quiet for a moment.

"Is there something you wanted to ask me, dear?"

"No," Shelby said hastily. "Reverend Mather wanted me to check to be sure you had everything you needed."

"Yes, dear, I'm all set. The cloth will be ready in a few weeks. I'm afraid I'm not as fast as I used to be."

"That's fine, then," Shelby said, itching to hang up. "If you need anything, let Reverend Mather know, okay?"

"I will, dear. You have a good evening, now."

Shelby breathed a sigh of relief and clicked off the call.

One more call left. Shelby stared at the numbers for a moment before punching them in. She mentally crossed her fingers as she waited for the ringing to start.

This time someone answered so quickly Shelby was startled.

"Hello?" The woman's voice was sharp and abrupt.

Shelby cleared her throat. This task wasn't getting any easier. She cleared her throat a second time. The woman's impatience was nearly palpable.

"I'm sorry to bother you," Shelby began, "but I was a friend of Prudence Mather's. It seems you were one of the last people to talk to her before she died."

"Worst day of my life," the woman answered.

"I'm sorry. I didn't realize you and Prudence were such good friends."

"We weren't. Her husband was the former rector of our church."

"Then what—"

"Listen, I don't want to talk about this on the phone. Can you come here?"

Shelby did some mental calculations. It would be late when she got back—she didn't want to leave Billy and Amelia all alone. She'd have to call Bert. "I think so. I need to call someone to stay with the kids, but I'm sure it will be fine."

"Good," the woman said with a certain bitter satisfaction. "It's quite a story."

23

Dear Reader,

I have a feeling that things are about to draw to a close. Although I hate going around asking questions of people, I think I am going to get some answers—answers that may lead to the discovery of Prudence's murderer.

Hopefully things will soon get back to normal in sleepy old Lovett. We've had enough drama to last a lifetime. I have been neglecting things a bit at the farm—despite my best efforts, my lettuce patch is over-run with weeds, and I have a batch of rhubarb that I've already picked but haven't gotten around to canning. I left a few leaves on the stalks to help retain moisture, but they won't last too much longer. You must be careful with the leaves, though—they're poisonous.

Bert came banging through the back door shortly after Shelby called her.

"Have you canned that rhubarb yet?" she asked before she even put down her purse.

Shelby felt guilt wash over her. "Not yet. Tomorrow."

Bert grunted. "Where did you say you were off to?"

Shelby wasn't going to tell Bert the truth about where she was going. She had the feeling Bert would not approve. "To Kelly's. She asked me to help her decide on a menu for a dinner she's planning with her future in-laws. She got herself into a complete panic over it, and I promised to come over and calm her down."

Bert grunted again. "You go on, then. I'll keep an eye out. Amelia is in her room, I assume?"

"Yes, and not likely to come down any time soon."

"She'll get over it—don't worry."

Shelby grabbed her purse, said good-bye to Bert, and headed out the back door. The sun was still bright—one of the benefits of living on the most western side of the eastern time zone.

There was little traffic on the roads—most people had long since arrived home from work, and few people were headed anywhere at this hour. Shelby made good time and arrived in Cranberry Cove a good fifteen minutes sooner than she'd anticipated.

The woman, who had said her name was Marcia, lived on a cul-de-sac a couple of miles inland from Lake Michigan. Shelby drove down the street, scanning the numbers as she passed houses that must once have looked all the same but were now distinguished by different landscaping, paint colors, and upkeep—or lack of it.

Marcia's bi-level was painted a subdued taupe with

brown shutters. Shelby parked on the street, being careful not to block anyone's driveway, and walked up the path to the house.

She rang the bell and waited, her heart thumping. The door was answered by a thin, middle-aged woman in turquoise capri pants, a white tank top, and white slip-on sneakers.

"Come in," she said, opening the door wide.

Shelby stepped into the foyer, where a small table was stacked with unopened mail.

The woman turned to Shelby and held out her hand. "I'm Marcia Swanson."

This couldn't be a coincidence, Shelby thought as she returned the handshake—two women with the same last name and both somehow involved with Prudence?

She followed Marcia into the living room, where a mauve sectional took up nearly all the space and matching elaborate mauve drapery blocked most of the light. There was a glass of wine with a smear of pink lipstick on it sitting on the coffee table.

"Would you like some wine?"

"No, thank you." Shelby wanted to get this over with as quickly as possible and head back home. She was suddenly bone-tired.

Marcia sat on the sofa, near her drink, and motioned for Shelby to take a seat.

"Your phone call took me by surprise." Marcia crossed one leg over the other, her foot swinging back and forth. "I heard about Prudence's murder—it's been all over the news in this part of the state. Is there anything new?"

"I'm afraid not."

Marcia contemplated her folded hands for a moment,

then looked up. "You asked me why Prudence called me the day she was murdered."

"Yes—I don't know if it's relevant to her murder or not, but I have a feeling it might be."

"Are you some sort of private investigator?"

Shelby felt her face turn red. "No. I'm only trying to find out what happened."

That seemed to satisfy Marcia. She sighed and looked down at her hands. "The phone call from Prudence was very strange to say the least." Marcia reached for her glass and took a sip of her wine. "Perhaps I should start at the beginning." She glanced at the ceiling as if expecting to find the story written there.

Shelby made an encouraging noise.

"I married later in life," Marcia began. "I'd been engaged in my early twenties, but we decided to break it off."

She gave a wry smile that suggested to Shelby that her fiancé had been the one to call it quits.

"After that, I didn't think I'd ever marry, but then Alan came along. He's a natural-born salesman and back then he worked for a paint company. It meant he was away, traveling, quite a lot, but I actually didn't mind. I'd been alone for so long I was used to it. And when he came home it was a . . . special time for us. Like a perpetual honeymoon." She smiled.

Shelby nodded.

"Alan joined a different company about five years ago, but the job still entailed a good bit of traveling, so life went on pretty much as usual." She paused and took another sip of her wine. "We attended church here in town, where Reverend Mather was the rector. That's how I met Prudence." Marcia shook her head. "She was always causing trouble—making accusations against people that weren't true, stirring up bad feelings—that sort of thing."

"I heard that's why the Mathers were moved to another church."

"Yes, that's what I heard, too, and frankly it didn't surprise anyone. We all felt sorry for Reverend Mather, of course—none of it was his fault. But I have to say Prudence's last stunt really took the cake—even for her!"

Shelby cocked her head. "What did she do?"

"As you know, Prudence called me. I was surprised to hear from her—we certainly had never been close and hadn't stayed in touch after she moved. I thought perhaps it had something to do with the church, but I soon found out the real reason." She gave a bitter laugh. "She tried to tell me that my husband . . . Alan . . . is a bigamist. Can you imagine? The nerve of the woman!"

Shelby nodded but kept quiet, and Marcia continued.

"Prudence claimed that Alan was at her new church's potluck with another woman—someone named Grace— who introduced Alan as her husband. I told her she was mistaken—Alan wasn't usually in town on Sundays, so he didn't attend church with me. Prudence had only met him the one time he'd picked me up from the Women's Auxiliary luncheon. She insisted the man she'd met with this Grace was my Alan. I refused to listen to any more lies, and I hung up. I was furious with her. She'd really gone too far."

"Have you talked to your husband about this?"

"No." Marcia shook her head and glanced at her watch. "But he's due home within the hour and of course I'll tell him about it. We'll both have a good laugh over it, I'm sure."

Shelby swallowed hard. Should she tell Marcia what

she knew? Would Marcia even believe her? Perhaps it would be better to go to Frank with this information and let him deal with it.

"I hope that answers your question," Marcia said, beginning to get up. "I don't mean to rush you, but I'd like to freshen up a bit before Alan gets here." She patted her hair.

Shelby thanked her and stood up to leave.

Marcia walked Shelby to the door and stood there for a moment, watching, as Shelby got into her car. Shelby waved and slowly pulled away.

She waited to turn out of the cul-de-sac onto the main road while a dark blue Buick made a right turn onto Marcia's street. Shelby glanced at the driver. It was Alan Swanson and he was staring straight at her.

||||||||||||||||||||||||||||

As Shelby turned onto the highway, she wondered what Alan planned to say to Marcia. Marcia seemed willing to believe him—eager even. Obviously Prudence had cried *wolf* once too often—no one believed her anymore. If that was the case, Alan might get away with his double life.

With Prudence conveniently dead, there would be no one to tell Grace the truth about her husband because there would be no one else who knew. Except herself, Shelby realized with a panicky start.

She glanced in her rearview mirror. There was a dark blue car behind her. It was too close for her to determine the make. How long had it been there? Shelby's palms suddenly felt slick against the steering wheel.

If Alan had killed Prudence to keep her from telling

anyone else about his double life, what was to prevent him from killing her? He seemed an intelligent man—he would have guessed why Shelby had been visiting Marcia.

Panic seized Shelby. She looked in her mirror again, but the car was no longer there. She felt a moment of relief and then realized it was passing her. It went by too fast for her to see the driver.

Was Alan heading to the farm to lie in wait for her return? Shelby was about to reach for her phone to dial Frank when a thought occurred to her—Liz Gardener had said she'd seen a woman go into the mudroom after Prudence. Alan couldn't be the murderer. All the stress and tension of the last week was getting the better of her common sense.

Shelby relaxed in her seat and switched on the radio. She had a weakness for cheesy pop songs and was happily singing along to one of them when another thought occurred to her. Liz Gardener often said that although she needed glasses, she was too vain to wear them all the time. She hadn't been wearing any the day of the potluck. Could she have mistaken a man for a woman because of it?

Panic welled up in Shelby again and she abruptly switched off the radio. What had sounded pleasant before was now stretching her nerves to the limit. She hit the gas pedal and the car jerked forward. She scrabbled in her handbag with her right hand and breathed a sigh of relief when her fingers closed around her cell. She flicked on her blinker, slowed down, and pulled over to the shoulder of the road. The sun was beginning to dip toward the horizon, and Shelby clicked on the car's interior light.

Her heart sank when she looked at her cell phone—there were no bars to speak of and the low-battery warning was on. Shelby tossed it back in her purse, turned out the overhead light, put on her left signal, and pulled back out onto the nearly empty road.

She would head straight to the police station as soon as she reached Lovett.

Shelby tried to quell her panic as she sped down the highway. It would abate slightly only to return with a vengeance, making her palms sweat and causing her to punch the accelerator aggressively. A few times she found herself drifting into the other lane without realizing it, and she prayed she would make it home in one piece.

A never-ending dialogue was on a loop in her head— one minute she was convinced that Alan was on his way to her house and the next minute she had convinced herself that her imagination was running away from her.

Would Alan hurt her children? The thought made Shelby sick to her stomach. Of course they weren't alone—Bert was with them, but although she was as feisty as they came, Bert would hardly be a match for a strong, healthy man and determined killer.

Shelby had never been so glad in her life to pass the sign stating LOVETT 5 MILES. She was almost there. She'd planned to head to the police station, but she had to make sure the children were okay. She couldn't bear the anxiety another moment. Besides, would the police think her an overwrought woman and drag their feet about sending a car around?

That decided, she made the left turn that would take her down the road leading to the farm. Mud created by the recent rain splattered up against her windshield as she flew down the road, her foot pressed to the gas pedal.

Finally Love Blossom Farm was in sight. Shelby's heartbeat sped up as she rocketed down the pockmarked driveway toward the back of the house.

24

Dear Reader,

I think I may have opened a can of worms. Is it too late
to swear off amateur detective work and concentrate
on learning to knit? Unfortunately I am afraid the damage may already be done. If you don't hear from me
tomorrow, you will know that the killer is onto me.

Shelby bolted from her car and headed toward the old
farmhouse, her heart hammering in her chest. Everything
looked normal from the outside—no unexpected cars in
the driveway or strange faces peering out the window.
Obviously she was overreacting. She was glad she hadn't
gone to the police station—she would have looked a fool.

The back door was open, as Shelby had expected, and
she let herself inside. The kitchen was empty and dimly

lit by the light over the sink. The dishes were all done and the table wiped down. For a moment Shelby smiled and silently blessed Bert.

Faint sounds drifted into the kitchen from the television in the living room, and music thumped overhead from one of Amelia's favorite YouTube videos, which she'd already played at least a thousand times. Everything was as it should be, with nothing out of the ordinary. Shelby's panic slowly began to subside, although a faint uneasiness remained. She tiptoed into the living room, half afraid she'd find Bert and the children tied to chairs and gagged, but Bert was snoring softly in the recliner, her knitting abandoned in her lap, and the children were obviously upstairs in their rooms. Jenkins was tucked in next to Bert on the chair, and Bitsy's chin rested on her knee, leaving a spot of drool on her capris.

Bert must have sensed Shelby standing there, because she woke with a snort. She pretended she hadn't been asleep and Shelby pretended to believe her—a game they'd played many times before.

"All's quiet on the western front," Bert said, snapping the recliner into position and levering herself out of it. She pointed toward the ceiling. "Except for that, of course." Thumping bass notes from Amelia's music drifted down the stairs to the living room.

"Was everything okay?" Shelby asked, unable to rid herself of the unease that prickled her scalp.

"Right as rain." Bert squinted at Shelby. "Is something wrong?"

"No," Shelby said hastily, shaking her head for emphasis.

Bert clearly didn't believe her, but Shelby was relieved when Bert let it drop with a grunt.

"Guess I'll be taking off, then." Bert tucked her knitting into a patchwork cloth tote and made her way through the kitchen to the back door.

"Thanks, Bert. I don't know what I'd do without you."

"Don't go getting all sentimental on me," Bert admonished. "You'll make me cry, and that will ruin my tough gal image."

Shelby laughed, closed the door behind Bert, leaned against it, and breathed a sigh of relief.

She moved around the kitchen restlessly—there wasn't anything left to do; Bert had taken care of everything. She drifted into the living room and turned on the television, but nothing held her attention. She was as jittery as someone hyped up on too much caffeine, and she hadn't had so much as a cup of coffee since early that morning. Finally she decided she would work on her knitting and retrieved her needles, wool, and half-finished scarf from the basket next to the recliner.

Dear Reader, whoever said knitting is calming must have been delusional. I have half a mind to chuck this project out the window.

Shelby continued to dutifully struggle with her knitting—she couldn't show up for the church knitting club not having made any progress at all. She held up the length of red scarf that descended from her needles. Could numerous holes from dropped stiches be considered progress? She was ready to stuff the whole thing back in the basket when she was startled by the sound of someone knocking on the front door.

A knock on the door at any other time wouldn't have fazed Shelby in the least, but tonight it froze her in her tracks. Who could be stopping by now at this late hour?

Maybe Alan had been lying in wait and was now coming after her hoping to catch her off guard? The thought made Shelby's stomach turn over. Her hands were trembling when she pushed aside the living room window curtain to peer outside.

But instead of Alan's dark blue Buick in the driveway as she had feared, it was Frank's beat-up pickup truck.

Shelby breathed a sigh of relief, unlocked the front door, and threw it open.

Frank stepped over the threshold. "Sorry about my boots. I can take them off if you want."

Shelby glanced at his feet. "Are you kidding? The kids track in more dirt than you ever could." She motioned toward a chair. "Can I get you a drink?"

"I don't want to trouble you."

"It's no bother. Iced tea?"

"Sure."

Shelby left Frank in the living room and went to the kitchen for the tea. Why had he come? Did he have some news about the case?

Shelby poured them each a glass of tea and carried both back to the living room.

She handed Frank his glass and took a seat opposite him. He seemed nervous. Was there bad news?

Frank downed his iced tea in one long gulp, wiped his mouth with the back of his hand, and put the empty glass down on the table.

"I came by to make sure you were okay," he said after looking at Shelby for a moment.

Shelby ran a finger around the rim of her glass.

Should she tell Frank that she thought Alan had been

following her? Probably not—most likely she had been mistaken.

Frank looked so like his brother sitting in the shadows by the television that for a second Shelby forgot he wasn't Bill and almost got up to go to him. When she looked at Frank, there was a yearning look on his face that startled her.

Frank tilted his head to one side. "You sure you're okay? You seem sort of . . . tense." He rolled his own shoulders as if he himself was tightly wound.

"I'm fine. Really."

"If you're sure . . ." He sighed, put his hands on his knees, and pushed himself out of the chair.

He walked toward Shelby. She couldn't move. She knew Frank wasn't Bill, but she couldn't stop the small leap of her heart as he came closer.

He put a hand on her arm. "Shelby."

Shelby tried to find her voice but couldn't.

Frank sighed again. "I'd better go."

He pulled his keys from his pocket and paused at Shelby's front door. "Call me if you need anything, okay?"

Shelby nodded and watched Frank retreat through the open door. She had the feeling there was more to his parting words than even he realized.

25

Dear Reader,

The fact that Frank looks so much like my Bill is playing havoc with my mind and heart. I know he's not Bill, but I can't help being drawn to him nonetheless. I know my future lies elsewhere—with Matt or Jake or someone I haven't even met yet.

Shelby stared at the closed door for several long minutes before collapsing in the recliner. What had just happened? Why was her heart beating so fast?

The sound of Billy calling out in his sleep pulled her out of her reverie. She knew he was fine, but she decided to check on him anyway. Perhaps the sight of his childish sleeping face would chase away the other thoughts that were going around and around in her head.

She tiptoed up the stairs, even though she knew both Billy and Amelia were sound sleepers. The old steps gave their usual creaks and groans and Shelby winced, but all remained quiet. The door to Billy's room was cracked, and Shelby eased it open the rest of the way. The room was softly lit from the glow of the night-light her parents had sent him that cast stars and moons on the ceiling.

He'd kicked off his covers and was clutching an old stuffed rabbit he'd had since he was a baby. Its fur was rubbed off in places, and it was missing both button eyes— Bert had applied some creative stitchery to make new ones in their place. Shelby reached out and smoothed a lock of blond hair off Billy's forehead before tiptoeing out.

There was no music coming from Amelia's room, but the strip of light beneath her closed bedroom door meant she was still up. Shelby had a vision of how Amelia looked sleeping when she was younger—spread out like a starfish, the blond curls around her forehead always a little damp with perspiration. Shelby started to raise her fist to knock but then dropped her arm to her side again. She'd let Amelia sleep on things first before tackling her in the morning.

Shelby went back to the living room and picked up a seed catalogue she'd been meaning to look through, but her earlier feelings of unrest returned. She flipped the pages without really seeing them and finally tossed the catalogue back on the ever-growing pile of unread magazines and old newspapers. Finally she decided she might as well go to bed herself—she would be up with the chickens, literally.

Shelby checked the front door to make sure it was locked, then went around to the back door and did the same. Not that the locks would provide much security if someone tried to break in—the house was as full of holes as a piece of Swiss cheese. It would be easy enough to cut a screen on one of the open windows or pry apart the doors to the cellar and find the way inside.

Shelby walked down the hall and glanced at the open windows in the living room. A deliciously cool evening breeze was wafting in and, along with it, the scent of the lilacs planted alongside the house. Shelby hesitated for a moment, then went over and slammed them shut. Even though she doubted she and the children were in any real danger, she wasn't taking any chances. The feeling of unease that had started when she saw Alan's car was still with her, hovering around the edges of her consciousness.

Shelby climbed the stairs to the second floor with Bitsy and Jenkins following close behind. The air was stuffier the higher she climbed, especially with the children's bedroom doors closed. Shelby left hers open, hoping to encourage some air circulation. Her own windows were wide-open, and the lace curtains billowed in the breeze like a blowhard puffing out his cheeks.

A four-poster bed dominated the room—it had been Shelby's grandparents', then her parents', and finally hers and Bill's. And now it was just hers, and it seemed so vast and lonely. She gave a mental shake, reminded herself that self-pity was horribly unattractive, and gave herself orders to lose it.

Shelby washed her face, brushed her teeth, and slipped into an oversize T-shirt—gone were the days when she would go online to order pretty nightgowns from JCPenney. She slipped into bed, threw back the light summer blanket she kept on the bed for those occasional cool summer evenings, and pulled the sheet up to her chin.

She heard Jenkins grunt and the crack of Bitsy's knees as they settled themselves onto their respective dog beds. Moments later, the soft murmur of Jenkins's snoring drifted on the warm air.

Barely a minute later, Shelby sat up in bed, her ears straining in an attempt to decipher the sound she was convinced she had just heard. The cracking of a twig as someone stepped on it? The specter of Alan Swanson creeping toward the house in the dark immediately rose to Shelby's mind.

She sat stock-still in bed, clutching the sheets, trying to sort out the noises coming in the open window—the croaking of crickets, the faint sound of a car in the distance, then another crack followed by a thump. Shelby pulled the sheet up to her chin, her breath ragged, beads of sweat beginning to form on the back of her neck. Another loud crack. Shelby bit back a cry and slipped out of bed. She knelt down beside it and swiped a hand underneath, stifling a sneeze as dust rose in the air and drifted toward her.

Her hand made contact with a baseball bat—a Louisville Slugger that Bill had wielded in Lovett's defeat of a team from Detroit in the playoffs his senior year in high school. She held it close to her side as she made her way toward the bedroom door. She whistled for Bitsy and Jenkins, who sprang to their feet as if they hadn't been deeply asleep only seconds ago. They followed Shelby as she made her way into the hallway toward the stairs. Halfway down the steps, Shelby suddenly realized how ridiculous she must look—creeping about in the night with a baseball bat for a weapon—all because some nocturnal animal had stepped on some dry twigs.

The glimpse she'd had of Alan Swanson's face as she drove out of his neighborhood had certainly set her nerves on edge. She sat on the bottom step, the bat held loosely across her lap, and listened intently. Wind whooshed through the trees and crickets chirped, but Shelby couldn't hear anything even remotely sinister—no one wiggling the door handle or sawing at the screen.

She was getting chilly and pulled her T-shirt down so that it covered her knees. She sat on the steps for another five minutes before deciding she was being ridiculous—no one was trying to break in. She might as well go back to bed.

Shelby tiptoed up the stairs, Bitsy and Jenkins on her heels, slid the baseball bat back beneath the bed, and crawled under the sheet.

⁣⁣⁣⁣⁣⁣⁣⁣⁣⁣⁣⁣⁣⁣⁣⁣⁣⁣⁣⁣⁣⁣⁣

Shelby finally managed to fall into a restless sleep, but when she woke in the morning, the bedclothes were tangled around her legs and her pillow was damp with perspiration—evidence of her night filled with frightening nightmares and restless sleep.

She sat on the edge of the bed and yawned. For once she was glad it was time to get up. She felt as if she'd been fighting in her sleep, and her bones and muscles ached with a combination of tension and weariness. Staying busy was always the best prescription for a troubled mind, her granny used to say, and many times Shelby had found her to be right about that.

The word *coffee* percolated through Shelby's mind as she pulled on jeans and a long-sleeved shirt—mornings were still chilly in Lovett in June, although by noon she'd be swapping her top for a T-shirt and her jeans for a pair of shorts.

She splashed some cold water on her face, patted her hair into semi-submission, and flipped off the bathroom light. She felt her way down the darkened hall toward the stairs, glancing at Amelia's and Billy's closed doors as she passed. She imagined she could hear soft breathing coming from both of them.

The stairs creaked in the same spots they always did—the second step from the top and the fourth one from the bottom—but the children didn't stir. Bitsy and Jenkins padded along in back of her—she could hear Jenkins's nails tapping on the wooden floor and the sound of Bitsy's constant panting.

Shelby stood in front of the coffeemaker for a moment, trying to force her sleep-addled brain to remember how it worked. Finally she pulled the coffee canister closer, emptied the basket of yesterday's grounds, and began measuring out a fresh batch. A few minutes later, the scent of brewing coffee began circulating through the kitchen. Shelby inhaled deeply and grabbed a mug from the cabinet.

Hot coffee in hand, she padded barefoot out to the sunroom and dropped into the old rocker. A piece of broken wicker poked the back of her leg, and she shifted around in her seat to avoid it. She rocked back and forth, reviewing all the things that needed to be done that day before the meeting of the knitting club later that afternoon.

Shelby mentally cringed when she thought about her knitting. She'd bought that red wool with such hope and enthusiasm and had utterly failed to weave it into the scarf she'd hoped to make for Billy. Thinking about the skeins of wool she'd brought home from the Lovett General Store reminded her of the scrap of yarn Frank and his team had found in the mudroom. When he'd showed it to her, she'd assumed it was hers, but now that she thought about it, she wasn't so sure. Wasn't that piece a darker red—verging toward maroon? She remembered someone in the knitting group using a similar color, but for the life of her she couldn't remember who it was.

She drained the rest of her coffee and heaved herself out of the rocker. The chickens weren't going to feed themselves. The sky was beginning to lighten to the east—they'd be squawking furiously and prancing around in indignation by now.

Shelby slipped her feet into her gardening clogs and headed out the back door. The drops of dew clinging to the lawn were cool against her bare heels as she brushed against the grass. The air, too, had that early-morning chill, which the sun would eventually burn away as it climbed higher in the sky.

The air was fragrant with the mingled scent of herbs and damp ground. Shelby inhaled deeply. As much as she hated leaving her bed so early every morning, she relished this time of day, when the world was quiet and still.

The barn was a shadow in the distance. Even before she reached it, Shelby heard the screeching and squawking of the chickens. Their chatter was interrupted by a vocalization from Jack Sparrow, the rooster. Shelby had learned to interpret his different crows, and this one signaled danger from above, like a hawk ready to swoop down on unsuspecting prey.

As Shelby approached, she watched the hens scurry

toward the shelter of the barn, their frantically flapping wings creating a maelstrom of flying feathers.

Shelby pushed the barn door open wider. It creaked loudly and she again made a mental note to oil the old hinges. The interior was dark, with the only light coming from the open door behind her. She felt along the wall for the shelf, retrieved her flashlight, and turned it on.

Dust motes danced in the beam of light as Shelby made her way across the barn. She set the flashlight down, retrieved the battered metal bucket from the hook in the wall, and began to fill it with chicken feed.

The chickens squawked and danced around, scratching at the barn floor as they waited impatiently. Shelby picked up the now-full bucket and headed toward the door. The chickens turned and followed her out of the barn, making her feel like a sort of Pied Piper of the poultry set.

Shelby stood in the middle of the yard and began scattering the grain in a wide arc. The chickens scurried after the feed, pushing each other out of the way as if afraid there wouldn't be enough.

"There's plenty for all of you," Shelby called to them as she tossed out the last handful.

She retrieved her flashlight, turned it on, and headed back into the barn. The sun was slowly rising and more light filtered into the barn now. Shelby switched off her flashlight—no need to waste the batteries when she could see reasonably well now. She reached the back of the barn, returned the pail to its hook, and turned around to leave.

Shelby jumped and stifled a gasp. Someone was standing in the doorway. The person was silhouetted against the light, making it impossible for Shelby to tell who he, or she, was.

"Bert?" she called out even though she already knew the silhouette was too tall and too slim to be Bert's.

"Who's Bert?"

The voice was female and tantalizingly familiar.

The person stepped farther into the darkened barn, moving away from the light. Shelby picked up her flashlight, switched it on, and aimed the beam at the intruder.

26

Dear Reader,

You know how they say people's lives flash in front of their eyes when they're drowning? I don't know if that's true or not, but in this case it did happen to me. I saw myself as a girl sitting in that old apple tree that Billy likes to climb, then dressed in the white wedding gown my grandmother sewed for me with fabric that originally came from her gown. Bill was at my side, looking impossibly handsome. We started giggling because we both knew we couldn't wait to be alone. Then the dash to the hospital through the pouring rain and the arrival of Amelia. It was sunny the day Billy was born, and we almost didn't make it in time. And now here I am, facing a killer in my own barn.

"Grace!" Shelby exclaimed.

"Were you expecting someone else?"

"No . . . no," Shelby said. She didn't tell Grace that she had been positive her husband, Alan, would be the one coming after her.

Shelby's mind raced, trying to piece together the facts she knew about Prudence's murder—Prudence's false accusations, Liz claiming to have seen a woman follow Prudence into the mudroom, Prudence's call to Marcia . . . and that bit of yarn Frank and his team found in the mudroom. Of course! It must have been Grace's. Shelby remembered now—Grace had been knitting a dark red sweater—more than once Shelby had admired the skill with which she'd followed that complicated-looking pattern of cables and bobbles. So Liz had been right after all—she *had* seen a woman go into the mud-room after Prudence.

"What do you want?" Shelby tried to keep the quaver out of her voice.

"I want you to be quiet," Grace said, slowly raising her arm. There was a gun in her hand.

Shelby involuntarily took a step backward. "I won't say anything," she said, even though she knew it was pointless—Grace wouldn't believe her.

Grace laughed. "Why should I believe you? Prudence refused to be quiet." She took a step closer to Shelby and smiled. "I'm not much of a shot, and I don't want to miss."

"I promise—"

"Prudence would have ruined everything—blabbing to everyone about Alan's other wife. I knew all about Marcia. He promised me he would divorce her as soon as the time was right. And then I would be his one and only." Grace's face hardened, reminding Shelby of a picture of a gargoyle she had seen once.

"I waited so long for someone to come along—I wasn't about to let anyone ruin it. Certainly not Prudence." She shook her head. "With Prudence taken care of, the problem was solved, but then you had to go nosing around, didn't you?"

"But I'm not going to say anything, I promise."

"I wish I could say I believe you." Grace aimed the gun and braced her one arm with the other.

Panic made Shelby's heart race until the blood pounding in her ears became deafening. She looked around, her head spinning like the girl's in the *Exorcist*. If Grace missed, it would give Shelby the opportunity to duck under the loft. If. But then what? *Move,* she screamed to herself. It was always harder to hit a moving target—and who knew how good a shot Grace really was?

Shelby thought of screaming, but who would hear her? Even if Jake was on the very edge of his field, her voice would be muffled by the walls of the barn, and it would be a miracle if he heard her. The house was too far away. Besides, the last thing she wanted was for either of the children to come running. The thought made her shiver.

"Cold?" Grace sneered. "Fear does that to a person."

Grace's finger was on the trigger now. Shelby was tempted to close her eyes, like a child facing something unpleasant, but that wasn't going to save her. She inched her hand toward the pocket of her shorts.

"Stop!" Grace commanded, waving the gun wildly at Shelby. "Put your hands where I can see them."

Shelby held her hands out in front of her in a gesture of surrender. Grace raised the gun again. Shelby was primed to throw herself to one side when Bitsy and Jenkins appeared in the doorway. Their heads were raised and their eyes narrowed—they obviously sensed danger. Jenkins bristled with indignation and even the normally placid Bitsy had pulled her lips back, baring her teeth. Both uttered a low guttural growl deep in their throats.

Grace looked over her shoulder at the dogs. "They're not going to save you. I'll shoot you first and then the two of them."

She pointed the gun at Shelby and put her finger back on the trigger. Shelby threw herself to one side as Grace squeezed the trigger. The bullet missed her but came a heck of a lot closer than she would have liked.

The sun was getting brighter and pinpricks of light lit the barn's leaky roof. The lighter it got, the better Grace's aim would likely become.

Grace raised her arm again, but before she could shoot, the dogs were on her. Jenkins bit her in the calf and Grace dropped the gun and howled in pain, grabbing with both hands at her leg. Before she could straighten up, Bitsy was on her, sending her flying backward. Grace hit the ground with a thud, sending up a cloud of dust.

Grace squirmed and thrashed this way and that, but she couldn't throw Bitsy off her. Jenkins hovered nearby, giving a low growl and baring his teeth.

"Get this beast off me," Grace screamed. "I'm bleeding. I need a doctor." Her tone was pleading now.

Grace stuck out her arm, swishing it back and forth across the ground in an attempt to retrieve her gun. Shelby had already started looking for it, but it was nowhere to be seen. She hoped that if she couldn't find it, Grace wouldn't, either.

Bitsy seemed to be doing an admirable job of restraining Grace, so Shelby reached into her pocket and pulled out her cell phone. She was dialing 911 when a voice came from the open barn door—a masculine voice this time.

"Drop the phone," it commanded.

Shelby looked up. Alan Swanson was standing just inside the barn with a gun pointed straight at Shelby. She was so startled that she dropped her cell phone. It hit the ground and bounced twice before landing facedown.

"What . . . ," Shelby stammered.

"Call off your dogs." Alan waved his gun toward Bitsy and Jenkins, who continued to stand guard over Grace.

Shelby gave a sharp whistle, and both dogs turned to look at her. "Bitsy, Jenkins, come," Shelby ordered.

They hesitated for a moment, reluctant to relinquish their prey. Shelby slapped her thigh, and they both left their position and walked over to where she was standing. The hair on Jenkins's back was standing on end, and Bitsy stood stiff and at attention. Both looked disappointed that Shelby had put an end to their fun.

Alan reached down and grasped Grace's hand, pulling her to her feet. "Are you all right, darling?"

"I'm bleeding," Grace snapped, pointing to her leg.

"We'll soon get you to a doctor—don't worry."

"It hurts," Grace whined.

"I'll just finish up here, shall I?" Alan raised his gun and pointed it straight at Shelby. "Too bad you didn't heed our warning," he said.

"You hung the squash from my porch roof," Shelby exclaimed.

"It was Grace's idea. Brilliant, don't you think? Too bad it didn't work."

Shelby had a flashback to the potluck. She remembered talking to Alan and Grace and noticing the blot of red sauce on Alan's white shirt—sauce that looked as if it had come from Prudence's slow-cooker meatballs.

"You're the one who killed Prudence," Shelby said. "Not Grace."

"Yes." Alan preened and threw his shoulders back. "I'm the one who killed Prudence." He put an arm around Grace and squeezed her. "Grace was only trying to protect me."

Grace smiled up at him.

"Prudence recognized me from their former church in Cranberry Cove. She called Marcia and told her all about it. I couldn't let her ruin things for me. I knew I could convince Marcia it was all a lie—Prudence was forever telling tales, and it was easy enough to convince Marcia that this was another one of them."

Shelby looked at Grace. "Doesn't it bother you that your husband has another wife?"

"I won't be married to Marcia much longer," Alan said before Grace could answer. "I need to take care of a few details and then as her spouse, I'll be getting the check from her rather hefty life insurance policy. When she took it out, I thought it was rather a waste of money, but now I'm glad she insisted."

"You mean you're going to kill—"

"Why not?" Alan shrugged. "Then Grace and I can be together legally."

Dear Reader, that's pretty rich of him, don't you think? Worrying about legality when he's already committed murder?

It was lighter in the barn now, making Shelby an even easier target for Alan. The phrase *shooting fish in a barrel* came to mind. Maybe if she kept Alan talking, someone would come along? Shelby knew that was a long shot, even as the thought crossed her mind. She wasn't going down without a fight, though—that was for sure. She couldn't leave Amelia and Billy orphaned. A sob caught in her throat, and she balled her hands into fists.

"And now it's your turn." Alan leveled the gun at Shelby.

27

Dear Reader,

Have you ever noticed how in moments of fear, all your senses are heightened—smell, for instance? I could smell both dogs—Jenkins smelled of damp fur, as if he had gotten into some water somewhere on the farm—and Bitsy smelled hot. I could smell Alan's aftershave, too—something musky and rather too heavy for summer. My hearing became acute as well. There was the sound of water dripping somewhere that I hadn't noticed before. I made a mental note to check it out before realizing how ridiculous that was. I was staring down the barrel of a gun and not likely to get away.

Alan gave Shelby an apologetic look. "I really am sorry about this. If you hadn't gone snooping . . ."

He raised the gun a fraction, steadied his aim, and moved his finger to the trigger.

Shelby was tense with readiness, shifting her weight to the balls of her feet.

Alan pulled the trigger.

Shelby threw herself sideways, and the bullet bit the dirt behind her, sending up clods of earth. The noise was deafening, and for a moment, her ears rang shrilly from the blast. Alan swore, and she knew he was taking aim again. Grace was scouring the ground for the other gun, dragging her injured leg behind her.

Shelby had made it under the loft, where it was considerably darker than the rest of the barn. She prayed the shadows would keep her hidden enough to make it difficult for Alan to aim at her. She saw him raise the gun again and quickly scuttled across the barn floor, closer to the ladder to the loft.

Both Bitsy and Jenkins had bolted—the two of them struggled to get under the beds when it thundered or firecrackers were going off. The chickens in the yard were squawking wildly, startled by all the unaccustomed noise. Jack Sparrow was crowing frantically, and she pictured them all running to and fro, flapping their wings uselessly.

Before Alan could take aim again, Shelby started up the ladder to the loft. She knew she was making herself an easier target, but if she could get to the top . . .

She was on the final rung when she heard the click of the empty gun—Alan was out of bullets. Shelby risked a look and saw him throw the gun on the ground and swear.

"Find that other gun, would you?" he shouted at Grace. "I never should have let you take it. You never do anything right," he added, a sneering tone to his voice.

Grace gave a whimper as if he had lashed out at her physically.

"Go on! Don't just stand there," Alan screamed at her. "Move."

Grace put her hands on her hips. "How dare you talk to me like that!"

"This isn't the time to discuss . . . Oh, never mind." Alan grabbed the ladder and began to climb. "I'll deal with this another way."

Shelby scurried to the farthest reaches of the loft. She could feel the structure shake as Alan climbed the ladder. By now she was pressed into the corner, wishing there was somewhere to hide.

Dear Reader, I'll be darned if I'm going to stand here cowering like some helpless female out of a Perils of Pauline *movie. I'm going to fight back—but how?*

Shelby scanned the loft for a weapon of some sort—anything she could use against Alan, who was considerably bigger and taller than she was. A motley collection of rusted gardening and farm implements were scattered across the floor. They'd been there so long they'd almost become one with the wooden boards of the loft. They were a testament to Shelby's grandfather's thrift—even if something was broken, he would save it in case it would prove useful later.

Shelby picked up a trowel that had a nicely pointed end. It would have to do. She decided it would be best if she took the offense, but when she turned to face the loft stairs, Alan was already there, startling Shelby, and she dropped the trowel. Alan kicked it out of reach with a wicked grin.

In no time, Shelby was backed against the wall. She felt the rough and splintered wood through the thin cotton of her T-shirt. Alan was so close she could almost feel his breath on her face. She tried to scuttle away—going sideways like a crab—but he put out an arm and pinned her to the wall.

Shelby felt panic choke her as Alan put his hands on either side of her neck and began to squeeze. Shelby stomped on his foot as hard as she could, but he didn't loosen his grip. She was beginning to feel light-headed and was convinced she was seeing stars.

There was no time to lose. She had to do something before she lost consciousness. Shelby swept a hand along the rough wooden wall in back of her. A splinter lodged in her thumb, but she hardly noticed. The tips of her fingers brushed something hard.

She managed to stretch her arm out far enough to get her whole hand around the object. It was a long wooden handle. Shelby remembered there was an old pitchfork up in the loft—she'd warned Billy numerous times not to touch it. She'd kept meaning to get rid of it, and now she was glad she'd never gotten around to it.

It was now or never, Shelby decided. She grasped the handle as far down as she could reach for better control, lifted the pitchfork off the floor, and swung it around until it made contact with Alan's body.

It wasn't an especially hard blow, but it was enough to make him let go of Shelby's throat. She moved away as quickly as she could, swinging the pitchfork in front of her to keep him at bay, much like a lion tamer waving a chair.

Alan's face was crimson with rage. He made a sound like a roar and lunged at Shelby. She jabbed at him with the pitchfork, forcing him backward and farther away from her. She caught a glimpse of Grace out of the corner of her eye. Bitsy and Jenkins had returned to the barn now that the noise was over. Jenkins stood in front of Grace, growling, as she pressed against the wall. Her hands were empty—she obviously hadn't found the gun, and with Jenkins guarding her, she wasn't able to continue looking.

Bitsy was staring at the loft as if sensing the danger to Shelby. She made a few futile lunges at the ladder, barking furiously. Shelby had taught her to sit, to stay—more or less—to roll over and beg, and now she only wished she had found a way to teach her how to climb a ladder. At least the two of them were frightening Grace enough to keep her from looking for the gun.

Shelby and Alan continued their cat-and-mouse game—thrust and parry, thrust and parry. Alan was panting, and Shelby felt sweat trickling down her back, causing the fabric of her T-shirt to stick to her clammy skin.

Alan lunged again and Shelby jabbed at him with the pitchfork. He pushed it aside and for a moment Shelby stood stock-still, thinking he was about to grab her. Frantic, she swung the pitchfork in a wild arc, striking Alan on the cheek. He howled and clasped a hand to the spot where the pitchfork had hit him.

The pain seemed to have enraged him even more.

"You're not getting away with this," he hissed at Shelby. "I had everything planned. If it hadn't been for you, it would have come off without a hitch."

And he lunged at Shelby again, trying to grab the pitchfork from her hand. She gave him a hard jab with it, and he stumbled backward. She jabbed again, as hard as she could, and the sharp tines connected with his stomach, forcing him backward a few more steps. He teetered on the edge of the loft for a moment, and Shelby held her breath. He stood there for a few more seconds, waving his arms frantically, then lost his balance and plummeted to the ground.

Shelby thought she would never forget the sound his body made when it hit—that and the sound of Grace's piercing scream. Shelby peered over the edge of the loft— she couldn't tell if Alan was dead or just knocked out. She thought she saw his chest rise and fall but wasn't sure. Grace leaned over him, crying and calling his name.

Shelby started down the ladder, keeping one eye on Grace as she descended. Bitsy and Jenkins immediately surrounded her. Bitsy put her paws on Shelby's shoulders, and for a second Shelby couldn't see past the dog's slobbering tongue. When Bitsy finally got down, having satisfied herself that her owner was okay, Grace was no longer leaning over Alan's body.

Grace was bending over with her back to Shelby, and when she whirled around it was clear she had found the missing gun. Her hand was quite steady as she leveled it at Shelby's head.

Shelby was exhausted from fighting Alan and barely had enough energy to think straight.

She watched, stunned, as Grace tightened her finger on the trigger.

28

Dear Reader,

When something intense happens, everything seems
to go in slow motion and time becomes telescoped so
that what may have taken a minute or two feels as if
it's taking hours. But then when it's over, time snaps
back again and you realize it's only been a short time
after all. It's a little disconcerting, though, when you
find yourself staring at a gun.

The dogs circled Grace, as if trying to decide what to
do. Grace paid no attention to them—her focus was riv-
eted on Shelby.

Shelby was bracing herself to jump out of the way—
Grace would probably still hit her, but perhaps it wouldn't
be the fatal shot Grace was hoping for.

"Police. Drop the gun," an authoritative voice came from the open door of the barn.

Grace's jaw dropped, and she spun around.

Shelby was just as surprised as Grace to see Frank standing in the doorway, his gun drawn but still at his side. The easy way he held himself made him look almost nonchalant, but Shelby could tell he was anything but. Like his brother, the unwavering intensity of his gaze gave him away.

Grace turned back to Shelby with lightning speed, grabbed Shelby's arm, and pulled her closer. She pointed the gun right at Shelby's head and maneuvered her so that Shelby was in front of her like a shield. She gave Shelby a push. "Move. My car is parked at the end of your driveway."

"Where are we—"

"Quiet," Grace hissed in Shelby's ear.

Shelby clamped her mouth shut. Grace was clearly delusional if she thought she could get away with this, but the look in her eyes scared Shelby. She was obviously crazy, and crazy people did crazy things—like pulling the trigger on a gun even when confronted by the police. Even the dogs seemed to sense that Grace was behaving erratically, and kept their distance from her although their stance remained alert and watchful.

Frank's eyes narrowed as he watched Shelby and Grace's progress across the room. He held his gun loosely, but Shelby could see the muscle jumping in his jaw.

She had to give Frank a shot at Grace somehow. She thought of giving her a shove, but Grace's finger on the trigger was so twitchy Shelby didn't want to chance it. If only she could trip her somehow. She had to bite back a gasp when the idea came to her. That hole in the ground!

It wasn't deep—just deep enough to throw someone off balance. How many times had she herself stumbled after catching her foot in it?

Shelby started to lead Grace as subtly as possible to the left. Fortunately they didn't have to go far, and luckily Grace didn't seem to realize Shelby had them crossing the barn at a slight angle—all her attention was focused on Frank and his gun.

At first Shelby thought they'd missed the hole when suddenly Grace gave a squeak like a mouse caught in a trap. Her body twisted and she went down on one knee. Her hand holding the gun slammed into the ground, and the gun went off.

Bitsy and Jenkins streaked past Shelby at astonishing speed—Bitsy, for once, giving up her characteristic lope in favor of sprinting like a racehorse.

Frank ran over to Shelby and grabbed her arm, pushing her to safety behind him. Two uniformed policeman with guns drawn burst into the barn, and between them they quickly subdued Grace and carried her off to the waiting police car outside. She screamed like a fishwife and her hissed curses could be heard even after she'd been removed from the barn.

A third policeman arrived and immediately ran to Alan Swanson, where he lay near the stairs to the loft.

Dear Reader, the entire Lovett police force must have come out for this. It certainly makes an exciting change from directing parking at the county fair and ticketing speeders.

Frank motioned to Shelby to stay where she was as he joined the uniformed officer who was kneeling by Alan's side. Shelby felt herself start to shake uncontrollably.

Frank leaned over Alan's body. "Is he alive?" he asked as he stuck his gun in the waistband of his jeans.

"He's knocked out pretty good, but there's a pulse," the cop said, removing his fingers from the side of Alan's neck. "Who knows what's broken, though?" He stood up and stared at Alan's twisted body. "I'll radio for an ambulance."

"The EMTs are already on their way. I was afraid we were going to need one, so I radioed ahead." Frank pulled a piece of gum from his pocket, tore off the wrapper, and put the folded piece in his mouth. He chewed calmly as he gave a last glance at Alan's body before turning and walking toward Shelby.

As soon as Frank reached her, Shelby's legs gave out. Frank put an arm around her, and she leaned her head against his chest, trying to stifle the tears that were gathering and threatening to spill.

"It's shock," Frank murmured against Shelby's hair. "It will pass."

Shelby nodded and gave a loud sniff.

"Shelby, are you okay?" a male voice came from the barn door.

Frank and Shelby jumped apart quickly.

"Jake!" Shelby said. "Yes, I'm fine. Or I suppose I will be."

"I heard the sirens, and when they stopped at your place, I panicked. I ran all the way here." Jake pulled out the tail of his shirt and wiped the perspiration off his face.

Shelby didn't know why, but she felt as if she'd been caught doing something she shouldn't have been. The look on Frank's face as he walked away told her he felt the same.

"What the . . . ?" Jake said, gesturing toward Alan's

body. He went to stand next to Shelby. "Are you sure you're okay?" he asked, his voice edged with concern.

"Positive."

Dear Reader, I'm as okay as anyone can be after being attacked in their own barn and having to fight off two people who were both intent on killing them.

||||||||||||||||||||||||||||

By the time Shelby left the barn, the sun had risen considerably higher in the sky. The EMTs had come for Alan, who had regained consciousness only to find himself strapped to a backboard. Judging by his attempts to free himself, he wasn't that grievously injured.

Frank had spent some time questioning Shelby. It had been a little awkward as she tried to gloss over the fact that she had been actively investigating Prudence's murder herself. That and the fact that she and Frank were both acting like two people who had touched a hot stove and been burned. Shelby vowed that in the future, she wouldn't let Frank's resemblance to Bill go to her head.

Amelia and Billy were up when Shelby got back to the farmhouse. Billy had his baseball cards spread out over half the breakfast table, and Amelia was still in her nightgown, hunched over her cell phone and a bowl of cereal.

"Bert!" Shelby was surprised to see Bert at the kitchen sink.

Bert spun around. "My neighbor's daughter works part-time as a file clerk for the Lovett Police Department. She got wind of what was happening here and called me. I came over in case you needed me."

Shelby sank into a kitchen chair, feeling as if all the

air had been let out of her. "Bert, I don't know what I'd do without you."

"And I don't know what I'd do without you." Bert dashed a hand across her eyes. "I was real scared for a minute there."

Shelby thought she saw some tears clinging to Bert's lashes, but she knew better than to ask—Bert would simply deny it.

Bert tilted her head toward the kitchen window. "So, what was going on out there?" She turned to Amelia and Billy. "You two, shoo. Go on upstairs and make your beds."

"I thought it would be better if they didn't hear," Bert said after Amelia and Billy left the room. "I put on some fresh coffee if you'd like some."

"Sounds great," Shelby said. It would give her time to collect her thoughts.

"Now," Bert said with relish as she set a mug of steaming coffee in front of Shelby and took a seat opposite. "Want to tell me what was going on out there? I've been dying of curiosity, but I saw Frank's car, so I knew you'd be okay."

Frank had said he'd look after her, Shelby thought. Maybe that frisson of attraction between them had been nothing more than the promise he'd made to his brother?

Shelby shook herself and looked over at Bert, who was eagerly awaiting what she had to say. She was giving Shelby the same look she gave the television set when waiting for her favorite program to start.

Shelby explained how she'd gone out to the barn to feed the chickens when suddenly Grace had appeared with a gun.

"So Grace is the killer?" Bert gasped, her cup of coffee forgotten at her elbow.

"No, not exactly."

"Then who?" Bert's voice was edged with impatience. "You remind me of that detective show I watched the other night when, just as the killer was about to be revealed, the show ended and the announcer said to stay tuned for part two next week."

"I promise you won't have to wait that long."

Shelby realized she hadn't eaten anything for breakfast yet and she was hungry. She got a loaf of bread from the bread box and popped two slices into the toaster.

"It wasn't Daniel, was it?" Bert said, obviously hoping to hurry Shelby along.

"No, it was Alan Swanson."

"Alan Swanson?" Bert echoed in disbelief. "But he and Prudence hardly knew each other. Now, Grace I could picture as the killer. Plenty of things happening at church to cause her to feel murderous toward Prudence."

"True," Shelby said as she transferred her toast to a plate and buttered it. "But Prudence knew something about Alan that Alan didn't want anyone to know." Shelby slid into her seat at the table. "Alan is a bigamist."

"No!" Bert nearly knocked her coffee over in her astonishment. "Does Grace know?"

"Not only does she know, she seems to be condoning it," Shelby said, taking a bite of her toast.

"And his other wife? Where does she live? Nearby?"

"She lives in Cranberry Cove, over by the lake. Prudence called her and told her about Alan and Grace, but she didn't believe her."

"I know Prudence was good at ferreting out secrets, but how on earth did she discover Alan's bigamy?" Bert frowned. "Unless Alan made a clean breast of it to Daniel, and Daniel then indulged in some pillow talk. Although that doesn't sound like Daniel." She frowned again.

"It doesn't sound like Alan, either. I can't picture him spilling his sins to the local rector. No, Prudence recognized him from their previous parish and knew he was married to a woman there. She called his other wife—probably to ask if they'd been divorced. And when it became apparent the other woman—her name is Marcia—was still married to Alan, Prudence filled her in on Alan's double life. Ironically Marcia didn't believe Prudence. It seems Prudence had cried wolf once too often."

Bert rolled her eyes. "That I can believe." She blew on her coffee and took a sip.

"From what I was able to learn, Alan planned to do away with his first wife and collect on a hefty insurance policy in her name. And Grace didn't seem to mind. She wanted to be married at all costs."

"And married to a man with money," Bert added. She was thoughtful for a moment. "So Alan is the one who did the deed."

"I think Grace followed Prudence into the mudroom and tried to reason with her—Alan must have told Grace he'd been recognized. But it was Alan who actually wrapped the cord . . ." Shelby pushed her toast away. Talking about the murder brought the horrific scene to mind and took her appetite away.

"It's like one of those soap operas," Bert said, getting up and putting her empty mug in the dishwasher.

They were both startled by a knock on the back door.

Shelby got up and walked over to push open the screen door, making a mental note to fix the small hole that had appeared in the upper right-hand corner.

Kelly burst into the room, bringing with her the scent of hay, warm animals, and manure. Her jeans had ominous-looking stains on the knees and there were some equally indecipherable spots on her T-shirt, which advertised a 5k run that had taken place seven years ago.

"I heard on the scanner that the police were headed to your house," Kelly said breathlessly. "But the Mingledorffs had another emergency, and I couldn't get away until now. I've been a nervous wreck." She looked Shelby up and down. "Are you okay?" She glanced around the kitchen. "And the kids?"

"Just fine on all counts," Shelby assured her.

Kelly collapsed into a kitchen chair and ran a hand through her unruly red hair. "So what happened?"

Bert cleared her throat. She took off the apron she'd retrieved from Shelby's cupboard and draped it over a chair. "I'll be off if that's okay with you. I promised to make some rhubarb pies for the St. Andrews Women's Auxiliary, so I'd better shake a leg, considering we're only going to get twenty-four hours today as usual. You gals carry on."

She turned to leave, then stopped in her tracks and pointed at Shelby. "Better check that patch of lettuce again. Thought I saw some spots of mildew on the butter oak. I know you sprayed, but maybe you ought to do it again to be sure."

Shelby groaned. She couldn't afford to lose her crop of lettuce. She'd better tend to it right away. She'd wasted too much time already looking into Prudence's murder.

Kelly exhaled forcefully as Bert left the room. "Okay, enough of that. I want to hear about what happened this morning. If you knew how worried I was . . ." She reached across the table and took a piece of the toast Shelby hadn't finished. "Do you mind? I'm starved. I never got breakfast this morning." She took a huge bite and wiped her mouth with the back of her hand. "First let me tell you my news. It's good. Seth didn't murder Prudence," she finished triumphantly.

"I know."

Kelly looked crestfallen. "How did you know?"

"Alan Swanson murdered her."

"Alan? Seriously?"

Shelby nodded. "But it sounds like Seth had an alibi—like you found out where he was when he was supposed to be at the potluck."

"He was having lunch with an old girlfriend." Kelly wrinkled her nose. "They dated when Seth was in medical school but broke up before graduation. I guess she looked him up and came to Lovett to see if she could rekindle things."

"That's awfully forward of her."

"I think it's typical of her and that's one of the reasons they broke up. Seth wasn't high-powered enough for her. She's on her way to finishing her training as a heart surgeon, and here Seth is—a family doctor in a small country town." Kelly shrugged. "Apparently she decided that that didn't matter to her anymore, though, because she came here determined to get Seth back. But he sent her packing. He said he'd tried calling me the afternoon of the potluck, but I'd left my phone in the truck. This Natalie turned up out of the blue, and by the time he got rid of her and was about to head to your place, he got called out on an emergency—some farmer had a nasty accident—got his foot tangled in a piece of machinery. The potluck was nearly over before Seth was finished there."

Kelly finished the last few bites of Shelby's uneaten toast. "So, tell me how you knew it was Alan Swanson who murdered poor Prudence." She glanced at her watch. "Rats! I have clinic in twenty minutes."

She got up from her chair and brushed the crumbs from the toast she'd filched from Shelby's plate into the palm of her hand. "You can tell me tonight over a glass of wine—how's that? I'll pick up a bottle of chardonnay and swing by here after work."

"It's a date."

Shelby had barely closed the door behind Kelly when the front doorbell rang. She scurried down the hall, through the living room, and flung open the door. With Alan and Grace in custody, there was no longer any need to worry about who was at the door.

Frank was waiting on the front steps.

He appeared ill at ease, his arms hanging limply at his sides, his expression serious.

"Come in," Shelby urged him as he hesitated on the front steps.

"Do you have more questions for me?" Shelby hoped that wasn't the case. She didn't want to have to relive the morning's events one single more time.

"No." Frank hooked a thumb through the belt loop on his worn jeans. "I just wanted to make sure you're okay."

For a moment Shelby's breath caught in her throat. Even Frank's voice was like Bill's—deep and mellow.

She was tempted to close her eyes. The moment passed. "Yeah, I'm okay. I'm just fine."

Dear Reader,

Something like Prudence's death certainly puts everything in perspective. Problems like Billy getting his head stuck in the banister become small in comparison. I can even view Amelia's sneaking out with Ned in a new light. Not that I'm going to allow it to continue, but I am willing to face the fact that she is growing up even if it breaks my heart. I think that will make her happy.

RECIPES

HOMEMADE MEAT LOAF

2 pounds ground beef
1 pound ground pork
3 garlic cloves, minced
1 large onion, chopped
1 teaspoon salt
black pepper to taste
½ teaspoon thyme leaves, crumbled
½ cup unseasoned bread crumbs
2 eggs
optional: bacon strips

Preheat oven to 325 degrees.

Measure all ingredients except bacon, place in large bowl, and mix thoroughly with your hands. Form into loaf shape and place in baking dish (or form smaller loaves and freeze some for another dinner.) Arrange optional bacon strips on top.

Bake for 1½ hours, basting occasionally. Let sit for 10 minutes before slicing.

‌‌‌‌‌‌‌‌‌‌‌‌‌‌‌‌‌‌‌‌‌‌‌‌

LOVE BLOSSOM
FARM BEET SALAD

2 large beets
grated zest of 1 lemon
juice of 1 lemon
2 teaspoons extra-virgin olive oil
1 teaspoon honey
½ small red onion, sliced into rings
⅓ cup chopped toasted walnuts or pecans
salt and freshly ground pepper, to taste
3 ounces crumbled feta cheese

Preheat oven to 400 degrees. Place beets in a roasting pan and cover tightly with foil. Bake until the beets are easily pierced all the way through with a paring knife— about 1 hour and 15 minutes, depending on the size of your beets. Let them cool slightly.

Whisk together the lemon zest, juice, oil, and honey to make the dressing.

Rub off the beet skins and slice the beets into thin

rounds. Place them in a salad bowl, along with the red onion, and toss with the dressing. Add walnuts or pecans, salt and pepper to taste, and toss. Sprinkle the feta cheese on top.

|||||||||||||||||||||||||||||||||

HOMEMADE SLOW COOKER YOGURT

½ gallon whole milk (not ultrapasteurized)
6-ounce container of plain unsweetened yogurt with
live cultures (check the label)

Pour milk into the slow cooker and heat to 180 degrees (approximately 1½ to 2½ hours, depending on your slow cooker).

Turn off the slow cooker and allow the milk to cool to 120 degrees (approximately 1½ to 2½ hours, depending on your slow cooker). Let the container of starter yogurt come to room temperature while the milk is cooling.

Mix the container of starter yogurt into the milk and stir.

Cover the slow cooker and wrap it in a beach towel or several smaller towels. Let it sit for 8 hours or overnight. Unwrap the slow cooker, remove the insert, and place in your refrigerator to cool.

To make thicker Greek-style yogurt, line a strainer with cheesecloth and set it in your sink. Place yogurt in the strainer and allow it to drain until the desired consistency is reached.

Save ¾ cup of yogurt to use as a starter for your next batch.

YOGURT CHEESE SPREAD

Place homemade Greek-style yogurt in a sieve lined with cheesecloth and drain, pressing out the whey, until the yogurt is the consistency of soft cream cheese. Mix in a combination of fresh herbs of your choice—parsley, dill, basil, oregano, or mint—and sea salt and freshly ground black pepper to taste. Use as a spread for crackers or crudités.

Also from
Peg Cochran

Berried Secrets
A Cranberry Cove Mystery

When Monica Albertson comes to Cranberry
Cove—a charming town on the eastern shore of Lake
Michigan—to help her half brother, Jeff, on his cranberry
farm, the last thing she expects to harvest is a dead body.

It seems that Sam Culbert, who ran the farm while Jeff
was deployed overseas, had some juicy secrets that would
soon prove fatal, and Jeff is ripe for the picking as a prime
suspect. Forming an uneasy alliance with her
high-maintenance stepmother, Monica has her hands full
trying to save the farm while searching for a killer.
Culbert made plenty of enemies in the quaint small
town…but which one was desperate enough to kill?

"Cozy fans and foodies rejoice—there's a place just
for you and it's called Cranberry Cove."
—Ellery Adams, *New York Times* bestselling author

pegcochran.com
facebook.com/PegCochran
penguin.com

Also from

Peg Cochran

Berry the Hatchet

A Cranberry Cove Mystery

The entire town of Cranberry Cove is popping with excitement. Monica Albertson is baking cranberry goodies by the dozen and shopkeepers are decking out their storefronts for the first annual Winter Walk—an event dreamed up by the mayor to bring visitors to the town during a normally dead time of year.

But it's the mayor who turns up dead during the grand opening ceremony, his lifeless body making its entrance in a horse-drawn sleigh. Monica's mother and stepmother quickly become the prime suspects when it's discovered that the mayor was dating both of them, and to make things worse, her half brother Jeff uncovers a clue buried near one of the bogs on Sassamanash Farm. Now it's up to Monica to find out who really put the mayor on ice.

INCLUDES CRANBERRY RECIPES

pegcochran.com
facebook.com/PegCochran
penguin.com

Penguin
Random
House
BERKLEY